LAST TRIP TO LONDON

REAGAN KEETER

Summithill Press
Atlanta, Georgia

FIRST EDITION

Printed in the United States of America

ISBN 978-1-7343945-6-6 (softcover)
ISBN 978-1-7343945-9-7 (ebook)

GET AN EXCLUSIVE COPY OF *THE LAYOVER*

Connor Callahan has been through a lot. More than anyone should. It has left him with an overdeveloped sense of justice. Perhaps that is why when he sees a man discreetly tag a stranger's suitcase with a black magic marker, he sets out to discover what is going on. It's a decision that will thrust Connor into a conflict far more dangerous than he could have imagined, and when it's over, he will know one thing for sure: You're not always safer on the ground.

Details can be found at the end of this book.

CHAPTER 1

AT CONNOR'S URGING, THE Uber driver sped down the London streets toward the Keaton & Ivy Hotel, a boutique establishment at the edge of the city. He ran through yellow lights, ignored stop signs, and dodged pedestrians with the skill of a stuntman.

All for good reason.

Moments ago, Connor had received a call from a man who claimed his life was in imminent danger, and the driver, who by now had taken Connor and Dylan across London and back several times, had been there to hear the conversation. Or at least Connor's end of it.

"Call the police," the driver said as he swerved around a woman who had just stepped into a crosswalk.

Connor already had his phone out with the intention of doing just that. He told the police about the call he had received, the address of the hotel, and that he was going there now. Then he hung up and heard the driver mumble, "This is crazy."

"Just keep going," Dylan said, who was sitting in the back seat next to Connor.

When the driver pulled up to the hotel, Connor and Dylan hopped out of the car and raced inside.

"Wait!" the driver shouted. "What are you doing? You've already called the police! Let them handle this!"

Connor didn't want to do that. Neither did Dylan. Things had not gone well from the moment they'd landed, and had only gotten worse since. If they did not step in now, here, somebody might die.

They ran through a beautiful lobby with white leather sofas and a bar, occupied only by a pair of clerks behind the counter. As Connor went for the elevator, Dylan headed for the stairs.

"This way," she said. "It'll be faster."

Connor immediately realized she was right and changed course. They took the stairs up to the fourth floor with Dylan in the lead. Connor resisted the urge to say he worried they might already be too late. Then again, he wasn't sure he could speak even if he tried. He was breathing hard, pushing himself as fast as he could go. There wasn't much air left in his lungs for anything else.

They reached the landing with a large number four by the door. Dylan pushed it open and, once on the other side of it, they both hesitated for a moment while they tried to decide which way to go.

Their options were straight ahead and to the right. Connor knew from experience the hallway had been constructed such that, whichever way they picked, they would end up right back where they were. So no matter what, they would get to where they were going. The problem was the wrong choice would take them longer, and right now every second mattered.

Just like all those seconds ticking away while they made up their mind.

"Screw it," Connor said and started moving straight ahead. Right now, either choice was better than none at all.

"You know where you're going?" Dylan said as she fell in beside him.

Connor did not answer. Not at first. He looked at the numbers on the doors they passed. Four-oh-one on the left. Four-oh-two on the right.

They were looking for four-ten.

"It's this way," he said and sped up.

He still wasn't sure they were going to make it to the room in time. He also wasn't sure they would be able to help if they did.

The only thing he was sure of—and it hardly mattered at the moment—was that this had all started four days ago because of a man named Chris Miller and a movie called *Wayward Strangers*.

FOUR DAYS EARLIER

CHAPTER 2

CHRIS MILLER CHARGED THROUGH the bank doors. He was dressed all in black, save the dramatic red overcoat and diamond-shaped sunglasses. A Glock in each hand.

This was the moment Maria Alexander had been waiting for. Although she felt like little more than a bystander while the action before her unfolded, she was not. She was the mastermind behind this event. An "architect of chaos," according to the people she worked with. She was practically giddy as she stared at the small monitor in front of her.

Chris fired one of the guns at the ceiling. "This is a robbery," he declared in his distinctive baritone voice.

Maria frowned a little. She knew that was what Chris was going to say, and she had never liked the line. But since nobody had been able to come up with anything better, it had stuck. To Chris's credit, he had delivered it as effectively as anyone could have.

There were fourteen people on the monitor besides Chris. Three tellers. Eleven customers. The customers screamed and ducked. A child started to cry. His mother pulled him close.

Chris turned the guns on the two tellers at the far ends of the counter and immediately pulled both triggers. The teller to his left, in his skinny tie and wire-frame glasses, collapsed to the floor. The teller to his right, a woman in a floral-print blouse, stumbled back a step, hitting the wall behind her, and slid slowly down it.

Then Chris tucked one of the guns in his waistband and pulled a garbage bag from his back pocket. He placed it on the counter in front of the only remaining teller, smiled. "Fill it up," he said softly.

The teller had a nametag pinned to her blouse that read "Brittany." Her hands were clasped in front of her. Maria could see them shaking on the monitor.

When the teller did not immediately move, Chris took a step back, aimed the gun in his right hand at her forehead, and shouted, "Fill it up, Brittany!"

Finally, she sprang into action, shaking open the bag and moving to the first teller station to withdraw the cash from the drawer.

Chris looked over each shoulder. "We don't need any heroes here, you got it? This is all going to be over in seconds. Nobody needs to get hurt."

Brittany moved from one drawer to the next. The whole thing was taking longer than Maria would have liked. That was just the way it was sometimes. She watched anxiously as the teller filled the plastic bag with cash, paying careful attention to the small sounds picked up by the mike: the squeak of a man's shoes, a woman clearing her throat, the child whimpering softly.

Brittany placed the garbage bag, now filled with cash, on the counter in front of her station and stepped back.

"Thank you, ma'am," Maria mumbled.

Chris tipped an imaginary hat. "Thank you, ma'am." He grabbed the bag, headed for the door.

He was almost gone when a voice from behind him said, "You know I'm not letting you leave with the money."

Chris spun around. On the far side of the bank was a man wearing a black-and-white pinstriped suit and holding a gun of his own. He was trim, with dark hair and movie-star good looks. His jaw was set, head tilted slightly forward. He looked like a man ready for a fight.

Chris raised his own gun in response. "Try it. I dare you."

The man in the pinstriped suit looked right at the camera. His eyes were an electric blue that was so crisp, so clear, they almost looked like they might glow in the dark. "He dared me," the man said.

It gave Maria chills. She leaned forward in her foldout chair.

Then the man in the pinstriped suit fired his gun. Chris fired back. The gunshots echoed through the cavernous lobby. Customers screamed and fell to the floor; most of them, anyway. Two men with slicked-back hair and wearing white suits stood and pulled guns of their own. They likewise began to fire at Chris.

Chris turned around and ran for the exit. Just as he reached the door, there was an explosion of blood from his shoulder, and then two more in the center of his back.

He staggered outside.

"Dammit!" Maria shouted. She pulled her headphones off, got to her feet. "Cut! What the hell was that?" She looked around. "Marty? Where's Marty?"

An overweight man with a gray beard and wearing a Grateful Dead tee shirt jogged over while the actors cast into various bank roles began talking among themselves. The two tellers who had been shot got to their feet and joined the conversation.

The man in the pinstriped suit said something to the other shooters in white, then they approached Maria, too.

"What was that?" Maria said to Marty once he was close enough to reach out and touch if she had been so inclined.

Maria's chair was positioned in the center of a raised platform to give her a better view of the bank. Marty looked up and shook his head. His cheeks turned a bright red underneath his thin beard. "I don't know. I only strapped one squib to Chris's jacket. Maybe it malfunctioned—"

"And went off three times?"

Now the man in the pinstriped suit was over there, too. Luke Cross. There was a reason he had movie-star good looks, and it was, quite obviously, because he was a movie star. He had been in forty-two films to date and was an A-lister by anyone's measure.

"Listen," he said to Maria. "I know you want to do this in one take. If we're going to have this sort of amateur-hour bullshit going on, then maybe we should break it up into multiple shots."

"I don't need your advice," Maria snapped. She was just as invested in the success of this film as Luke was. Maybe more. Unlike Luke, who was already on top, Maria was still climbing the ladder. This was her first big-budget film, and she did not intend for it to be her last.

Around them, the teeming organism that was a film set buzzed with activity. Cameramen, gaffers, electricians, assistants, actors, costumers . . . and on and on it went—all of them hurrying about, engaged in the nebulous myriad of tasks that had to be performed when the cameras weren't rolling.

Wayward Strangers was being shot in a real bank on the outskirts of London. The bank had been closed down six months earlier, and Maria considered herself lucky to get it. The location lent authenticity to the scene that she felt could not be achieved on a sound stage. The only problem was it meant the space was tight, so there was nowhere Maria could take Marty to discuss the matter privately. Which meant she was stuck dealing with not only Marty's screw-up, but Luke's criticism, as well.

"Fine," Luke said, waving a hand dismissively. "You don't want the help of a seasoned professional, I guess that's up to you. It's your film to ruin."

"Luke!"

Luke rolled his eyes and walked away. "Call me when you need me," he said over his shoulder. "I'll be in my trailer."

Maria took a deep breath, then turned her attention back to Marty. "Look, someone on your team wired up multiple squibs. Find out who it was and make sure it doesn't happen again."

Marty nodded and scurried back the way he had come, gesturing to get someone else's attention.

Maria fell back into her chair. "Hannah!"

A petite young woman with a shaved head and too many piercings appeared beside her. She was the PA assigned to her by Nightbird Studios, the production company footing the bill for this Hollywood blockbuster. She was competent, although not extraordinary. However, hiring her had been non-negotiable, according to the studio.

"Yes, ma'am?"

"We're going to have to go again. Make sure everyone's ready. Get Chris back to wardrobe. Makeup, too, if he needs it."

"Yes, ma'am." She looked around. "Where is Chris?"

Suddenly, Maria felt uneasy. She remembered the horror story of a death on set some twenty years before, when defective ammunition had cost a film its lead actor.

I only strapped one squib to Chris's jacket.

Could it have happened again?

This time, when Maria rose to her feet, she did so slowly. She tried to see through and over the crowd, looking for Chris's distinctive red overcoat.

She had last seen the actor stumbling through the bank doors just before the scene ended. Was he still out there? Dead on the old stone stairs that led up from the street? Heart pounding, she was just about to step off the platform to go find out when she heard his distinctive baritone voice coming from behind her.

"I guess we're going again, huh?"

It was a voice made even more distinct by Chris's British accent, which he rarely used when on camera and still sounded artificial to Maria's ear. Perhaps because she had watched him in so many movies before meeting him.

She spun around, relieved to see Chris standing there. He shifted his weight to one foot and cocked his head slightly in the opposite direction. She had seen that stance many times by now. It usually accompanied a carefree smile that Maria figured was easy to flash around when you weren't still clawing your way to the top. Today, though, he looked like something was bothering him.

"Yeah, we have to," she said, pulling herself together and feeling a little foolish for jumping to the conclusion that he had died on set. "Those damn FX guys."

He waved a hand dismissively. "It's fine. These things happen." Then, in a more serious tone, he added, "But I'm flying out of here tomorrow. So we need to make this next one count."

Maria nodded her understanding. Although Chris wasn't in charge, he carried enough clout to have some authority.

Chris responded in kind and turned to the PA where he repeated the gesture—this time, a nod of acknowledgment. "Hannah."

She, too, repeated the gesture. "Chris."

"I'll be in wardrobe."

The Crown was a small and dingy bar on an equally small and dingy street. It was not on any tourist maps. Nowhere close to Big Ben or

Piccadilly Circus or any of the other tourist traps that dotted the London landscape. All that was fine with the people who frequented the place. There was even a sign on the back wall that read "Locals Only."

Chris had been there many times growing up, and always assumed the sign wasn't meant to be taken seriously. But since tourists never found their way inside, it hardly mattered.

The squibs had been hooked up correctly for the second take, so it had gone off without a hitch. Still, he was two hours late. It took time to clean the suit, reset the squibs, get everyone back in position.

He had texted Steve Thompson to let him know about the delay. Steve had been a friend from the Waterton Theatre, where Chris had gotten his start many years ago. The first show they had worked on together was *Hamlet*. Chris had played Rosencrantz, a minor part, especially when compared with Steve's coveted role of the title character.

Even back then, Chris's natural talent was obvious, and Steve had told him quite candidly that if he had been as plugged in to the local theater scene as Steve was, he would have been cast for the role instead. Actually, Chris remembered, he hadn't said *would*. He had said *should*. *You* should *have been cast for the role instead.*

"Get involved," Steve had told him. "Run lines with other actors. Build sets. Do whatever you can to help out. The more you help the community, the more it will help you."

Chris took the advice to heart. From that day forward, every minute he wasn't busy working construction, he was at one theater or another looking for ways to—as Steve put it—"get involved."

Within less than a year, he was regularly getting cast for lead roles.

Mia Edwards, whom he had also met at the Waterton Theatre

(albeit on a different production) and whom he was also meeting at the Crown tonight, insisted it would have happened anyway.

Chris wasn't sure if that was true, but he was sure it didn't matter. All those hours working behind the scenes had given him an appreciation for the theater he might not have had otherwise. It had also led to lifelong friendships that certainly wouldn't have happened otherwise.

And, regardless of how he had gotten those roles, they had led to a TV show that had been far more successful than anyone had expected, which had in turn brought Hollywood calling.

So maybe Steve was right, and it mattered. Maybe Mia was right, and it didn't. Either way, as far as Chris was concerned, none of it was time wasted.

Chris stepped out of a cab and hurried into the bar. He was glad to see it was the same wood-paneled shithole he remembered, with an old dartboard on the wall by the bathroom and the only other entertainment coming from a bottle or a tap.

The place was loud. Nineties rock pumped out of speakers along the ceiling while, at crowded tables, patrons talked over each other to be heard.

Chris scanned the room, looking for his friends. He found them at a table near the back. They were all there—Steve, Mia, and Ryan, a playwright from the same London theater scene that had brought together the other three. They were wrapped up in some sort of intense conversation, with Steve forcefully tapping his pointer finger on the table, Ryan shaking his head, and Mia clearly amused by all of it.

Chris could feel a warmth blossoming in his chest at the sight of them. He hadn't been back to London in—What? Three years? More or less, he figured. Even so, he hadn't seen his friends in five. Such was the life of a sought-after actor in Hollywood.

Not that it was any excuse. He should have made a point of getting back here more often. After all, when he was here, his was just "Chris." Nobody gave a shit about his on-screen success. In fact, the only people who even looked at him were the ones he had to squeeze past as he made his way across the room, and even they did so with a look of annoyance.

It was a nice change of pace, and part of the reason he was thinking to make this his last movie. He'd had enough of the film industry and was ready to get out, perhaps live a quiet life in New England raising horses. Of course, that had been complicated by the information he had uncovered earlier in the day.

On the way over, he had tried to decide whether he would tell his friends about it and still hadn't reached a decision. Chris had a complicated history with all of them for one reason or another. Those complications had given their relationships depth and were perhaps inevitable in friendships that had lasted so long. But none of those entanglements, none of that drama, could even compare to a secret like this. This was big—massive, even—and it reached back so far through the years that, in one way or another, it touched every one of their lives.

On its face, Chris realized, it seemed obvious he should tell them. But like everything else in his life, the decision was not so simple. He hoped that, after a couple of pints, he would know what to do.

Steve saw Chris first and greeted him with a hug. He was tall and skinny, like a scarecrow with most of the stuffing pulled out of him. Which was to say he looked exactly like he always had, sans the goatee he had shaved off sometime over the last several years.

Mia, who also stood for a hug, had transformed in even bigger ways. She had been the very essence of punk rock when they last met. Now she dressed in designer labels. She was, to be blunt, on the fast track to marrying money, Steve had told him on the phone weeks earlier, and she had decided to fully embrace this new identity.

Ryan, who was all sharp edges and had lost most of his hair, stood only enough to reach across the table and shake Chris's hand. He was wearing a black hoodie and massive, bass-thumping headphones hung around his neck. In addition to working in the theater, he would DJ at a club called the Circle a few nights a week.

"Things seem to be getting heated over here," Chris said as he took a seat. "What are you two talking about?"

He glanced from Ryan to Steve when he asked the question, clearly directing it to them. Nonetheless, Mia was the one who spoke up. "Same as always. Ryan here is complaining that TV is killing the theater—especially with on-demand everything these days—and Steve is insisting that if Ryan just wrote something good, people would come anyway."

Steve slammed his pint down on the table. "I didn't say that!"

"It's what you meant."

Ryan scoffed. "How would you know?" he said to Steve. "You haven't been working in the industry for a long time."

That was true. When Steve had found out his wife was pregnant a year earlier, he'd started thinking about all the costs that came with raising a child, and realized he needed a more stable income than he could get from the theater, especially since he already had to supplement said income waiting tables just to pay the bills. These days, he made a decent living working in the administration office at the University of London. To his surprise, he actually enjoyed it.

Nonetheless, these sorts of passionate conversations about the industry—and the friendly fire that followed—were to be expected whenever he and Ryan got together.

Chris smiled despite his sour mood. It was good to be back among old friends. He reached for the pitcher of beer in the middle of the table, and Steve swiped it up before he could get his hands on it.

"This thing's shot. Barely enough for one glass left in it. I'll get us a new one."

When Steve returned, he did so carrying a tray with a pitcher of Guinness on it as well as four shots of tequila. "We got to catch Chris up," he said, passing the shots around the table.

Chris did not bother to point that if they all did a shot, he wasn't exactly "catching up." But he also understood that was just the pretense for ordering the shots to begin with, and who was he to complain? He needed a drink.

As the evening wore on, Chris began to loosen up. His sour mood retreated a little at a time. He smiled and then laughed as his friends retold stories from their theater days and discussed what they were up to now. And he thought less and less about his problems, until he was not thinking about them at all.

It was a much-needed break from the stress, a moment to clear his head before he got on the plane tomorrow.

That's right—the plane. He looked at the time on his phone. The digits were blurry. He had to concentrate to read them. It was already past midnight, he realized. He shouldn't be staying out so late.

But that wasn't the only problem, was it? He was also feeling sick. Had been for a while, to be honest. Only now it was getting worse. He felt like he was going to vomit.

Without warning, he charged through the crowd toward the bathroom, shoving people out of his way as he went. This was no time for courtesy.

Chris barely made it to a stall before everything he'd consumed that evening came back out. He leaned against the wall. His stomach was starting to cramp and, despite having vomited, he was feeling worse.

He reflexively looked down at the mess in the toilet, perhaps if only to see how much he might still have in his stomach. He saw something in the bowl that disturbed him and leaned in closer, trying to focus.

Is that blood?

Chris couldn't be sure.

His stomach cramped again. This time the pain was much worse. He collapsed back against the stall divider and gritted his teeth.

He heard the restroom door open.

"Chris? Mate? You all right?" It was Steve.

"I'll be all right," Chris said, although he sure didn't sound like he would be—not even to himself.

"Too much alcohol, huh?"

"Just give me a minute."

"Do you want me to bring you some water?"

"I'll be fine." Another stomach cramp. "Just give me a minute!"

"All right, all right. Just come on out whenever you're ready."

Chris listened to Steve cross the grungy tile floor. He heard the door open and close. He was once again alone.

Alone. In this disgusting, graffiti-covered bathroom.

He vomited again. But the nausea and the pain continued to get worse.

How long can this possibly go on? he wondered, which was followed by a darker thought: *Am I dying?*

CHAPTER 3

ONNOR WAS PARKED ALONG a curb outside an apartment building close to North Saxton Road. He had a digital camera, complete with a telephoto lens, in his lap.

It had taken almost a week of work to get him to this moment—and that only accounted for his time. Dylan and Olin had also logged hours looking for Lance Casey.

He was not easy to find. But that was the job.

Actually, to be specific, the job was to figure out who was stalking Jackson Hart—or "Jax" as he was known to his fans—and report back with a name and a face so the actor could take appropriate legal action and make sure to stay clear of him.

It was the fifth case they had worked since Connor and his friends had become licensed PIs, and the third that had been sent to them by Maddie Thompson, the daughter of the famous artist Andrew Thompson.

Getting the name had not been without its challenges. It would also not be the most difficult thing Connor and his friends would have to do to close the case. That honor went to getting the man's picture. Lance did not have any photos online, which meant they'd had to go old-school.

The building was a dilapidated eyesore that seemed to be holding onto its status as a functional apartment complex by sheer will. Connor had spent enough time looking at it now that he could probably reconstruct the entire thing in his mind's eye, right down to the loose gutters that hung free of the roof and the wood rot eating away at the siding.

Perhaps none of that should have been a surprise.

North Saxton Road was in a shady part of Atlanta, populated largely by strip clubs and second-hand stores. Here, gangs operated freely and drugs were available on every other street corner.

If the Riverbrook Apartments building had been located directly on North Saxton Road, Connor would have had to call his stakeout quits an hour ago. It had gotten dark, and this was not the kind of place you wanted to find yourself in after the sun went down.

But here, a mile off North Saxton on a quaint two-lane road, Connor had not seen the sort of spillover that might alarm him. Sure, the occasional homeless person shuffled past his car. Connor was used to that. He had, after all, lived in New York City.

The front door to the building opened. A man in jeans and a gray sweatshirt stepped out, lit the cigarette clamped between his teeth. Connor lifted the Nikon to his eye so he could get a better look. Unfortunately, the light hanging above the stoop flickered like it had been doing all night, and by the time the camera focused in on his subject, he was already heading toward the parking lot at the back of the building.

When Connor had first arrived, he'd knocked on Lance's door pretending to be a magazine salesman, both to make sure the man was home and so that he knew what Lance looked like. While a physical description was not going to cut it when it came to closing the case, it would be invaluable when it came to making sure he snapped a picture of the right person.

That is, assuming he could *see* the person he wanted to take a picture of.

Well, Connor figured, if the man was planning to leave by car, he would know soon enough whether this was Lance.

Connor watched the driveway that led out of the lot. A minute passed. Then two. Finally, a 1980 Plymouth Gran Fury rolled onto the street like some slow-moving and ancient leviathan. Connor could safely assume the driver was the man who had exited the building a moment ago. And even though he couldn't see his face in the darkness, Connor knew what kind of car Lance drove.

This was that car.

Even if the vehicle wasn't rare, Connor recognized the number on the license plate. Dylan had gotten it for him two days earlier.

Connor had two choices at this point. He could follow Lance and try to get a picture of him when he got out of the vehicle, or come back another day. Coming back another day seemed like a bad choice. He couldn't exactly knock on the man's door again to see whether he was home if he did. Besides, he was ready to call this case closed.

He started his engine and pulled out onto the road behind Lance.

Connor's CR-V was about as inconspicuous as a car could get. He didn't worry much about Lance noticing he was there.

Lance turned into the parking lot at an Italian restaurant called Gianna's.

Perhaps he was meeting someone, Connor thought as he pulled in behind him. He hoped he would be able to snap a picture of his target before Lance stepped inside. But Gianna's had valet parking, and Lance was already passing through the restaurant's door by the time Connor was able to bring him into focus with the Nikon.

Shit.

He waved off the valet and parked his car as close to the door as he could get.

The restaurant had a fireplace on each end of the dining room. Red-and-white checkered tablecloths with white linens on top. Exposed brick walls.

A hostess led Connor straight past Lance to a table near the back.

"Actually," Connor said, pointing to another, "do you mind if I sit there?"

"Whatever you like," the hostess said, and led him to his preferred location.

The table he had selected put him face-to-face with Lance, albeit with a pair of diners between them. But at the right angle, Connor could still get a decent picture with his phone. (He had left the Nikon in the car for obvious reasons.)

Lance had a menu in front of his face. When Connor leaned to the left, he could see the man's eyes scanning its contents. A waiter appeared beside him and they had a quick exchange, during which Lance pointed to something on the menu.

So, if he was waiting for someone, he wasn't waiting for them to arrive before placing his order.

The waiter smiled. Lance smiled. Then the waiter took the menu and left.

Lance's smile struck Connor as insincere and smug. Then again, maybe that was how Connor saw it because of everything he knew about the man.

Lance's first contact with Jax had come via Twitter. It had read simply "You suck @realjax." Jax, wisely, had not responded. Most of the time, that would have been enough to shut down a troll like Lance. That was not the case here. Lance had sent another message, and then a third. And when Jax had finally decided to engage, it had only made things worse. They had exchanged barbs online, and things had quickly escalated into a battle nobody would win until Jax reported the abuse and Twitter had suspended Lance's account.

Lance had then taken his battle offline, delivering angry, hate-filled letters to Jax's home, along with a disturbing assortment of packages that included everything from a broken DVD of Jax's last film to magazine pictures of Jax with his eyes punched out or his head cut off.

Neither Connor nor Dylan had been able to find a reason for the abuse, but that was hardly what mattered. All Jax cared about was stopping it.

Connor watched Lance for a while. The stalker drummed his thumbs on the table, straightened his man bun, looked around aimlessly.

It's now or never.

Connor pulled out his phone, leaned to the left, and snapped a picture. It was a great shot. Too good, actually, because Lance had been looking right at him when he clicked the button.

Lance's pale complexion reddened almost immediately and his lips clamped together so tightly they turned white. Without taking his eyes off Connor, he slid his chair back, stood up.

Connor likewise got to his feet.

"Hey!" Lance shouted. "What the hell was that?"

Everyone in the restaurant looked at him. Everyone except Connor, who tried to make his way to the exit without drawing attention from anyone else.

"I said, what the hell was that?" Lance shouted again. Then he, too, began to move.

Connor wasn't sure if he heard Lance coming or sensed it. Either way, once he looked back and saw Lance gaining on him, he broke into a run. He weaved around the tables, dodged a waiter coming out of the kitchen with a tray full of food, and pushed through the front door.

The hostess made a sound as he passed—surprise or shock, maybe.

Lance sped up. "*What the hell was that?*" he demanded again.

Connor sprinted to his car, fishing in his pocket for his keys as he ran. He was feet away when he found them and pressed the center button to unlock the doors. The lights on the CR-V flashed. He grabbed the handle, and just as he started to pull the door open, a hand from behind slammed it shut.

Lance grabbed Connor by the shoulder, spun him around. "Why are you taking my picture?"

Dylan had offered to come with Connor tonight. He had told her to go home and relax. "It's just a picture," he had said. "Easy-peasy." Now he wished he had some backup.

He looked around for help and saw none was coming. A few people had stepped out of the restaurant to see what was going on. However, they remained on the far side of the parking lot.

Screw it.

Connor kneed the man in the balls.

Lance groaned, collapsed to the ground. Kneeling, hands between his legs.

Then Connor pulled open the car door, hitting him in the face. He heard Lance groan as he fell onto his side, then hopped into his car and took off.

CHAPTER 4

CONNOR PULLED UP TO the callbox outside Jax's house, and Jax buzzed him through.

The driveway was almost long enough to be a road in and of itself. It meandered through a pleasant, wooded area and opened onto a gorgeous three-story contemporary that would have looked out of place among the neighboring colonials and Cape Cods, if you could actually see it from the street.

Jax Hart was not the biggest celebrity to have had a residence in Atlanta. However, Connor had learned, he was among an increasing number who were choosing to call the city home.

There were a dozen or more cars parked along the driveway. Connor got as close to the house as he could and then hiked the rest of the way on foot. He could hear music blasting from inside once he was within sight of the front door—a large, steel monstrosity that reminded Connor of the kind of thing you might see on a safe.

Jax swung the door open. He had deep-set blue eyes and a strong chin. He was wearing a tailored black suit with a matching black shirt underneath. Jax was always ready for company. It looked like tonight he had good reason to be. The living room behind him was crowded with guests. "Come on in," he slurred.

As Connor stepped past him, he noticed Jax was holding a drink in one hand. A bourbon, he suspected. It was what the actor had been drinking the last time they had met.

"Can I get you anything?" Jax said, holding up the glass. Then, before Connor could answer, he shifted his attention to a small group of people nearby. "Honey!"

A woman turned around. It was Melissa Hart, Jax's wife. She was wearing an elegant white evening dress and more diamonds than Connor would have thought one person could own. She, too, was an actress. Or an aspiring one, anyway, who—despite her husband's connections—had not been able to get her career off the ground.

"Make Connor a drink," he said.

Melissa smiled at Connor. "What would you like?"

"Nothing. Really." Connor directed Jax's attention toward the manila folder he was carrying. "Are you sure you want to do this now?" he said, shouting to be heard over the music.

Connor had called Jax after he had left the restaurant to give him an update and schedule a meeting for tomorrow, but Jax had insisted he come over right away. "I've lived with this asshole long enough," he had said. "If you know who he is, I don't want to wait until tomorrow to find out."

Connor had understood and reluctantly agreed. Of course, he did not know he would be walking into something that—best he could tell—was more or less equivalent to an upscale college kegger.

"You bet I want to do this now." He gestured for Connor to follow him. "Come this way." Then he led Connor down a series of hallways, dodging partygoers as he went, while Melissa turned back to her guests.

The house had felt like a maze the first time Connor had been here. With all the people, it seemed even more like one now.

When they finally ended up in Jax's office, he regained his bearings. Although the route they had taken to get here was not the one he would have expected, he had been in this room before.

There was a lot to like about the space—from the hand-knitted geometric rug to the built-in bookcases to the fourteenth-century swords mounted on either side of the door. But the focal point was clearly intended to be the custom executive desk that stood right in the middle of the room.

"Not another one like it in the world," Jax had declared proudly the first time they'd met. It was based on designs Jax had drawn and was handmade in Italy by a master craftsman.

Jax closed the door, cutting the volume of the music to a tolerable level. Then he plopped down in the leather chair behind the desk and left Connor standing on the other side. "So is that it?" he said, pointing to the folder in Connor's hand.

"It is, although—"

"Let me see."

"Before I give this to you—"

Jax held out his hand. "Oh, come on. Let me see."

Connor sighed. This wasn't the way he wanted the conversation to go. He wanted to share the contents of the folder one item at a time, explaining the significance of each document as he went. But Jax was the client. If he wanted it all now, Connor might as well give it to him.

Jax snatched the folder out of Connor's hand when Connor offered it and immediately began flipping through the contents.

The first page was a printout of one of the emails Jax had received, with an IP address highlighted near the top.

"We used the IP address to—"

"Yeah, yeah, yeah," Jax said, flipping past it.

He moved just as quickly through all of the pages. Connor didn't try again to explain any of the documents. Jax clearly wasn't interested. Finally, Jax looked up.

"Where's the picture? You were supposed to get a picture."

"That's at the back."

Jax smiled his movie-star smile. "Saving the best for last, huh? I like it." He flipped past the remaining pages all at once and finally found the eight-by-ten glossy he was looking for.

With Lance sitting at the table in the Italian restaurant and staring straight at the camera, the picture almost looked staged.

"So there you are, you son of a bitch," Jax said to himself.

"His name's Lance Casey."

The actor's gaze shot to Connor. "You have an address?"

"Back one page."

Jax flipped back, scanned the paper until he found what he was looking for. Then he pulled out his phone, entered the address into Google Maps, and slipped the piece of paper into his pocket. "That's a pretty shitty part of town."

Although Connor agreed, he did not respond.

Jax hopped up before he could have if he had wanted to, anyway, and headed for the door, his bourbon abandoned on the desk. "Stay, if you want. Have Melissa make you a drink. Seriously. I won't be long."

"Where are you going?"

Jax turned the phone around so Connor could see the screen. "Here. I'm going to put a stop to this once and for all."

Connor quickly moved to block the door. "That's not a good idea. This guy is dangerous."

"So am I."

"Think about this for a second, Jax."

Jax moved to the left to get around Connor and Connor mirrored the step.

"Get out of my way."

"Take this to the police. You have everything you need for a restraining order now."

Jax scoffed. "Like I'm going to wait around for that." Then he tried to push Connor out of the way, and Connor pushed back. Hard.

Jax spent four hours a day in the gym. Connor was pretty sure if he managed to move the man at all it would take every bit of force he could muster. But the alcohol had compromised Jax's balance. He stumbled back and fell, dropping the phone in the process. "Dammit, Connor!"

Connor wasn't sure what he should do. Part of him thought he should apologize. Then again, that might undermine his position. He had pushed Jax away from the door to make a point. "Don't go to his house, okay? At least not tonight. Sleep on it. I'm sure in the morning you'll know the right thing to do."

Jax stared at Connor for ten or fifteen seconds, perhaps considering what he had said. "All right. If it means so much to you that you'd be willing to do this"—the actor gestured to the space between them—"then I suppose the least I can do is wait until morning."

"Yeah?"

"Yeah," Jax said as he started to stand.

Connor leaned over and offered him a hand. Jax took it. Once he was back on his feet, he added, "You know I could kick your ass, if I wanted to."

"I know."

Jax nodded. "All right. Just so long as we're on the same page."

CHAPTER 5

NO MATTER WHAT JAX said, he wasn't really on the same page with Connor. Not about seeing Lance tonight, anyway. Lance didn't seem like the kind of guy who would respect a restraining order. If Jax wanted to get through to him, he was going to have to do it in a more personal way.

Not that Jax minded getting up close to that son of a bitch. In fact, as he stood on the porch watching Connor drive off, he thought he might even enjoy it.

Jax had been born into a working-class family in Adel, Georgia. Population: 5,289. His father had been a mechanic at a gas station called Bartow's. His mother had been a waitress at a Waffle House a quarter of a mile away. While they had not always worked the same schedule, that proximity had still made things easier to manage, since they'd only had once car.

"Which is one more than we can afford," he had overheard his father say once during a heated conversation between his parents.

Jax still remembered that discussion clearly. He had been eight years old. And right then and there he had sworn he was not going to live his whole life in that town, struggling and scraping just to make enough money to eat.

He wanted more.

To get it, he had first focused on his studies, bringing home As and earning a full ride to Georgia State University. His parents had been proud. So had he. But the scholarship had dried up during his sophomore year after several restrictive changes to the program collided with his GPA, which, although excellent, was no longer good enough.

Jax had then packed up everything he owned and headed out to California, where he promised his mom and dad he would make his mark.

It took ten long years. A lot of stage plays. A handful of commercials, background roles, and bit parts. Finally, he had scored a lead role in an indie film that made it big, signed with an agent, and never looked back.

Once he was established, he had moved back to Atlanta to be close to his family. His parents still lived in Adel because, for reasons Jax couldn't understand, they liked it there. At least they no longer had to work. Jax sent them ten thousand dollars a month to make sure of it.

In short, he had worked too hard—for himself and for them—to have someone like Lance in his life.

Jax stepped back into the living room. He found his wife talking with a different group of guests, gently pulled her aside. "I've got a name."

Melissa should not have been surprised. Connor had practically said as much when he'd arrived. Still, her eyebrows went up. "Really?"

"I'm going to go take care of this now. Keep everyone entertained. I won't be long."

Unlike Connor, Melissa did not put up any resistance. Jax did not think she would. She liked it when he acted tough. Sometimes she even encouraged it. Besides, she was as tired of dealing with Lance as he was. She might not have been the man's target, but Jax knew she nonetheless felt threatened.

Melissa squeezed Jax's hand. "I'll see you when you get back."

Jax made his way to the five-car garage and grabbed the keys for the Porsche off the wall. A Lamborghini, a Tesla, and a Jaguar were also parked there. But the keys for the Porsche were closest to the door and, right now, he didn't care which car he drove. He just wanted to get to Lance's apartment as soon as possible.

He cruised past the strip clubs on North Saxton Road, looking for the street that would take him to Lance's apartment building. When he had been a college student at Georgia State, he had been down here half a dozen times with friends. Everything about Atlanta had been new and exciting in those days, the strip clubs in particular.

Now he looked at them with disgust. The dealers and homeless he looked at with even more. This was a part of Atlanta that could burn down and not be missed, as far as he was concerned.

When Jax came to a light, a man in a ragged black tee shirt approached, carrying a sign that read "STRANDED. NEED MONEY FOR BUS FARE."

Yeah, right.

The man waved to get Jax's attention, and Jax pretended he couldn't see him, which took more of his acting skill than he might have expected. It was all he could do not to roll down his window and tell the man to get the hell away from his car.

But Jax didn't need a confrontation right now. He needed to save his energy for the one he had coming.

Finally, he found the street—and then the building—he was looking for. Jax recognized it from one of the many pictures Connor had given him.

He parked around back. There was a sign that read "Residents Only," which he disregarded. There was no way he was leaving his

Porsche on the street. He didn't even like leaving it in the lot.

Before he got out of the car, he double-checked the apartment number on the piece of paper Connor had given him: 22B.

Jax went straight to the front door, worried he might have to be buzzed in, and instead found absolutely no security at all. He bounded up the stairs two at a time and hurried down the hall, scanning the numbers on the doors to each unit.

When he reached Lance's, he knocked hard, then stood to the side so Lance would not be able to see him through the peephole. His heart was pounding. Jax could feel his blood coursing through his veins. He curled his fingers into fists, released them, and curled them back up again.

While he waited, he noticed the hallway had a stench to it he couldn't quite identify. It was musty and stale. An insidious odor that he doubted any cleaning crew could get out.

He looked down at the carpet. Perhaps there was mold growing underneath it, he thought.

A minute passed.

Jax knocked again, harder. He began to worry Lance might not be home. Then again, it was just as likely Lance checked the peephole, saw no one outside, and did not bother to open the door. If that was the case, all Jax had to do was keep knocking.

Which he did.

Knock, knock, knock.

Knock, knock, knock.

Knock, knock, knock.

Each was louder and more insistent than the one before.

Soon enough, the effort paid off. The door swung open. Lance stepped out, looking left then right. One side of his face was bruised and starting to swell, Jax noticed. Maybe this man had more than one enemy.

"*You*," Lance said when he saw who it was.

"That's right. *Me*."

CHAPTER 6

RED SKY INVESTIGATORS WAS located on the third floor of a midtown office building that was home to a wide range of small businesses, none of which Connor had ever heard of.

He arrived early and, per usual, was the first one there. Olin would show up an hour later and—if past was prologue—he'd come armed with a Starbucks for both of them. Dylan would roll in around ten.

It was going to be a quiet day. Jax had been their only active case.

The suite included a waiting area with a row of plastic chairs that, so far, no one had ever used, and a wilting fern in one corner. The large room beyond it was modestly furnished with three desks and a small, round table where they could hold meetings or talk with clients.

Connor used the coffee maker that sat on the filing cabinet by his desk to brew a pot. He stood by the wall of windows opposite the waiting room, looking out at the bumper-to-bumper traffic below until it finished. Then he filled the plain, blue mug he kept on his desk, took his first sip, and began browsing the internet.

The coffee he made in the office always seemed to taste a little stale, and normally, he would wait until Olin arrived with the Starbucks. But Connor hadn't slept well last night. He hadn't been able to shake the feeling Jax was going to do something he shouldn't.

And he was right.

Articles from a whole variety of outlets carried the story. Most were reprints from the original in the *New York Post*. It was top-shelf tabloid content.

A few minutes later, Olin entered with—as expected—a Starbucks for Connor, and Connor took it gratefully, setting the remains of his own mug of swill aside.

"How'd it go last night?" Olin asked him. He had always been fastidious in his appearance, and today was no exception. Unlike Connor, who was happy as long as his hair wasn't sticking out every which way, Olin's was carefully parted. His pressed white dress shirt was tucked into a pair of pleated gray slacks, and his shoes were almost shiny enough for Connor to see himself in.

"Got the picture," Connor said.

Olin's expression shifted subtly, indicating surprise. "Good job."

"Yeah, well, it wasn't without its challenges."

Olin slid a chair back from the table in the middle of the room and sat down. Connor joined him.

"What do you mean?" Olin asked.

Connor filled him in on the entire series of events: knocking on Lance's door, trailing him to the restaurant, getting chased back to his car after he snapped the picture, talking to Jax.

"Wow. That was much more eventful than you were expecting, huh? Maybe you should have had Dylan come with you."

Connor shrugged.

Olin looked him over. "It seems like you came out of it okay."

"It could have been worse. But that wasn't the end of it." Then he filled Olin in on what he had read online.

Dylan entered in time to catch the tail end of the story. Like she always did, she had her long red hair neatly clipped back from her face with a pair of bobby pins. "What's going on?" she asked, likewise sitting down at the table. She leaned back and propped her feet up on it.

"Jax got himself arrested last night."

"Really?"

Connor filled her in on last night's events as well, then said, "Jax promised he wasn't going to do anything stupid. Unfortunately—"

"He did," Olin interjected.

"After I met with him to give him the info on his stalker, apparently he went over to Lance's apartment to confront him in person. Beat the crap out of him. I don't know if Jax meant to land him in the hospital; that's what happened, though. He should have just taken the information to the police like I told him to."

Dylan put her feet back on the floor and leaned forward. "I don't know. Maybe."

"Maybe?"

Then she got that mischievous twinkle in her eye. "He got the message, right?" she said to Olin. She was no doubt thinking about the handful of times Olin—who was normally not a confrontational person—had been driven to violence by circumstance.

"Funny," Olin said.

There was one phone in the office. It sat on Connor's desk. They planned to add a second if they ever got a receptionist, which was looking less and less likely. As things stood, they were barely getting by. Perhaps that was normal for an agency like theirs.

Either way, the phone rang so infrequently, it took all of them by surprise when it did.

Connor went over to answer.

"I'm looking for Mr. Callahan," a man said. His voice sounded like he had been a heavy smoker for many years.

"Speaking."

"Jax gave me your number."

Must have been before he was arrested, Connor thought.

"I've got something I need to talk to you about. You know Cafe de Flore?"

"Yes," Connor said. He knew it well. Dylan had worked as a waitress at the restaurant when she had first moved to Atlanta and had taken Connor and Olin there on a number of occasions.

"Can you meet me there in an hour?"

"Sure."

"Great. See you then."

"How will I find you?"

"Ask the hostess for Hudson Davis." Then Hudson hung up.

"What was that about?" Olin asked.

Connor shrugged. "I guess I'll find out. Some guy named Hudson Davis wants to meet. Jax gave him our number. I suppose it's about a job."

Dylan's eyes grew wide. "Hudson Davis?"

"Yeah, why?"

"*The* Hudson Davis?"

"Who's Hudson Davis?" Olin said.

Dylan looked from one man to the other. "You two don't know anything, do you? You remember all those *Night Fire* movies? If it's the same guy, he produced them. I mean, it must be him, right? If Jax is the one who recommended us?"

Connor returned to the table. "Well, whoever he is, I'm meeting him at Cafe de Flore in about an hour."

"Not without me, you're not," Dylan said.

CHAPTER 7

CONNOR AND DYLAN ENTERED Cafe de Flore. The hip midtown restaurant billed itself as a French-style eatery. The waiters wore tuxedos. Every table had a candle on it.

The man behind the hostess stand was named Mike and he looked like he was in his early fifties, but Connor knew from Dylan he was quite a bit older than that. This was his retirement gig—something to get him out of the house. He had been here when Dylan started and would likely be here until he died.

Connor and Dylan exchanged pleasantries with Mike. Then, just before Connor could ask him where Hudson Davis was sitting, Dylan grabbed Connor's arm and pointed. "Look. That's him." She pulled Connor forward. "Let's go."

Connor shook her loose.

She looked back over her shoulder and waved. "Good seeing you, Mike!" Then she hurried past Connor like Hudson might disappear if she didn't get to him fast enough.

Connor followed after her, then shook his head as Dylan sat down in a chair across from the producer, startling him.

"Hi," she said, holding out a hand. "It's great to meet you. I'm such a big fan of your work."

Hudson had a long face that seemed to be locked in a perpetual frown and a neatly trimmed salt-and-pepper beard. Having regained his composure, his eyes moved from Dylan's hand to her face in a way that suggested he was both bored and annoyed. "Miss . . ."

"I'm sorry," Connor said, taking a seat. "She's with me." He looked directly at Dylan. "She doesn't normally act like this."

"We also don't normally meet somebody like Hudson," she replied.

The producer turned that same bored look on Connor. "And you are?"

"Connor Callahan. This is Dylan Naese."

Finally, Hudson reached across the table and shook Dylan's hand. "I was only expecting you," he said to Connor.

"I know. But she's a big part of the reason we found Jax's stalker as fast as we did. I thought she might be a valuable part of this conversation." That was only half true. Dylan *was* a big part of the reason they'd found Jax's stalker so fast. But she was only here now because she had insisted on coming. Still, at least it explained her presence in a way that didn't make her look quite so much like some sort of crazed fan.

Hudson settled back in his chair and took a sip from the small cup of coffee in front of him. As Connor watched, he wondered if he should have another one himself.

"I have a problem," Hudson said, setting his cup back on the table. "I think you may be able to help. I'm shooting a movie in London right now." His perpetual frown grew deeper. "I *was* shooting a moving in London. Yesterday, my lead actor died."

Connor listened without showing any emotion. He was glad to see Dylan, now that she was done being starstruck, seemed to be doing the same.

"The police are looking into it. I don't know how long that will take. Or how much they will tell me. So far, I have been able to keep the whole thing under wraps. I won't be able to do that for long, though. Sooner or later, somebody will talk to a tabloid." He sighed. "It's sad, but it's also predictable. It's the way it is these days."

"So somebody killed him?" Dylan said, sounding once again like the woman Connor knew.

Hudson shook his head. "I don't know. It happened in a bar after we were done for the day. He was found crumpled up in a stall on the bathroom floor. That's all I can say for sure. I would like you to go there and see what you can find out for me. I need to get ahead of this thing. I need to be able to control the fallout if I'm going to save this movie."

Dylan looked at Connor. She seemed to be thinking the same thing he was and spoke first. "I don't mean to be callous. It sounds like a drug overdose or something like that. It's not like there was some horrible accident with the production. Why should this put the movie at risk?"

Hudson shifted his gaze once again to her. "Listen, ma'am—"

"Dylan."

"Do you want the job or not?"

Connor thought about it and realized he seemed to be missing one key piece of information. "Who died?"

Hudson mulled the question over, as if he wasn't sure whether he wanted to answer it. Then he casually glanced over each shoulder and leaned in. "Chris Miller."

"*Chris Miller?*" Dylan repeated, much louder.

Connor shot her a look, and Hudson said, "Keep your voice down." Then, to both of them: "Are your passports current?"

Now Connor leaned in. "You want us to go to London?"

"You're not going to be able to figure out what happened from here, are you?"

41

CHAPTER 8

LANCE WOULD HAVE TO change buses twice to reach the
Garder Museum, where he worked as a night watchman. But
driving wasn't an option. It wouldn't be for the next six to eight
weeks. His 1980 Plymouth Gran Fury was a stick shift. With his right
arm in a cast, driving would be impossible.

Every time the bus stopped, he watched the passengers get on and
off, imagining their sad little lives, their petty concerns. They worried
about bills; they worried about being alone; they worried about their
jobs and their cars and their apartments and all the little things that
could happen to them from the time they got up until the time they
went to bed. They had no idea how bad life could really be.

Lance worried about all those things and more.

When Lance was young, he had been destined for great things. His
mother (who had lost her life to lung cancer two years ago) had said so.
Now he worried he might never achieve them. That was far worse than
just worrying about your car and your job and your bills, because every
day, when he woke up and looked at the ceiling of his shitty apartment,
his first thought was, *I'm not supposed to be here.*

To be fair, his apartment wasn't "shitty." It just wasn't meant for
him. If he had reached his full potential—if this was as far as he could
go—he might actually be able to enjoy his life. He wasn't unattractive.
He could find a girl, if he wanted to. He could settle down and do all

the things so many other people did to pass the time: reading books, going to movies, seeing friends.

But this wasn't his full potential. Not even close. And the problem was, whenever he got close to achieving it, someone came along and clawed it away from him. Almost as if life itself did not want him to be happy.

Lance shifted his attention to the window to try not to think about the day everything first started to go wrong. He watched streetlamps flicker to life as the sun eased behind the midtown buildings. Drivers turned on their headlights. Shadows grew long. Something about it was almost Zen-like.

Still, he thought about that day. Maybe it was inevitable. The cast reminded him of the hospital, and one hospital reminded him of another.

When Lance was in high school and still living in LA, he had decided to take up running, joined the track team, and excelled. He pushed himself as hard as he could, going for miles at a time—always farther, always faster. He loved the wind in his face, the way his heart pounded so hard it felt like his chest might explode. He imagined, if he kept it up, he might one day be able to participate in the Olympics.

His chest never did explode, of course. But, it turned out, that wasn't the risk he'd needed to be worried about.

The date was June 2. Lance was as certain of that as he was that it had happened on a Tuesday. These were facts that would likely be etched into his brain forever. Just like the weather: crisp, cool— unusually so for a summer afternoon.

Lance was out for a run, determined to beat his personal best. That meant going just over twenty-one miles. He had already driven the route to make sure there were no surprises. Now all he had to do was run, and that was just a matter of putting one foot in front of the other until he reached his goal.

He could do that.

Or so he thought.

At an old cathedral he had used as his twelve-mile marker, Lance began to feel lightheaded. He suspected it was because he had skipped breakfast that morning. At twelve miles, he was closer to the end of his route than the start, so he kept going. He figured he would overcome it. What doesn't kill you makes you stronger, and all that.

Unfortunately, sometimes there's a third option.

Two miles later, Lance passed out. Everything else that happened between that moment and when he woke up at the Southern California Hospital in Hollywood he had pieced together from the various nurses and doctors who attended to him.

From what he gathered, he had fallen into the street, hit his head on the cement hard enough to bleed and had one leg crushed under the wheel of a taxi. He was rushed into emergency surgery, where they had performed a procedure he now knew as a ventriculostomy. Basically, the operation meant cutting a small hole in his skull to drain the cerebrospinal fluid with the intention of relieving pressure on the brain.

It had, according to the staff, saved his life.

But he had sustained damage, and no one could say for certain exactly how much, or whether he would make a full recovery. That was the nature of a brain injury, it seemed. Either way, with his leg crushed under the taxi, he would likely never run again—at least, not like he had before.

It had been devastating, and not long after that, he had started to spiral. He began drinking too much and taking whatever he could get his hands on to dull the pain—both physical and emotional.

"Tenth and Peachtree," announced the bus driver.

Lance slid into the group of people who called this their stop, disembarked, and waited on the bench for his next bus.

He remembered the nurse from last night shaking her head when he had relayed the story. "A broken leg and now a broken arm. That's some bad luck," she had said.

He did not disagree. He also knew it could have been worse. When Jax had shown up last night, Lance had been expecting him. He figured the guy who had tried oh-so-hard to discreetly take his picture at the restaurant had to be a PI or something like that, and he was certain once Jax had the photo in hand, he would not hesitate to come to Lance's apartment to confront him.

That's just who Jax was.

It was why it had taken Lance a while to come to the door. After Jax had knocked repeatedly, Lance had gone in search of a weapon. He'd found a baseball bat in the back of his closet. That would do.

He'd grabbed the bat and jerked the front door open, looking left, then right. He was certain this was not a ding-and-ditch situation. This wasn't just a group of kids out for a good time.

And he had been right.

"*You*," Lance said.

"That's right. *Me*," Jax responded.

Lance had been holding the bat by his side, more for convenience than anything else. Jax didn't see it until Lance raised it over his shoulder, getting ready to swing. The actor's gaze shifted from Lance to the makeshift weapon, and his eyes grew wide. Lance thought he remembered Jax saying something like "Oh, shit!" But he wasn't certain. Everything had happened fast.

When Lance swung the bat, Jax jumped back, and the bat punched a hole into the drywall.

Lance thought Jax deserved every bit of pain coming to him, and swung again. His long hair hung in his face, obscuring his vision. Perhaps that was why he missed the second time, again taking a bite out of the drywall.

Either way, this time Jax was ready for it. When he jumped back, he also reached out and grabbed hold of the bat as soon as it hit the wall. With a quick jerk, he pried it from Lance's hands, spun it around.

It was his turn to start swinging.

Jax, it turned out, had better aim. Cursing the entire time, he went low, first hitting Lance in the leg (his bad leg, and Lance was certain that wasn't an accident). When Lance dropped to the ground, he hit him again in the shoulder. Lance reached out to try to grab the bat, and Jax hit him in the forearm.

Bone cracked—Lance could hear it—and pain shot up his arm like a lightning bolt. He screamed as Jax raised the bat again.

Lance was certain the actor was about to kill him.

Maybe he would have, too, if reason hadn't gotten the better of him at the last second. Jax froze mid swing, with Lance cradling his bad arm in his lap and holding up his good arm to try to protect his head.

Then, instead of continuing the physical assault, Jax proceeded with a verbal one. That must have gone on for ten minutes or more. Lance couldn't remember what Jax said then any more than he could anything else the actor had said that evening. He didn't much care, either.

This whole confrontation proved to Lance what he already knew to be true about the actor.

It didn't matter to Jax who he stepped on, who he hurt. Jax was about Jax, and no one else.

The whole thing finally came to an end when a voice at the end of the hall called for his attention. "You there! What do you think you're doing?"

Still holding the bat, Jax turned around to see two police officers coming toward him. They were both bigger than Jax, and one had his hand on the butt of his holstered gun.

Jax looked from the officers to the bat in his hand and back. He tossed the bat on the floor. "It's not what you think."

"Thank God you're here!" Lance screamed. "This man would have killed me."

Jax tried to explain that Lance had been stalking him, that he was just defending himself, and on and on.

Nobody was listening, least of all the police. They handcuffed Jax, read him his rights, and dragged him, fuming, toward the stairwell.

Once he was gone, Lance saw an old woman standing in the doorway of an apartment not far away. "You okay, sonny?" she asked.

Lance gently placed his hand on his broken arm. "I think so." Then he winced as he pushed himself back to his feet. "I will be."

"I can't believe what he did to this place."

Lance looked at the smashed drywall on both sides of the hall. Some of it had caved in, exposing the insulation behind it. The rest had fallen to the floor in chunks.

He didn't see any reason to correct her about who had done the damage. There were no cameras on this floor. So he not only let the assumption stand, he parroted it to the police when they asked about it later.

That was not enough to balance the scales. Not nearly. But it was a start.

CHAPTER 9

OLIN AGREED TO STAY behind to man the firm. As far as Connor could tell, he did not want to go to London, anyway. Connor wasn't sure if it was the long flight or if being in Europe would bring him too close to memories he would rather forget. However, it didn't matter, so he didn't ask.

Connor and Dylan booked the first flights out they could get.

Dylan slept most of the way there. Connor tried but found sleep elusive. After his meeting with Hudson, he had scoured the web for anything he could find on Chris's death. Just as the producer had told them, word about it had not leaked. Yet.

But the more time he had spent looking into Chris's death, the more he began to wonder about Hudson. Something about the producer's explanation for hiring them had seemed, well, *off*.

Sure, Connor didn't know the industry. Maybe Chris's death in a bar *could* cause problems for the movie. But he doubted it. Not any more trouble than they would already have after losing one of their main actors. That would likely mean re-shoots with someone new, or script changes, or maybe both. Nothing that would shut the movie down.

So what was Hudson's real reason for hiring them?

A general search of the web did not provide any clues. Hudson did not appear to have any deep, dark secrets. Upon Connor's request,

Dylan searched the dark web and didn't find anything there, either.

That only made Connor more intrigued.

The plane landed at Heathrow on schedule. Connor and Dylan found a woman near the baggage carousel holding a placard with Connor's name scrawled on it in black magic marker. She had a shaved head, a piercing in her nose, another in her eyebrow, half a dozen up one ear, and more in the other. She was skinny in a way that bordered on unhealthy, Connor thought, and looked just as unhappy as she was thin.

He went over and introduced himself, then Dylan.

The woman dropped the sign. "Hannah," she said in her Mancunian accent, and nodded toward the baggage carousel. "Keep an eye out for your bags. Once you've got them, I'll take you to the hotel. Maria's there waiting. She's anxious to talk to you."

"Who?" Dylan said.

Hannah shot her a sideways glance. "The director. I'm her PA. Didn't Hudson tell you who she was?"

Connor vaguely remembered the name. Maybe he had told them. Regardless, he knew Dylan wouldn't react well to Hannah's tone. He could already see her revving up to say something she shouldn't and decided he had better jump in before that happened. They didn't know who was a friend and who wasn't. Best not to alienate anyone yet.

"Yes, of course. We're looking forward to talking to her."

Now Dylan glared at him, but at least she kept her mouth shut.

Traffic in London was as bad as New York. Connor had moved from the Big Apple to Atlanta a year ago, and although there were things he missed about the city, the relentless crush of cars was not one of them.

They inched their way along under a dark and cloudy sky toward the Keaton & Ivy Hotel, located on the opposite end of the city.

"So, you're here to investigate what happened to Chris, huh?" Hannah asked, glancing in the rearview mirror at Connor as she spoke. She had stacks of binders and boxes of various sizes in the front passenger seat—presumably movie related—and had not offered to move them.

"Something like that," Connor said. "Have you heard anything about it?" He had checked the internet again for news when the plane landed. There hadn't been any. That didn't mean the police hadn't been by to give the director and her team an update.

Hannah shook her head. "I hope they get this sorted out soon, though. Chris was my mate from way back. He got me this job. I can't believe this happened."

The woman had seemed a little edgy—morose, even—from the moment they had met. At first, Connor had chalked it up to the tragedy in general. Anyone who lost a coworker that way would be upset. But Chris was more than that to Hannah, it turned out. He was a friend. That would no doubt be devastating.

"How long have you known him?" Dylan said.

"Since secondary school."

"When?"

"That's 'high school' to you."

"Long time," Connor responded.

Hannah shot him a look in the rearview mirror again. "That's what I said."

Connor could feel her annoyance. He waited a beat to let it pass. Then, to lighten the mood: "So, did you always want to be in the movie business?"

"Me? No. I couldn't care less about all that. I hardly ever even go to the pictures."

"Then why did Chris get you the job on set?"

Hannah did not answer. She followed the traffic onto Tower Bridge, where two massive Victorian towers rose up from the River Thames, one on each side of the drawbridge. The traffic light in front of the closest tower turned red. Hannah, along with everyone else, came to a stop.

"Shit," she said as she looked out onto the water. A large boat was coming their way.

The drawbridge rose slowly.

Hannah sighed. "We're going to be here for a minute." Then, after another long pause, she said, "I was in rehab not too long ago. Doesn't matter why. At any rate, when I got out, Chris said he'd help me get back on my feet. So he got me this job. Sometimes it feels like I'm a glorified gofer. Maybe I am." She shrugged. "It's a job, and I appreciated him doing it for me. That's just the kind of guy he was." This time, when she made eye contact with Connor, she actually turned around to do it. "Happy?"

Connor nodded, and Hannah turned back around in her seat and stared out at the river again.

Dylan mouthed *Wow* in his direction.

Connor decided perhaps he should keep his mouth shut until they reached the hotel. He hadn't meant for the conversation to be much more than idle chit-chat. But this edgy, morose woman was in no mood for conversation of any sort. Perhaps if his friend had just died, he reasoned, he wouldn't be, either.

The drawbridge came down, and traffic started to move. They were clear on the other side of London, where the city's iconic architecture had given way to uninspired brick tenements, before anyone spoke again. This time it was Hannah who started the conversation.

"Frankly, I'm kind of surprised you're here."

"Why's that?" Dylan asked.

"Well, right now, all we know is Chris is dead, right? If it turns out someone killed him, don't you think this is a job that would be better left to the police?"

There it was. Whether or not the death was natural, that was the real reason for her annoyance. They were PIs, coming into an active investigation. Some people didn't like that. They worried the PIs would make it harder for the police to do their job by scaring off witnesses the police had yet to talk to or tampering with evidence the police had yet to find, only to come up empty-handed when they were done.

No doubt, there were PIs out there who did just that, but Connor and Dylan were not among them.

Connor tried to assuage Hannah's concerns, but nothing he said seemed to have much impact. Eventually, she raised a hand in the air as if to silence him and said, "Look, just forget it, all right? I shouldn't have said anything."

She turned a corner. "Hotel's right up there." Then she pointed to her right. "Most of the filming is happening in that bank. You probably know we're on hold until someone shows up to replace Chris, but if you're looking for anybody who's not in the hotel, odds are still good they'll be over there. At least if it's anyone on the crew. With the actors—who knows?"

Connor turned to look at the bank. It was a beautiful stone building with half a dozen cement steps leading from the sidewalk to the double doors that marked the entrance. In the parking lot surrounding it were large white trailers emblematic of a film set.

CHAPTER 10

THE HOTEL WAS AN unassuming brick building from the outside. Painted blue with white trim. Inside, it was an homage to 1920s decadence, with a working fireplace in the lobby, a bar to one side, and plenty of places to lounge.

The clerk at the front desk gave Connor and Dylan their keys, and a bellhop disappeared with their luggage.

"He'll run it up in the lift to your rooms for you," Hannah explained. She had stayed with them the whole time to ensure the process went smoothly.

Aside from a couple of guys at the bar, there were no other guests within sight.

"Just take a seat somewhere over there," Hannah continued, waving in the general direction of the lobby. "Maria will be down in a minute." Then she started toward the elevator.

"How will we know her when we see her?" Dylan asked.

"She'll know you," Hannah called back. "We have the whole hotel to ourselves. You'll stick out like a fly on a wedding cake." She pressed the button for the elevator and the doors opened immediately.

Once they were alone, Connor looked around the room. "How about there?" he said, pointing to a group of plush leather chairs in one corner.

"As good as anywhere else, I suppose," Dylan said.

They were barely seated a full minute before the elevator doors opened again and, this time, another woman stepped out. She had long blonde hair that appeared to be haphazardly parted to one side and was wearing a red wool sweater and a pair of blue jeans. She nodded at Connor and Dylan, then walked over to the bar where the men were sitting.

"Think that's her?" Dylan asked.

"I guess we'll find out in a minute," Connor said.

The woman gestured to the bartender. Then she exchanged some words with the two men. Connor had barely given them a thought the first time he'd seen them. Now that he knew everyone here worked on the film, he took a closer look.

One of the men had a gray beard and was wearing a Grateful Dead tee shirt; probably in his fifties, if Connor were to guess. The other was twenty years younger (and at least as many pounds lighter).

The bartender handed the woman a drink. The woman turned and said something to the men, and the one in the Grateful Dead tee shirt responded with a casual salute. Then, as she crossed the lobby, they turned back toward the bar.

She took a seat in one of the chairs facing Connor and Dylan, placed her drink on the table between them.

It's always five o'clock somewhere, Connor thought, looking at the ice cubes bobbing in the dark liquid. Then again, that "somewhere" was here. No matter what time his internal clock told him it was, the one on the wall read eight p.m., late enough for a drink regardless of who you were.

In this case, the "who" was indeed Maria Alexander. There was no doubt about that, since she introduced herself as soon as she sat down.

"So, you're here about Chris, huh?"

"That's correct," Connor said.

"I know Hannah probably did not give you the warmest welcome. She's been pretty upset since it happened. We all have, but she has history with him, you know? Anyway, I, for one, am glad you're here. And I'm the only one who counts."

"Good to hear," Dylan said.

"What do you think happened?" Connor asked.

Maria took a sip from her drink. "So far, the police aren't telling us anything. At first, I thought it was just an accident. But they still haven't issued an official cause of death, so now I'm starting to wonder. At least with you here, we won't all be stuck in the dark."

"Hudson told me a thing like this could really screw up your film."

"I don't know. Maybe."

"You don't know?" Dylan asked.

"This is my first time working on a film of this size. I have no idea what this could mean for the movie. If Hudson says it could really screw it up, he probably knows what he's talking about. Worst part is—none of this had to happen."

"What do you mean?" Connor asked.

"Hudson didn't tell you?"

Connor leaned in. "Tell us what?"

"Chris was one of a dozen actors Hudson and I were considering for the role of Habersham. Neither of us were particularly keen on him— mostly because there were rumors he might retire from acting soon, and Hudson and I both thought this film could be the beginning of a franchise if it did well. Then, all of a sudden, Hudson did a complete one-eighty. Chris was no longer simply an actor to consider—he was the man for the role. I tried to reason with him, but there was no changing his mind. At some point he told me flat out that without

Chris, there'd be no movie."

"I bet you didn't like that," Dylan said.

Maria sighed. "This is the real world. You don't always get what you want. Hudson was the money man. If he wanted Chris, we were getting Chris. I just don't understand why he changed his mind. Not that it matters now, I guess."

She finished her drink and, leaving the glass on the table, stood up. "I'll be having breakfast with several key members from the cast and crew tomorrow morning. Stop by if you can. I'm sure they'd love to meet you. It will be right back there behind the bar." She pulled a card from her pocket and handed it over. "Stay in touch, all right? I think we'd all like to know what happened as soon as possible."

"Wait," Connor said, standing as well. "Before you go, can you tell us the name of the bar Chris was at when it happened?"

Maria pursed her lips. Her brow furrowed. Then she shook her head. "No. I'm sorry. I can't. Not for sure. Hannah might be able to, though."

Dylan rolled her eyes.

"I know," Maria said. "But if she can help you, she'll do it." She pulled her cell phone out of the same pocket she'd had her card in. "Let me get you her number."

CHAPTER 11

HANNAH TOLD CONNOR CHRIS had gone to the Crown. "It's a dingy little bar. Nothing you'd find if you didn't already know it was there."

"Do you know who he was meeting?"

"Some friends from his theater days, I think. That's about all I know. Sorry, I can't help you there."

Connor thanked her and hung up. He and Dylan were once again alone in the lobby. "You feel like going to a bar tonight?"

"Why not? We might as well get started right away."

Connor used his phone to summon an Uber, then he and Dylan went outside to wait for the driver. The bank was in full view from where they were standing. Connor wondered briefly if anyone was inside those trailers right now before turning his attention to more pressing matters.

"Did you hear what Maria said about Hudson insisting they hire Chris?" He asked the question without looking at Dylan, and she responded without looking at him.

"What are you thinking?"

"I don't know yet. It feels weird, doesn't it?"

Dylan nodded. "Yeah, it does."

"Something about this whole thing feels weird."

This time, Dylan did look at Connor. "What do you think we should do about it?"

"For now, nothing, I guess. Let's just see what we can find out at the bar, and we'll go from there. But it doesn't smell right to me. First, Hudson doesn't want to use Chris. Then he insists on it. Then Chris dies. Then Hudson sends us out here to investigate the death, as if the police aren't going to reach the same conclusion we will. It's almost as if he knows something."

A blue Honda Civic pulled up to the curb. The driver rolled down her window. She was a middle-aged woman with an accent so thick Connor could barely understand her. "Ya Connor?"

"Yeah."

"I'm rue ber."

"What?"

"Ya deaf? I'm rue ber. Come on, let's go."

Finally, Connor figured out what she was saying: *I'm your Uber.* By concentrating, he could also understand what she said next: "You just going to stand there? You're not the only ride I got tonight. Get in."

"Let's just take it one step at a time," Dylan said to Connor.

Then they both climbed into the back seat.

The bar was indeed dingy and small. And it was indeed located in a part of town Connor would not have stumbled upon on his own. Even the Uber driver didn't know the bar was here. But a lot of other people did. The place was packed—every table full, every stool at the bar taken.

"Guess it's standing room only," Dylan said as they squeezed their way inside.

A small group of people within earshot—huddled close together and all holding beers—shot them a look. Connor wasn't sure what it meant, but it made him uneasy.

"Where should we start?" she asked.

"Let's try the bartender."

Dylan gestured for Connor to lead the way, and he did, pushing a path through the crowd. The bartender was busy with a swarm of patrons who had gotten there before them. It took several minutes to get his attention. Dylan slipped around Connor and flashed a smile. "Hiya."

At first, Connor was annoyed. He already had his questions lined up. Once he understood what she was doing, however, he was glad she had pushed her way in. The guy looked like he was more muscles than brains. She'd get further with him than he ever would.

The bartender smiled back. "Where are you from?"

"Not here."

"What can I get you, girl-from-not-here?"

She pointed to the tap in front of her. "I'll take one of those." The handle read *Magic Rock*. Connor had never heard of the brand. It was most likely a micro-brewery of some sort. Of course, he knew that wasn't why Dylan had ordered it. If he was a betting man, he'd wager she didn't know the brand either. She had ordered it because it would keep the bartender's feet planted right where they were for a few seconds longer. Sometimes, that was all it took.

"You normally here?" she asked, while he filled a glass.

"Most nights. What are you doing in London?"

"Working on a movie," Dylan said casually.

The bartender slowed his pour. His smile fell away. "What movie?"

"Were you here last Tuesday?"

The bartender placed the glass down in front of Dylan hard enough for beer to slosh over the rim, soaking his fingers, which he then wiped with a towel. "That'll be four pounds. I suggest you drink it and get out of here."

"Wait, wait, wait," Connor said, finally joining the conversation. "We're just trying to find out what really happened to Chris. Don't you want to help us with that?"

"You want to know what happened to him? I'll tell you what happened to him. He died in that bathroom right over there. That good enough for you, you fucking vulture? Now pay up and get the hell out of here."

After Connor's parents had been abducted years earlier, a string of reporters had made their way up to the house and hounded him for information. He suspected something similar had happened here. Maybe not reporters, since there hadn't been a story published on Chris's death yet. But looky-loos, perhaps. Friends of friends who had heard about what happened from someone who had been at the bar. If that was the case, reporters were bound to get hold of the story soon, no matter how much Hudson wanted to keep it under wraps. And when they started traipsing their way in here, the bartender would undoubtedly get more hostile than he already was. Connor and Dylan needed to make this trip count.

"It's not what you think," Connor said, lowering his voice. "We're private investigators." He flashed his PI license.

That seemed to calm the bartender down a little. "Who sent you?"

"Hudson Davis," Dylan said. When she didn't get a reaction, she huffed, then added, "The guy producing the film. He's responsible for *Night Air* . . ." No response. "*Out With a Bang? Lost in the Underworld?*" To Connor: "It's like I'm the only one who knows who he is."

Instead of responding, Connor directed his attention to the bartender. "Can you please help us?"

The bartender sighed, but he didn't tell them to fuck off, and Connor took that as a good sign. The man looked down the bar at all the patrons clamoring for his attention, waited a beat, then shouted, "I'll be with you in a minute!" He turned back to Connor. "So you don't think it was natural, huh?"

"We don't know."

"I thought it might be a drug overdose, myself."

"What makes you think that?"

"Celebrities—you know how they are."

Connor shrugged. "Maybe."

"Well, if it wasn't natural, we might as well piss the truth down the drain if we leave this in the hands of those Scotland Yard fuckers." The bartender held out his hand. "Name's Ed."

Connor shook it and introduced himself and Dylan in response.

"All right, what do you need to know?"

"Anything you can tell us," Connor said, relieved Ed was willing to help.

"I don't know much. He was sitting with some friends over there." Ed nodded to indicate a nearby table. "Then, some point, he just got up, went to the bathroom, and never came back out."

"Any unusual behavior? Was he in and out of the bathroom a lot that evening? Anything like that?"

"Couldn't say. You see how this place is. I noticed him because—you know, he's Chris Miller. But the bar was packed. Just like this. It's not like I was sitting there watching him the whole time."

"What about the people he was with?" Dylan asked. "You know who they were?"

Ed shook his head. "Can't say I do." Then he snapped his fingers. "One of them was buying drinks before Chris showed up. As you might imagine, Chris started paying after that, being a big-shot Hollywood star and all. Anyway . . . hold on." He disappeared through a door at the back of the bar and was gone so long Connor began to wonder if he was ever coming back.

When he did, he had a slip of paper in one hand and did not look particularly happy. "The first guy opened a tab. When you do that, we put a credit card on file. Scan it through the system. Link the tab to a name. It's all very fancy. Way over the top, if you ask me. I always thought writing the drinks down on a slip of paper worked just fine. Then again, I don't own the place."

"You have a name?" Dylan asked.

He shook his head. "All that razzmatazz isn't going to help you here." He placed the slip of paper down on the bar. It was crinkled and stained, with a list of drinks digitally printed on it. Ed directed their attention to the top of the paper, and it became immediately clear what he wanted to show them. The name "Steve" was visible in the top left corner. Large print. Dark ink. It was easy to make out. Unfortunately, the last name, which started with a "Th" was not. The ink had been smudged beyond the point of readability.

"Someone put a drink down on it," Ed explained. Then he folded up the paper, put it in his pocket. "Sorry I can't help you."

When the bartender had first disappeared through the door behind the bar, Connor had been certain he was going to come back with news that would push their investigation forward. But Steve was a common name. Even knowing the last name started with a "Th" might not be enough to get them to a real person.

Then Connor had an idea. Hannah had told Connor Chris was meeting people from his "theater days." That had to be from when he was just starting out. Maybe if they could locate the playbooks from the shows Chris was in all those years ago . . .

Yeah, right.

Or maybe they could talk to the staff at the theater. Maybe somebody there would remember him.

It all seemed like a long shot. The odds of finding anything online seemed just as slim. If there had even been a website advertising any of the shows back then, it had surely long since been taken down or gobbled up by the internet, buried under all the bits and bytes of data getting pushed out every day.

There might be another way to find out the man's name, though. And it might get them more than just that.

"Do you have any regulars?" Connor asked.

"Got a few," Ed said. "You see the guy with the red ball cap over there?"

"Yeah."

"He's one. And that guy in the blue shirt."

Connor nodded.

"He's one, too."

In all, Ed pointed out roughly a dozen individuals.

"You thinking one of them might know who Chris was with?" Dylan asked Connor after Ed had stepped away to help another customer.

"Maybe."

Dylan shrugged. "Let's find out."

"You work the left side of the room, I'll work the right," Connor said. "We'll compare notes when we're done."

Dylan nodded and stepped into the crowd, leaving the glass of Magic Rock where it was. Connor pushed his way toward the small group of men and women with whom he had made eye contact on his way in. That group, Ed had indicated, was composed of more regulars than any other and was here more often. "Excuse me," he said once he got close. No response. He wasn't sure if they didn't hear him or were simply ignoring him. He tried again, louder. "Excuse me!"

This time, they stopped talking. A man with a crew cut and his back to Connor turned around. "What do you want, mate?" He was wearing a leather jacket zipped halfway up, a white tee shirt, and a pair of blue jeans that were way too tight. Dylan might have told him he looked like he had stepped right out of 1985 if she was around.

Connor suspected most people wouldn't dare speak to him that way and wondered if he might have been better served starting with someone else. But since he had already gotten their attention, he asked, "Were any of you here Tuesday night?"

The man with the crew cut looked at his friends, then back at Connor. "Who's asking?"

Connor had never needed to show anyone his PI license before tonight, but like with the bartender, he got the feeling simply saying he was a private investigator would not be enough. He pulled out his wallet and flipped it open.

The man leaned in uncomfortably close to read it. "You're a good long way out of your district, aren't you? What interest do you have in a dead Brit?"

"So you were here."

"What about it?"

"Chris was sitting with a guy named Steve. Unfortunately, the bartender can't tell us his last name. I was wondering if—"

"Listen," the man said as he pushed his finger into Connor's chest. "I'm not talking to you." He gestured to his friends. "They're not talking to you." He looked around the bar. "In fact, I bet you won't find one person in this place who's interested in talking to you. So why don't you piss off?"

Connor stood his ground, trying to ignore the hammering in his chest. On the far end of the group, there was a young woman clutching her beer in front of her chest with both hands, and something about the way she was looking at him suggested she might be willing to talk. Still, she wasn't likely to do it as long as the man with the crew cut was nearby. The best thing Connor could do was move on to another patron who might be more accommodating.

"I'm sorry for bothering you," Connor said as he took a step back.

The man with the crew cut sneered at him, then turned away. The group's conversation resumed instantly. It was almost as if Connor had been an apparition, forgotten as soon as he was gone. Forgotten by everyone except for the one woman clutching her beer to her chest, that was. Since there was no getting to her right now, Connor sank deeper into the crowd, in search of someone who would actually speak to him.

Connor tried to approach several other people with no more success. Most said flat out they hadn't been there Tuesday night. All of them looked annoyed.

When he and Dylan had finished working their way through the regulars, they met back at the bar.

"Any luck?" he asked.

"No. You?"

Connor shook his head.

"Wonder if that has anything to do with it?" Dylan asked, pointing toward a sign on the back wall that read "Locals Only."

Connor had not noticed it when they came in. Even if he had, he wouldn't have taken it seriously. But who knew? Maybe Dylan was right.

Then a voice from behind said, "Thompson."

Connor and Dylan turned around. The woman Connor had seen clutching the beer to her chest earlier was standing barely two feet away from them. She was wearing a plain blue dress that hid her figure and had a flat, round face. Her stringy hair had been parted down the middle and hung limply around her cheeks.

"His name is Steve Thompson."

Instinctively, Connor glanced toward the corner of the room where she had been standing earlier. He couldn't imagine Crew Cut would be too happy about her coming over to talk to them. But the crowd had shifted, and Connor couldn't see Crew Cut and his friends anymore.

"You're sure?"

"I'm sure. He and I—we used to be . . . a thing." Finally, she lifted the beer from her chest to her lips and took a small sip.

"You were here?" Dylan said.

The woman nodded.

"How many people were at the table?"

"Three, I think." She looked away, trying to remember. "Yeah. Three. There was Steve and one other guy I don't know. Plus a girl. Well, four if you count Chris."

"Do you know where we can find Steve?" Connor said.

"Sure I do. He has a place over on Hillcrest Way. It's walking distance from here. Thirty-two Hillcrest. Just head out the door and go right. You shouldn't have any trouble finding the street."

Connor was about to ask how far away the place was when movement from the corner of his eye drew his attention. It was the bathroom door opening. In a place this busy, that shouldn't have meant anything. But he was on high alert and, it turned out, he had good reason to be. Because the movement that drew his attention wasn't just the bathroom door opening. It was Crew Cut stepping out of it.

So that was how the woman had managed to slip away from the group and come talk to them.

Crew Cut began moving back toward the corner of the room where Connor had encountered him. Then his face changed in some subtle way that was hard to identify from this distance. Still, Connor knew what it meant. Crew Cut had realized his group was short one person.

The man stopped, scanned the crowd. He was taller than most of the people by a good three inches, which made it easier for him to take the lay of the land from where he was.

No doubt, Crew Cut not only knew who was missing, he also likely knew about the woman's relationship with Steve, and more than likely suspected she had sought Connor out to talk to him.

If he spotted them together, things could get ugly.

"Thank you for your help," Connor said quickly. Then he told Dylan they had to go. It was too late. Crew Cut *had* spotted them . . . and was headed in their direction.

CHAPTER 12

"**W**E HAVE TO GO *right now*," Connor repeated, this time adding the last two words.

Dylan looked confused. "What's the rush? This woman clearly wants to talk to us." She turned back to the woman. "Excuse me, I didn't get your name."

Perhaps because of Connor's behavior, the woman had started to look around as well. And she must have caught a glimpse of Crew Cut coming their way, because she spun on her heel and slipped back into the crowd without answering Dylan's question.

When Connor had gotten his PI license, he had taken self-defense classes. Although they had served him well when he'd been confronted by Lance several days earlier, he wasn't eager to put them into practice again. A fight for fight's sake was pointless. Most people came out worse off than they went in, and rarely was there a clear winner.

He grabbed Dylan's wrist. "Trust me. Let's go."

If she was dead set on staying, she would have protested, pulled back, wrenched her arm free; she would have told Connor he could go if he wanted, but that she was staying right where she was.

However, she did none of those things, which Connor took to mean she understood the gravity of the situation.

Not that it did any good.

With Dylan at his heels, Connor pushed his way through a tightly packed group of patrons—and ran straight into Crew Cut.

"I told you, nobody wants you here," Crew Cut said.

"We're just leaving." Connor tried to step around him.

"Let's make sure of it," Crew Cut said. Then he grabbed Connor by the shirt and pulled him toward the door.

Behind him, Connor heard Dylan shout, "Hey! Meat head! What do you think you're doing?"

Connor thought of a dozen ways he could turn the tables on his attacker. He could twist around, sweep his legs out from under him, and knock him down. He could punch him in the larynx or the ear. He might even be able to lunge on top of him, knocking him off his feet. In every case, he was certain Crew Cut would let go. But where would it go from there? Crew Cut would be enraged. A fight to break free might turn into a fight to stay out of the hospital. What would be the point?

Besides, they were already at the door. Crew Cut swung it open and, with one good shove, Connor was suddenly outside, stumbling along the sidewalk as he tried to keep his balance. Dylan ran out after him and grabbed his arm to steady him.

"Go where you're wanted," Crew Cut said.

"You're an asshole," Dylan spat back.

He glared at her. "You're lucky you're a woman."

"Too afraid to take on a woman? What's the matter? You afraid I'll kick your ass?"

Connor could practically see the steam coming out of Crew Cut's ears. "Dylan. Let it go."

Without further comment, Crew Cut stepped back into the bar, slamming the door shut behind him.

"You all right?" Dylan asked Connor.

"I'm fine," he said, straightening up.

"What was all that about?"

"I have no idea. Some people are just jerks. Guess he didn't want us in his bar." After taking a moment to collect himself, he added, "You remember what that address was?"

"Thirty-two Hillcrest Way."

Connor nodded. "Right," he said to himself. "Steve Thompson."

"You thinking to go see him now?"

Connor pulled out his phone. It was just after nine p.m. He opened the Maps application and requested walking directions. "The address is ten minutes from here. I think we should."

In a normal investigation, Connor might have waited until morning. Most people were more accommodating if you didn't knock on their door late at night. But someone had died—someone famous— and, as Connor had told himself on several occasions already, it was only a matter of time until the press got ahold of the news. They needed to make as much progress as they could before that happened. Regardless of what Hudson wanted, Connor knew that once the press got their hands on the story, the investigation would become exponentially more difficult, and not just when it came to questioning the obvious targets, like the bartender. Steve would be hounded as well, likely making him just as uncooperative.

They followed the directions down a two-lane road lined with small storefronts selling all sorts of goods. There was a dry cleaner, a mini market, a sub shop. Most were closed at this hour, and not a lot of people were on the street.

"I feel like this case is getting stranger by the minute," Connor said.

"What do you mean?"

"First we find out about Hudson—that about-face he did on hiring

Chris. Then there's that guy who just threw us out of the bar."

"I thought you said you didn't know what that was about."

Connor shrugged. "I don't. Not for certain. While you were over on the other side of the room, I talked to him and the group of people he was with. That's why that woman approached us with Steve's name. She was with him. I could tell she wanted to say something earlier, but she didn't want to do it in front of him."

"So he's like their ringleader or something."

"Something like that. At first, I thought he didn't want us around because of that whole 'Locals Only' thing. Maybe he just didn't want anybody talking to us about Chris."

Dylan shoved her hands into pockets, presumably to keep them warm. They walked a while in silence. "You think he was involved?"

"I don't know, but I think we'd better operate on the assumption that Chris's death wasn't natural or even self-inflicted. At least until we know otherwise."

They turned onto a street lined with narrow shotgun houses, each sitting on a plot of land not much wider than the house itself. Connor followed the numbers on the mailboxes until they found the one they were looking for.

The yard—more weeds than grass—was no bigger than a postage stamp and surrounded by a picket fence that had not aged well. Unlike most of the houses on this street, the porch light was out. The blinds were half-closed. Were it not for the soft glow of a lamp somewhere deep in the back of the house, Connor might have thought Steve was away.

He still might be.

Connor decided to knock. When he did, the lamp went out, plunging the house entirely into darkness.

"Did you see that?" he asked Dylan.

She nodded.

Connor knocked again. Two minutes passed, and still, whoever had turned off that light had not come to the door.

"You're right," Dylan said. "I don't know what's going on here, but it's strange, for sure."

CHAPTER 13

SOME MIGHT CALL THE Garder Museum creepy at night, with its darkened, cavernous galleries and the eyes of so many paintings following you as you crossed underneath the dim glow of the security lighting. Lance would have called it magical.

He and his partner, Ned Holland, took turns patrolling the massive three-story building every hour. Lance enjoyed these trips around each floor. It was like stepping back in time, traveling first through the Renaissance, then the neoclassical period, and finally ending on the third floor, among the artists of today.

Sometimes, with his flashlight aimed at a particular painting, he could almost believe he was there, standing among the flowers and fields so prevalent in the paintings of old, or floating through the endless swirling colors in the paintings of new. Especially if he blurred his vision a little. When he did that, the features even seemed to move. Rain would shimmer on streets. A woman's smile would tick up as if beckoning him toward her. A breeze would push an umbrella to and fro.

Sometimes on these patrols he would linger longer than he should, and afterwards Ned—a short, stocky man who was as wide as he was tall— would ask what had taken him so long. Lance always responded by saying it hadn't been as long as it seemed.

Most nights, their conversation revolved around Ned's troubled home life. His teenage daughter was failing two of her classes, and, even worse, his wife was cheating on him—he was sure of it.

"Lots of people cheat," Lance had said the first time Ned mentioned it. He had been thinking about a particular memory that he preferred not to discuss.

"Sure. Sure they do. But not my wife. What am I going to do?"

Lance didn't have a good answer to that. In fact, he didn't have any opinion on it at all. Nobody had ever cheated on him, because he had never been in a relationship long enough for anyone to cheat.

Tonight, Ned did not mention his cheating wife or his failing daughter. He seemed fixated on Lance's injuries. Perhaps, Lance figured, because it made his own problems seem smaller.

They were seated behind a long mahogany desk with monitors mounted to the top of it, midway between Lance's last patrol and Ned's next one. So far, Ned had only asked about the broken arm, to which Lance had simply replied, "It was an accident."

But Ned kept looking at it—it, and the bruises on Lance's face—and Lance finally decided he might as well tell Ned the truth. After all, Ned was as close to a friend as Lance had ever had. And sitting here, in this dark space, it almost felt like they were the only two men in the world, as if any story he told Ned could travel no further because there was nowhere for it to go.

Lance scanned the monitors one last time for trouble before starting his story. There were no signs of any. There never were.

"All right," he said. "You want to know what really happened?"

"I tell you about my wife, my daughter. So, yeah. I want to know. That's how this works. I tell you stuff. You tell me stuff. So, out with it. What happened? Bet the other guy got it worse than you did, didn't he?"

"Not quite." Then Lance told Ned about the night Jax came to his house and broke his arm with a baseball bat.

The one part he left out was that he had been stalking Jax for a long time before that. So it wasn't surprising when Ned asked the following questions: "Jax? You mean the actor? What would he be doing at your apartment? And what would you be doing answering the door with a baseball bat, anyway?"

"Jax isn't as nice as he pretends to be in the movies. He and I have . . . history."

"You two? What sort of history could you have?"

Lance shot an angry glare in Ned's direction. It was a knee-jerk response to the memory of the history that he and Jax shared—the reason he was obsessed with Jax to begin with, the reason he was intent on ruining his life. No, not just ruining his life. Not anymore. Not after the broken arm. Now it had to be much more than that.

"I wanted to be an actor," Lance said after taking a sip from the bottle of water on the desk in front of him.

"No shit? I guess under all those bruises and that hippie hair of yours, you might have the look for it. If you cleaned yourself up a little bit."

"Yeah, well, you're not the only one who thinks so." Lance had already told Ned he used to live in Los Angeles and about the broken leg that had put an end to his dreams of being a professional runner. He hadn't mentioned, however, the drugs and alcohol he had started consuming following the injury. (Ned had learned about those thanks to Lance's recent stay in rehab.) He also hadn't mentioned that after his dreams of running were squashed, he had decided to seek fame and fortune as an actor instead.

He had scored some cheap headshots from a friend studying photography at UCLA and landed an agent because, as he was told, he had "a look." More specifically, the agent said, "Some of those sharp angles on your face might not come across well in person, but the camera sure loves them."

Then, finally, the day came. He hadn't landed as much as a commercial so far. Nonetheless, his agent phoned to tell him he was one of two people being called back for a lead role in a major motion picture. "I told you you had a look," the agent said before he hung up. "It might not sell cereal, but it will get people in seats."

True to form, Lance had celebrated that night with a bottle of vodka and an assortment of pills.

"I was a pro," he said to Ned. "You saw me before I went into rehab. I always came in, did my job. You'd never know. It was just the same on that day. I was fresh as a daisy. That's when Jax and I met. It was him and me at that callback. Neither of us was anybody then. And you know what he did?"

Ned's only response was to pull a box of toothpicks out of a drawer and start working one of them between his teeth, but Lance could tell he had his attention.

"He started screwing with me. They had us read some scenes together as Rick and Tom. You remember? The two main leads in that movie he was in back then?"

Ned looked confused.

"*Descendant.*"

Then Ned nodded to indicate he remembered the film.

"Sometimes I was Rick and sometimes I was Tom. But Jax—he kept feeding me lines that weren't in the script, throwing me off my game. I couldn't understand it. The casting agents didn't bother to stop and correct him or anything. If *I* tried to improvise, though, it was an immediate 'Cut' and 'Try it again' and 'Stick to the script, will ya?'"

Lance leaned forward, resting the elbow of his one good arm on his knee and looking straight at Ned. "I'm not good at improvising like that. I got flustered. Jax knew what he was doing, too. He was trying to knock me off my game. I could see it on his face. You obviously know how it turned out.

"If that had been all there was, it might have been okay. I could have lived with that. In that kind of industry, you know, you don't always get the role. Later, I figured out he must have connections. That whole thing was just a show. They just brought me in to screw with me. They weren't ever going to cast me. And you know how I know he has connections?" Lance could feel himself getting worked up. "Because right after that, my agent dropped me and nobody in the industry wanted anything to do with me anymore. I was like a pariah.

"I wasn't going to put up with it, you hear me?" Lance slammed his fist down on the desk hard enough to shake his water bottle. "I wasn't going to put up with it!"

Ned slowly lowered the toothpick. He looked alarmed.

Lance took a deep breath to calm himself down. "He came back to my apartment the other day just to rub it in my face again. How he was a big success and I was nothing."

"You mean all these years later, he came to Atlanta just to do that to you?"

"He lives here now." As soon as Lance said that, he realized he shouldn't have.

"Really? That's a hell of a coincidence. Both of you moving to Atlanta like that."

It was not a coincidence, of course. Lance had followed Jax here, looking for revenge. But like so many other parts of the story he had excluded, he had left this one out, too.

CHAPTER 14

SINCE THEY COULDN'T STAND around outside Steve's house for too long without looking like creepers, Connor and Dylan returned to the hotel. Their rooms were side by side on the third floor, each a little different from the other, with adjoining doors that could be opened to extend the space for families that wanted to give their kids privacy but still keep them close.

Connor's was larger, with a fireplace that had been bricked over and a pair of antique chairs parked on opposite sides of an equally old table.

Dylan opened the adjoining doors so they could pass back and forth between the rooms without having to go into the hall. Then she got her computer while Connor got his and the two set up camp at Connor's table.

They had decided they needed to find out more about Steve Thompson. Per usual, Connor started his search on the various social media platforms while Dylan dove into the dark web.

It didn't take long for Connor to find out Steve was married with one child and working in the administration office at the University of London. The man posted so many pictures, his life was practically an open book.

"That's not the sort of guy you'd think would hide out in his house, is it?"

"No," Dylan said, still intensely focused on her own work.

"Especially with a wife and kid. If I was his wife, I wouldn't stand for it. Can you imagine hiding out in the dark with your baby like that?"

Connor browsed through some more of the pictures. Steve had been easy to identify because he showed up in more of them than anyone else but the baby. In each one, the man looked happy.

"Don't forget," Dylan said, "those pictures you see online are curated to be the best of the best. That's not what his life is actually like."

Connor knew this, and said as much with a simple, "Of course." Then he added, "Still . . ." and let his doubt hang out there.

Dylan finally looked away from the screen. "Well, whatever the hell he's gotten himself into, I'd tell him that was his problem. I'd take the child and get out of there."

Connor scrolled down and saw a picture of Steve and his small family standing in front of a house that was not the one they had visited tonight. It could have been anybody's house, but Connor had a feeling it was theirs, and, with that, he had a new theory. "Maybe that wasn't him at all in that house tonight. Maybe he was renting that place. Or maybe he owned it at one time and had since sold it. We never found out how long ago Steve was dating that woman, but it was long enough for him to find somebody else, get married, and have a child."

Dylan had already returned her attention to the computer when he said, "Could you find out if he actually owns the place?"

"That's exactly what I'm doing."

While Connor waited, he thought about Hudson. If they were going to assume Chris had been killed, they had to consider everyone a suspect. Even the person who'd hired them.

Connor already had doubts that Hudson had hired them for the reasons he claimed. What Connor hadn't considered was that Hudson might have had something to do with Chris's death. Maybe he figured if Connor and Dylan found anything, the police would find it, too, and he was hoping any news he got from Connor would help him stay one step ahead of them.

Connor wasn't sure how much he bought into that theory, but he couldn't entirely dismiss it, either. He needed to find out why Hudson had changed his mind when casting the role. But he couldn't just call up the producer and ask. He'd never get a straight answer.

So how would he find out?

Connor was still stuck on that question when Dylan said, "He owns the place. Had it for years now."

Shit. There went that theory.

"However, it's not the only one in his name," she continued. "He has another place with his wife."

"You have an address?"

She read it off to him, and Connor used Google Maps to get a look at the house. It was the same one he had seen in the photo on Instagram.

"I guess we've got two possibilities," he said. "First, that wasn't him in the house—"

"Or, second, his wife kicked him out of the other place," Dylan finished saying for him.

"Something like that."

"I guess we should go by there tomorrow and see what we can find out."

"I think we have to." Connor closed the lid on his laptop. "We have to find out why Hudson changed his mind about Chris, too."

"How are we going to do that?"

"I don't know."

"I don't suppose you want to call him and ask him, right?"

"I already considered that, and no."

Then they were silent for a moment. Connor could see Dylan's wheels turning. Finally, she said, "We could ask Olin to go talk to him."

"How would that be any better?"

Dylan got a sly smile and, without answering, dialed Olin's number. "Looks like you're going to be a part of this investigation," she said when he answered. Then she filled him in on her idea. Olin didn't like it, but she pushed him until he agreed. When she got off the phone, she said to Connor, "What do you think?"

Connor frowned. "It's probably the best chance we've got."

Then Dylan's eyes shot toward the door. "What's that?"

"What?"

Dylan pointed toward the crack underneath the door. Connor could see two shadows that might be feet, like someone was standing outside listening to them.

CHAPTER 15

DYLAN RAISED A FINGER to her lips, motioning for Connor to be quiet. She crept to the door, looked out the peephole, then signaled for Connor to come over.

At her direction, he also looked out the peephole. There was indeed someone there. The man had his head turned to the side and his ear close to the door. Connor was unable to see his face. He gestured to Dylan: *What do you want to do?*

Dylan quietly turned the lock.

Connor waved his hands in front of him and shook his head. Maybe confronting this man was the best course of action, but he wanted time to think. Too late. Dylan swung the door open.

The man outside was an inch or two shorter than Connor, with curly black hair that looked like it hadn't seen a brush in a while. He was wearing a blue polo shirt and tan slacks. His head whipped around fast—first, in their direction and then down the hall as he turned to run.

"After him!" Dylan shouted, as she, too, started moving.

Connor cursed and followed.

The man pushed through a door that led to the stairs, and they did the same. The hallway was carpeted; the stairs were not. Their footsteps echoed around them in a cacophony of thumps and squeaks as rubber-soled shoes hit and slid along tile.

The man had a good lead, and he was fast, reckless even—jumping the steps three and four at a time, leaping from one landing to the next, and then, when he was near the bottom, vaulting over the railing.

He sprinted through a door that led into the lobby. Connor and Dylan followed seconds later, nearly slammed straight into Hannah. She was carrying a bottle of beer in each hand and, near as Connor could tell, had been heading for the elevator. She jumped back, startled, as Connor and Dylan came to an abrupt stop.

The man they had been chasing was nowhere to be seen.

"Did you see anyone come out this way?" Dylan said, pointing back at the door to the stairwell.

Hannah, who seemed like she was still collecting herself, paused, then quickly nodded.

"Where did he go?"

She cocked her head toward the main entrance. "That way."

Dylan started running again, and Connor, panting, took off after her. Without being hampered by the confined space of a hallway or a stairwell, she moved even faster than she had before. Connor had to struggle to keep up. However, he no longer doubted whether confronting this stranger was the right course of action. This man clearly knew something. If they could catch up with him, they might be able to put an end to their investigation tonight.

The sliding glass doors parted.

Connor and Dylan burst onto the sidewalk and then stopped to look around, searching for their target. The area was deserted. Streetlamps shone down on empty roads. To the left, there was a four-way stop with no cars at it. To the right, there was the bank and the movie trailers in the parking lot. At first, it seemed like the man they had been chasing wasn't there, either.

Then Connor saw a figure move from shadow to light, stepping carefully between two trailers. The person was too far away to pick out any detail, but Connor was sure that had to be him. "There he is!" he said.

They raced across the street with Connor now in the lead, scrambled around the trailers, and saw their target cloaked in shadow only feet away. He looked back when he heard them approaching and, oddly, only then did he start to run.

When they grabbed him, Connor understood why.

Although he had only caught a glimpse of the man's face outside the hotel room, he had seen enough to know this wasn't him. This man's hair was straight, not curly; his shirt was a Queen tee, not a polo; and he was wearing jeans, not slacks.

The man cursed, twisted, tried to break free. He demanded to know what they were doing.

"That's not him," Connor told Dylan, as if it needed to be said. They had both already let go.

The man produced a switchblade from his pocket as he retreated several steps. "Stay back, you hear me? Stay the fuck back."

Connor and Dylan raised their hands in the air.

"I'm sorry," Connor said.

"I just came to have a look at the set. What's the matter with you?"

"We thought you were someone else."

The three of them stood in an uneasy standoff for several seconds. Connor watched the man's knife hand, worried he might come charging at them, blade out. The man eyed Connor and Dylan just as warily. Eventually, he took several more steps back and then turned to run.

Connor and Dylan lowered their hands, looked at each other.

"Remember you said we should assume Chris was killed until we know otherwise?"

"Yeah."

"I don't think we have to assume any longer."

Connor nodded in agreement. The simple fact was—no matter where the curly-haired man had gone, there wouldn't have been anybody skulking around outside their hotel room if Chris hadn't been murdered.

CHAPTER 16

CONNOR AWOKE TO HIS alarm at seven a.m. He was exhausted. Going to bed late hadn't been a problem because his internal clock was five hours behind. But getting up at seven (two a.m. Eastern, he groggily reminded himself) was no easy task. Especially since he hadn't slept well.

He must have spent half the night watching the crack underneath his door for those feet to return. At some point, he began to worry the man might be as good a lock pick as Dylan was, that he might sneak into Connor's room in the middle of the night and kill them both.

When morning came, he realized how crazy that sounded. Especially with the door chain in place. But in the middle of the night, with only the shadows for company, it had not seemed so unreasonable. At some point, he had even gotten up, taken one of the antique chairs from the table, and propped it under the door handle. It had been all he could do not to go into Dylan's room and do the same thing.

He moved the chair back to where it belonged now.

As he stood under the shower, hoping the warm water would work miracles, he ran through all the ways Chris might have died. At least, all the ones he could think of. The top three contenders were strangled, suffocated, or poisoned.

He clearly hadn't been stabbed or shot. Nor had he been beaten to death. Those would have been obvious to anyone who found him.

86

Connor pulled a wrinkled tee shirt out of his suitcase and slid it on right before Dylan knocked on the door that separated their rooms. Connor turned the lock, then the handle. Dylan pushed the door the rest of the way open and stepped inside. She looked far more refreshed than Connor felt. He wished he, too, had been able to nap on the plane.

"You look like shit," she said, using a pair of bobby pins to clip her hair back from her face.

"Thanks for noticing."

"You ready to go to Steve's?"

Connor took a seat at the small table by the fireplace and put on his shoes. "Before we go there, let's stop off in the restaurant to meet Maria." She had invited them for breakfast with key members from the cast and crew when they spoke in the lobby the night before. It seemed like an opportunity they should not pass up. The group was bound to have some stories about Chris, and every story they heard now might be something they could use later.

"I guess it won't hurt," Dylan said, clearly not sharing his optimism.

Connor stood up. "Maybe we can even find out a little something about the guy who was spying on us last night."

Dylan smiled. "Now you're talking."

They took the elevator to the lobby and circled around the bar to the restaurant behind it. Maria was already there, sitting at a long table with a dozen other people. He quickly scanned each of them and determined the person who had been outside his room was not among the diners.

When Maria spotted them, she swallowed a large bite of something and waved them over. "Connor! Dylan! Come here." She was already introducing them by the time they reached her. Then she gestured to each of the people around the table, rattling off a series of names and titles. The two names Connor caught were those he knew already: Laura Hackett, famous for playing tough, no-nonsense female leads; and Luke Cross, an equally big star in the action arena. Apparently, Chris wasn't the only household name starring in this movie. It really was meant to be a blockbuster.

There was also the cinematographer, the head of the FX department (who might have been named Marty), and somebody from wardrobe.

The rest faded into a blur of information Connor could not keep up with. He figured if anything important came up, he could sort out the associated names later.

"Get a plate and come join us," Maria said, referring to the buffet along the back wall.

Connor and Dylan did. As they moved past a wide assortment of dishes, Connor whispered, "Don't get starstruck." They needed to come across as professionals, especially now. He did not want a repeat performance of their meal with Hudson.

Dylan used a large spoon to scoop scrambled eggs onto her plate. "Oh, ye of little faith."

"I'm serious."

She cut her eyes toward him. He got the message: *We didn't know anybody was dead when we met Hudson.* Then, after stopping by the coffee dispenser long enough to fill a cup, she took her plate of bacon and eggs to the table. Connor followed with the same meal and a large cup of coffee.

Everyone had shuffled a little this way or that to make room for two additional chairs beside Maria. Connor and Dylan sat down.

"You're here investigating Chris's death, huh?" Laura said. She was far thinner in real life than she looked on film—practically a waif of a woman, wearing a long black dress that cut straight down between her breasts. Flawless makeup. Gold earrings. She looked like she was dressed for an evening out, not a breakfast with coworkers, and Connor suspected that might be for their benefit. If he was right, she was every bit as vain as the tabloids said she was.

"That's right," Connor said.

"Do you have any clues so far?"

"They just got here, Laura," Maria said.

"Sometimes, these people, you know, they already have an idea," Laura replied. She turned her attention back to Connor and Dylan. "So do you? Do you have an idea?"

"It's too soon for that," Connor said. "We prefer to let the evidence take us wherever it leads."

Laura's face fell with disappointment. Not in a way that made Connor think she truly cared whether the case was solved, though. Rather, it seemed like she was looking for gossip, a nugget of excitement she could retell to others to help her pass the time until they started shooting again.

"Whatever happened to him, it's sad," the overweight FX guy said. Marty, wasn't it? Yes, Connor decided, that was right.

Luke leaned forward so he could look straight at Marty. "What are you talking about? You were just saying last week you wished he wasn't working on this movie."

"That's just because he planned on retiring soon."

The woman from wardrobe shushed him.

Laura rolled her eyes. "It's an open secret, Meg," she said, and Connor made a mental note of that name, too.

Meg, however, did not seem satisfied with Laura's response until Maria chimed in: "It's fine. I already told them Chris was thinking about retiring."

"Well, I, for one, am glad he's gone," Luke said. "If he really did retire, he was going to gum up the works for sequels and everything else. They might have even had to retool the whole franchise, and then all of us would have been shown the door. I don't know about the rest of you, but I like my character. Better this than playing some two-dimensional asshole that spends most of his time shooting stuff up. At least now we can make this movie with someone who might stick around awhile." He sat back and folded his arms.

"Have you had a chance to do any work on the case yet?" Laura said, directing the conversation back toward Connor.

"A little," Connor said.

Suddenly everyone stopped talking and leaned in close to see what he would say next.

Connor wasn't sure how much he wanted to tell them. Dylan did not have that problem. "We went to the bar where he died," she said.

"Really?" Maria said. "Already?"

"Last night."

"And?" Laura asked.

Dylan shrugged. She seemed reluctant to tell them more than she already had. Connor wasn't sure she should have even told them that much.

"What do you know about him?" Connor asked the table. "Are any of you aware of problems he was having? Anything like that?"

The diners turned and looked at each other, then looked back at Connor. There were a few *Nos* and *Not that I can think of*s. Then Marty said, "He seemed upset about something the day he died, which wasn't like him. He was normally an upbeat guy. I didn't ask him what it was about. We weren't close or anything."

A couple of people nodded to indicate that they had noticed the same thing.

Dylan swallowed a bite of bacon and casually said, "Then I take it none of you would know anything about the guy hanging around outside our rooms last night?"

This got more reactions from around the table. These had a very different vibe than those Connor had witnessed only moments ago. Some people seemed shocked: "Oh my God!" Others were doubtful: "It was probably just somebody going to their room." And a few seemed to get exactly what Dylan was driving at: "If you think I had something to do with this, you are mistaken."

"That's not what she meant," Connor said.

"Oh, I know exactly what she meant," Laura replied, aiming her butter knife at Dylan. "If that's the kind of shitty investigation you're going to do—throwing out baseless accusations like that—we're better off waiting to see what the police come up with."

Connor could tell there was no way to bring this conversation back down to a civil tone, and since this would not be the last opportunity he had to talk to these people, he decided the best thing he could do for now was to get out of there.

He lifted the cloth napkin from his lap, wiped his mouth, and got to his feet. "I'm very sorry," he said. "We will let you all eat in peace. We have someone we need to talk to, anyway."

"Good," Luke snapped. "Good riddance. Hope you treat them better than you treated us."

"Come on, Dylan," Connor said.

She was still sitting, her fork in midair, not yet ready to go. She looked up at him, back at Luke, and huffed. She grabbed the last piece of bacon off her plate, shoved her chair back, and stepped away from the table.

"What was that about?" Connor hissed as they moved across the lobby.

"I wanted to see how they'd react."

"Did you get what you wanted?"

"You saw how heated Luke got, didn't you? That could be something."

Connor had been heated as well, but his temper dissolved as he realized Dylan might be right. "Maybe. Let's give them some time to cool off before we go any further down that road, though. Besides, we need to go see if we can talk to Steve. I want to know what was going on at that house last night."

CHAPTER 17

LANCE TOOK THE LONG bus trip home from the Garder Museum. At his front door, he fumbled with the key as he tried to get it into the lock using his left hand, dropping it once as he did so. He suspected he might well be ambidextrous by the time his right arm came out of the cast. Clearly, he was not there yet.

He cursed Jax's name as he turned the deadbolt.

His uniform was black slacks, gray shirt, black tie. As he stepped through the door, he loosened his tie (which had also been difficult to get on without his right hand) and struggled to free the top button on his shirt.

The apartment was small, with a kitchenette attached to the living room and a tiny bathroom off the short hall that connected to the bedroom. Still, it was a mess. Lance's mom would no doubt have said it looked like a bomb had gone off in here. There were clothes everywhere, not to mention stacks of unread newspapers by the door, piles of mail everywhere, and take-out cartons littered across the kitchenette that were weeks old.

Like Lance always did, he had grabbed a newspaper from the gas station across the street from the museum when he got off work. And, like he always did, he tossed it on top of the others, convinced he would get to it sooner or later.

He never would, and what did it matter? Most of the news in that stack was so old as to be out of date. If someone were ever to come into the apartment to clean it up, that stack would be the first thing to go.

Lance went in search of something to eat, starting first with the take-out cartons on the kitchenette counter. A roach crawled out of the first carton he opened. It dropped to the floor and raced into a crack between the wall and the cabinet.

Lance did not even flinch, but he did have enough good sense to turn his search toward the fridge, instead. There he found a half-eaten sandwich wrapped in tinfoil. Turkey and tomato. He smelled it, determined it had not yet gone bad, and called it his dinner.

When he was done, he sat down at the computer to check his email before going to bed. Lance's refurbished flip phone was old and inexpensive. It could not download any of the latest apps and did not support email. Not that he cared. He almost never got anything important. He checked it for the same reason he checked his physical mailbox—because you never knew what was there unless you did.

The computer was a desktop as old as his phone. The CRT monitor—which was deeper than it was wide—sat on top of a small desk in the bedroom. The machine itself sat on the floor. Lance was certain if he tried to place both on top of the cheap desk, it would have collapsed under the weight.

The computer whirred to life. Lance navigated to his Gmail account. At first, all he saw was exactly what he expected to see: junk, from companies who had somehow gotten his email address and added him to their mailing list. There was a sale on jeans at the Gap, a Redbox special "good for this weekend only!", and other more suspect emails promising specials on everything from electronics to ice cream. He never opened them. He also chose not to unsubscribe. Without them, he figured, he might not know if the account was working.

Then he saw an email that *was* worth opening—an alert from Facebook that he had received a message. There was likely only one person it would be from. He navigated to the social media site and read the message twice.

CHRIS IS DEAD.

CHAPTER 18

OLIN DROVE TO DOWNTOWN Atlanta and found a paid lot a block from his destination, then walked to the towering glass skyscraper. Hudson's film company, Nightbird Studios, was headquartered out of the thirty-second floor. He announced himself to the security guard in the lobby and took the elevator up.

The elevator opened onto a posh waiting room with black leather sofas, a coffee table made of nickel-plated metal, and a crystal water pitcher with matching glasses on a drink cart in the corner.

Three people were huddled close together on one of the sofas: a woman and two men. The men were wearing suits, the woman jeans and a tee shirt. Perhaps only because of how they were dressed, Olin decided the woman must be an actress and the two men with her were agents or lawyers or perhaps some combination of industry professionals with titles he'd never heard of. Whoever they were, they were engaged in an intense conversation and pointing to a stack of papers in the woman's lap. Olin suspected it was probably a script, but he could be no more sure of that than he could anything else about the group.

They paused briefly to look at Olin. Once they determined he was no one of consequence, they returned to their hushed conversation.

Olin asked the receptionist to tell Hudson he was there and, to the dismay of the group in the lobby, was immediately shown to the producer's office.

"Can I get you anything?" she said, leading him down the hall.

On the way here, Olin had wondered if someone would offer him any sort of refreshment. Since he wasn't sure, he'd stopped at convenience store to grab a Coke and had brought the bottle up with him. "I'm good. Thanks."

The space was expansive, with floor-to-ceiling windows behind a large desk and an unobstructed view of the Georgia State Capitol. Framed movie posters lined one wall. A variety of awards sat on floating shelves mounted to the other.

Hudson eagerly got up from his desk. "Close the door," he called to the receptionist on her way out. Once they were alone, he pulled a pack of Pall Malls out of his coat pocket and turned his attention to Olin. "Connor has something already?" he asked as he lit the cigarette.

Olin did not care for the smoking. He had long since embraced the philosophy that his body was a temple. He also wasn't in a position to ask Hudson to put it out. He was here to ask some uncomfortable questions. Best to let the man smoke if he wanted to.

"He has a lead," Olin said, still standing halfway across the room.

Hudson gestured to one of the chairs in front of the desk. Olin sat down, and Hudson took a seat on the chair next to him. He took another drag from his cigarette, and exhaled it in Olin's direction as he asked, "What is it?"

Olin did his best to suppress a cough. He unscrewed the cap from the bottle of Coke and took a sip. "It's too soon for that. But something has come up—something Connor wanted me to ask you about."

"Okay," Hudson said, sounding less enthusiastic than he had before.

"Why did you hire Chris for this role?"

"What do you mean? He's a great actor. Why wouldn't I hire him?"

"He wasn't your first choice. There are rumors he was going to retire soon. Couldn't something like that mess up the plan to turn this movie into a franchise?"

Hudson took another drag off the cigarette. "Where did you hear I was looking to do that?"

"Maria said something about it to Connor."

"She's an amateur," he said dismissively. "This is her first big film. She doesn't know what she's talking about. With a story like this there are all kinds of things the writers can come up with to explain a new actor if we have to. Sudden physical transformation. Body swapping. Mutation. The possibilities are endless. Do you know the show *Bewitched*?"

"That was from the sixties, right?"

"Ended in seventy-two. At any rate, Dick York was originally cast to play the leading man, Darin. Unfortunately, he had to step down because of an old back injury and was replaced by Dick Sargent. The audience didn't care."

"That was a long time ago."

"Okay, what about *Two and a Half Men*? They replaced Charlie Sheen with Ashton Kutcher and kept right on chugging."

"But they did that by killing him off. Besides, didn't it end a season or two later?"

"My point is, you don't have to kill a franchise because you change an actor. Take *Doctor Who*, for example. How many leading men has that show had? How many people have played James Bond?" Another drag from the cigarette. "I'll grant you, it's better to keep the same actor when you can, but there are ways to work around it if they leave."

Olin coughed again and took another sip from his Coke.

Hudson crossed to his desk and stubbed the cigarette out in an ashtray. "Satisfied?"

Olin wasn't sure if Hudson was referring to the cigarette or his explanation for hiring Chris. If he meant the latter, Olin was not. "He wasn't your first choice. You knew he might leave. You hired him anyway. Why?"

"I changed my mind!" Hudson bellowed. "I'm the producer. I have the right to do that. I can hire and fire whoever I damn well want. And if you guys keep coming to me with dumb-ass questions like this, I'll fire you, too!"

Olin didn't respond, didn't lift the soda to his lips, didn't even breathe. Not for several seconds. Not until Hudson took a deep breath of his own, ran his hand down his beard, and said, "I'm sorry. I shouldn't have exploded like that. I'm seeing a therapist about it. He's given me some deep breathing exercises and crap like that." He pulled out another cigarette. "Which is kind of the same thing as smoking, isn't it?" Not even Hudson's own joke brought a smile to his face. "Seriously, focus on the case. It doesn't matter why I hired Chris."

Olin had been reluctant to come to Hudson's office, and even more reluctant to do what Dylan wanted him to do next. She lived in a morally gray area Olin had not embraced. She and Connor both did. It was becoming clear, however, that without joining them in that morally gray area, Olin was not going to get to the truth.

The director was hiding something—there was no doubt about that—and the more fiercely someone fought to protect their secret, the more important it was to bring it to light.

Olin brough the bottle of Coke to his lips again and, this time, let it slip out of his hands in a way that looked accidental. He jumped to his feet, cursing as the sticky black liquid spread across a rug that was worth more than Connor, Olin, and Dylan had paid to furnish their entire office.

"What's the matter with you?" Hudson shouted.

Olin grabbed the bottle. "I'm so sorry! Do you have some paper towels?"

Hudson was already hurrying across the room, likely in search of something that would soak up some of the soda. He threw open the door hard enough for it to bounce off the doorstop before disappearing down the hall, shouting for his secretary.

Olin didn't have long. Seconds, probably. He had to make it count. Every nerve in his body was signaling for him to stop as he stepped into the morally gray area where Connor and Dylan seemed so comfortable.

He circled the desk, scanning the top for anything of interest. There were two large monitors connected to a laptop via a docking station, a fancy pen holder filled with fancy pens, and a thin leather mat covering the working surface with a stack of papers on top of it. At a glance, those papers appeared to be a contract. He guessed that the contract had something to do with the group in the lobby and did not spend any time on it.

He pulled open each drawer, glancing between the contents and the door. There was nothing that jumped out at him. Had he found anything, he would have tucked it under his windbreaker so he could discreetly ferry it out of the office for later review.

And that was all he had time for. Hudson was coming down the hall again, cursing Olin, his voice getting louder as he approached the office.

Then, as Olin was closing the center drawer, he saw one thing that might be useful. He grabbed it, certain Hudson wouldn't notice, and rushed back around the desk. The item was small enough to fit in his front pocket, where he placed it before dropping to his knees. He had brought a handkerchief with him just for this moment and used it to dab the carpet.

Hudson dashed over and pushed him out of the way. "Take care of that!" he shouted at his secretary, who was right behind him. Immediately, she sprayed the stain with some sort of chemical in an unmarked blue bottle and began working on it with a white cloth. To Olin's surprise, it seemed to be coming up.

"Go on! Get out!" Hudson told Olin. "Come back when you have something worth telling me about."

Since he had done everything he could here, Olin took that as his cue to leave. He slunk out the door without a word, glad to be finished with Dylan's task.

Once he was back on the street, he called Connor. "Is Dylan there, too?" he asked when Connor answered.

"Yes," Connor said, and transferred the call to speaker.

"What did you find out?" Dylan asked.

"He said pretty much what you expected him to say. Listed off some other cases where a show or movie had started with one actor and then pivoted, so it isn't unheard of. If Chris retired, it wouldn't kill the franchise, but I could tell there was more there."

"Did you find anything in his desk?" Dylan asked. "What about on his computer?"

"No. I didn't have a lot of time to look. One thing may have come out of it, though." He pulled out of his pocket the item he had taken from Hudson's desk. It was a business card, with simple black lettering against a white background. "Hudson is seeing a therapist."

"Patients tell their therapists everything," Dylan said.

It was exactly what Olin was thinking. If there was an answer to be had, the doctor might know what it was. However, asking him would be no more effective than asking Hudson. Doctor–patient confidentiality and all that. They might be PIs, but they weren't the police. (And even if they were the police, the doctor still might not give up his patient's secrets without a warrant.)

But he definitely would have been taking notes during the sessions with Hudson, and there was a good chance those notes might be digital.

"Do you know his name?" Connor asked.

"I do," Olin said and looked back down at the card. The simple black lettering read "Dr. Harris Brown, Psychiatrist." It included an address and phone number. Olin read off the doctor's name and said he would text the rest.

"Sounds good," Connor said. "We are on our way to talk to someone who might have information about Chris. We'll call you back soon."

They said their goodbyes and Olin hung up. He had made it to his car over the course of the conversation. Before getting inside, he turned back to look at the tall glass building housing Nightbird Studios and mumbled, "What is it you're hiding?"

CHAPTER 19

CONNOR SLID HIS PHONE back into his pocket and swiveled his head toward Dylan. They were both sitting in the back seat of their Uber driver's Ford Fiesta. "What do you think?" he asked, referring to the information Olin had just given them.

"Sounds like there's something there," Dylan said.

Connor nodded in agreement. His phone vibrated in his pocket. He didn't have to check it to know it was the text Olin had said he would send with the psychiatrist's information. He turned back toward the window. They had been in the car for half an hour already. Traffic was moving significantly slower than it had been last night, and the address they were going to was farther from the city than the bar. The driver was doing the best he could, cutting through side streets and ignoring the directions provided by his navigation app in favor of routes he claimed would be faster. But they were still going to get there later than Connor had expected when they left.

As he watched the world pass by outside his window, Connor weighed several options for getting onto the doctor's computer and decided to try the simplest option first. He retrieved his phone from his pocket and began composing an email.

"What are you doing?" Dylan asked.

"Writing the good doctor."

"What for?"

"If he replies from his computer, I'll have his IP. That's all I need to get onto his machine."

Connor's message was short. He said he had heard good things about the psychiatrist and wanted to find out if he was taking new patients. "Less is more here," he said to himself, as he pressed SEND.

He put the phone back in his pocket and realized Dylan had a look on her face he couldn't decipher. It was some weird mix of befuddlement and suspicion. "What?" he asked.

"Is that how you found me?"

Connor had met Dylan not long after she had sent him an email telling him to stay out of her computer. And, yes, her IP address had been exactly how he had found her. She had asked before how Connor was able to locate her, and he had only told her about the tracking app that had led him to the mall. Now, it seemed appropriate to tell her about the IP, as well.

"Yes, that's how I found you."

She nodded, impressed. "Good job."

The driver pulled up to a beautiful two-story house with a thatch roof. The brick walls had been painted yellow, the trim white. A picket fence cordoned off the front yard, separating Steve's property from the other widely spaced houses on this country road.

"It's going to be hard getting a car out here when we want to go back," Dylan said.

"Good point." Connor leaned forward, grabbing hold of the headrest in front of him. "Would you mind waiting?" he asked the driver. "We'll pay you for your time."

The driver was a young man. Connor had noticed textbooks on the passenger seat and suspected he was working his way through college. He might be grateful for some paid study time.

The driver seemed reluctant at first. Once they negotiated a price, he pulled off the road and cut the engine.

Connor and Dylan crossed the street, stepped through the gate in the picket fence, and followed the stone path from it to the porch. "Here's hoping," Connor said, right before he knocked. Neither one of them wanted to make the long trip out here later if no one was home.

Fortunately, Connor did not find himself in suspense for long. A woman opened the door right away. Connor recognized her from the Instagram photos. She was Steve's wife. She looked frazzled, tired. Somewhere in the house, their baby was screaming.

"Is Steve home?" Connor said.

The woman did not answer directly. Instead, she turned and moved deeper into the house, calling Steve's name as she went.

"I guess that's a yes," Dylan said.

"I guess so."

The door opened onto a living room with a pack-and-play on the floor and an assortment of baby toys everywhere. Another doorway— this one arched—separated it from the dining room. The woman went through that doorway and turned to the right. A moment later, a man stepped through it, entering from the left, and walked over to where Dylan and Connor were waiting.

He was tall and skinny, and looked as frazzled as his wife. He was wearing sweatpants and a white undershirt with a stain on it that might have been vomit. The baby was probably sick, Connor figured. From the way his parents looked, she had kept them up all night.

Assuming they were able to sleep at all, Connor thought. Chris's death may well have already robbed them of that.

"What can I do for you?"

Connor did not want Steve to react the same way the bartender had when he'd introduced himself, so he immediately informed the man he was a PI and, just to make sure there was no doubt, flashed his identification. "We were hired by the producer to look into Chris's death."

Steve looked back into the house, then stepped onto the porch. "Aren't the police doing that?"

"Doesn't hurt to get a second opinion," Dylan said, and Connor nodded in agreement.

"Sure. All right, I guess not." Steve closed the door. "How can I help?"

"Do you have a few minutes to talk?" Connor said.

"Sure." Steve gestured toward the stone path. "You mind if we walk? My wife's been through enough already. She doesn't need to hear about Chris again right now. Especially not with little Julie in there, sick as she is."

Connor and Dylan stepped out of the way, then followed Steve to the street.

"Your wife knew Chris?" Connor asked.

"No."

Connor wasn't sure what to make of that. He could understand why Chris's death would have been hard on Steve. But why would it have been hard on his wife if she didn't know him?

Perhaps that confusion showed on his face, because when Steve turned to close the gate behind them, he looked at Connor and said, "You're not married, are you?"

Connor shook his head.

"Trust me—if it's hard on one of you, it's hard on both of you." Steve turned to his right. With his hands in his pockets, he meandered slowly down the road with Connor and Dylan beside him. "I take it you've been by the Crown?"

"What makes you think that?" Dylan said as Connor looked over at their driver and noticed he was intensely focused on a book he had propped open on the steering wheel.

"Why else would you be here?"

"Do you mind telling me who else was with you that night?" Connor said.

"Sure. Ryan and Mia. We had all been friends for years. Met at the Waterton Theatre."

"Last names," Dylan said.

"Oh, right. Ryan Clarke and Mia Edwards."

"Do you know how we can get in touch with them?" Connor said.

Steve stopped walking. He pulled his cell out of his pocket and read a pair of phone numbers off to Connor, who dutifully copied them down into his phone. Then Steve provided his own as well. "In case you need to get in touch with me again."

"What happened that night?"

"Same as always. Had some drinks, talked a bunch of crap. That's how it started out, anyway. But Chris didn't seem like himself. It was like something was bothering him. Then, all of a sudden, he ran into the bathroom, sick as a dog. When I went to check on him, he said he wanted to be left alone. He was gone for a long time."

"You weren't worried?" Dylan interrupted, incredulously.

"We figured he had had too much to drink. It wouldn't have been the first time it's happened."

"Were you the one who found him?"

"I wish. No. Some guy came out of the bathroom screaming his head off about a dead body. I don't think he realized who it was."

"So you didn't see Chris then, after he died, did you?" Connor asked.

"Oh, I saw him," Steve said. He looked out at the grassy field that separated his house from his neighbor's like he was seeing it for the first time—probably lost in the memory of that night—before abruptly turning back toward the road and continuing his slow, meandering walk. "It was awful. He had been sick all over everything."

"Was there any indication of how he died?" Dylan asked.

"Not that I could tell."

"No signs of strangulation? Nothing like that?"

"I didn't see any." He sighed. "I'm not sure if I'd know, though, either. You'd probably have to ask the police if you want to find out something like that."

Earlier in their conversation, Steve had said Chris didn't seem like himself. Some of his coworkers had also noticed he was upset. They had not been able to tell Connor why. Maybe Steve could.

"Sorry," Steve said. "He didn't want to talk about it."

So that was it. Steve had been there. He had seen the body, no doubt talked to the police afterward. But Connor was almost certain that was as far as his involvement went. Which begged the very question Dylan asked next: "Why did you hide from us when we went by your place last night?"

Steve turned to her, visibly confused. "What are you talking about?"

"You've got a place near the Crown, don't you? We stopped by there last night. You might remember, since you turned off the light when we knocked."

"That wasn't me. My wife and I moved out of that place a year ago. We wanted something with more room. Once the real estate market picks up, I'm going to dump it. Unfortunately, if I tried to sell it now, I'd still end up owing money. In the meantime, I've been letting Ryan stay there."

"Why?" Connor asked.

"He told me he was evicted and needed a place to crash while he figured stuff out."

Connor and Dylan looked at each other.

"Why didn't he answer the door?" Dylan said.

"You'd have to ask him. You probably won't get him to come to the door now, though. He's probably asleep. Frankly, he probably won't take your phone call, either. He doesn't answer numbers he doesn't know. Your best chance of talking to him would be at the Circle tomorrow tonight. It's a club. He DJs there a few times a week."

"I'm surprised he's not taking some time off after everything that happened."

"He needs the money." Steve looked back down the road towards the house. "I'd better get back. We're taking it in turns to look after the baby."

On their walk back to the house together, someone shouted, "Steve!" Startled, Connor spun toward the voice, expecting any manner of trouble, only to realize the man calling for Steve was their Uber driver.

The driver was already out of the car and coming toward them. "I can't believe it's you. How are you holding up?"

Now Connor was even more confused than he had been at the sound of the man's voice. "You know him?" he asked the driver, looking from him to Steve and back again.

"I ran into him a couple of times at the university."

The driver had to mean the University of London, which Connor knew was where Steve worked. Since he had also suspected their driver was in college, he shouldn't have been surprised they'd met before.

The driver turned his attention back to Steve. "I'm so sorry to hear about what happened. That really sucks. Are you alright?"

"What are you talking about?" Dylan said to him. Chris's death wasn't public knowledge yet. Then, before he could answer, she turned to Steve. "What is he talking about?"

"Chris. Chris Miller," said the driver impatiently. "I didn't know you knew him. I can't believe what happened."

"You know what happened to Chris?" Connor said.

"I got an alert." The driver held up his phone, screen out. Connor hadn't noticed he was carrying it until now. On the screen was a news story. The body text was too small to make out, but the headline was clear: A-LISTER DIES UNDER MYSTERIOUS CIRCUMSTANCES.

CHAPTER 20

"**I** GUESS WE DON'T need to keep it a secret anymore," Dylan said to Connor, as she, too, read the headline.

The driver let the phone fall back to his side. "What do you mean? Are you here because of Chris?"

"We're investigating his murder," Dylan said, while, at the same time, Connor said, "Can I see your phone?"

The driver handed his phone to Connor and directed his next question to Dylan. "Are you like police or something? Real US detectives? Like from *CSI: Miami*?"

"PIs," Dylan said.

Connor caught none of this exchange. He was scanning the article for any news about Chris's death they might not have already uncovered. At first, there didn't seem to be much to it. Then he ran across the line that mattered: "The police suspect Mr. Miller may have been poisoned." It said tests were being conducted by the lab and results were expected soon.

Connor passed the phone back. At least that answered the question of how Chris had died.

"I'm sorry," the driver said, talking again to Steve.

"It's fine," Steve said. "If it's all right . . ." He trailed off as he pulled one hand out of his pocket and pointed at the house.

"Yeah, go ahead," Connor said. "Thanks for your help." He didn't think there was much else the man could tell them. If they needed Steve again, they knew where to find him.

"So who hired you?" the driver asked.

"Do you mind?" Dylan said, gesturing toward the car.

All three of them crossed the road and climbed back into the vehicle. Connor checked his email for a response from the psychiatrist, then looked up Mia's address online. Steve might have been able to give it to him if he went back and asked, but he clearly had his hands full, and, by matching Mia's phone number with her name, Connor was able to find her without much trouble.

While he looked, the driver pulled out onto the road and continued to drill Dylan with questions. At first, she was evasive, managing a level of tact Connor had rarely seen from her. Once she'd had enough, she reminded the driver that that was all he was—a driver—and suggested that he should keep his questions to himself.

For most people, that would have been enough to shut them up for the rest of the drive. However, once they were moving at a good pace, the driver was back at it. The faster he drove, the more questions he asked, as if the gas pedal was controlling not just the speed of the car but his mouth as well.

Connor answered the questions he thought were harmless and said he was not at liberty to discuss the others.

Mia lived in a large house in Notting Hill. She answered the door in a tight red dress that tied at the waist. When Connor told her who they were, she invited them into the sitting room to talk. "My fiancé's at work, and the maid is off for the day, so we have the whole place to ourselves."

She directed Connor and Dylan through a pair of large double doors, indicated a pair of crushed velvet wingbacks, and took a seat on the matching sofa facing them. On the wall opposite the sofa was a fireplace with a fire burning inside it and built-in bookshelves, packed full of books, covering the wall on each side.

Her story matched Steve's in all the ways that mattered (she had not gone into the men's restroom when someone came out screaming about a body), and she seemed appropriately distressed by the situation. Twenty minutes in, and Connor knew he wasn't going to get anything from her he didn't know already. Dylan shared a look with him that suggested she agreed.

Suddenly, Mia said something neither of them expected. "I don't know what was bothering him. He had beaten out some good actors for that role. We talked a few months ago. It was right after he found out he was being considered for the part. He said his agent had warned him they were leaning toward Jax Hart."

"Jax Hart?" Dylan repeated, perhaps to make sure she had heard the name correctly.

"That's right. Why?"

Maybe it's not so strange, Connor thought. Jax had passed Connor's name to Hudson, so clearly the men knew each other. Still, something about it didn't sit right with him.

"He should have been happy," Mia said. "His last film was a flop, and he wanted to go out on top. 'They can push you out the door or you can leave on your own terms,' he liked to say. Chris wanted to leave on his own terms."

"One more stop," Connor said to the driver—whom they'd since learned was named Dean—when they climbed back into the car.

"Anywhere you want to go," Dean said. He sounded enthused to be part of the investigation, no matter how small his role in it might be.

Connor gave him the name of the bar and then directed him down the narrow streets to the house where Ryan was staying. Connor and Dylan both knocked as hard as they could. There was still no answer.

"I'm going to try calling," Connor said and dialed the number Steve had given him.

Ryan did not pick up.

"Looks like Steve was right. If we want to talk to him, we're going to have to do it at the club," Dylan said, stepping away from the front door.

Connor nodded in agreement, and they returned to the hotel to regroup. Just before getting out of the car, the driver passed back a slip of paper torn out of one of his textbooks. Even without taking hold of it, Connor could see the letters "OLOGY" on the left and the number "232" on the right, indicating the paper had come from page 232 of a science book. Between them, Dean had written a phone number in blue ink. "Take it," he said. "Call me if you need to go anywhere else. Consider me your personal chauffeur while you're here."

Connor reluctantly took the slip of paper, doubtful he would ever use it. Then, as he got out of the car, he felt his phone vibrate, indicating the arrival of a text or email. He pulled the phone out of his pocket. The doctor had finally written him back.

CHAPTER 21

DYLAN FOLLOWED CONNOR TO his room. The door between the adjoining suites was still open, and both laptops were still set up on the table near the fireplace. There was a lot they wanted to know about both Chris's friends and Hudson's doctor.

Dylan took a seat in the same chair she had occupied the night before. "Do you think Steve and Mia might have coordinated their stories?"

Connor had considered that possibility on the drive back. He didn't think so. Their stories felt genuine and varied enough for Connor to believe they were not rehearsed. After he said as much to Dylan, he added, "But Ryan—that bothers me. Not answering the door when we knocked."

"Turning off the light," Dylan added.

Connor grabbed a bottle of water from the mini fridge and offered one to Dylan. She frowned and shook her head. "Maybe he had something to do with the murder and maybe he didn't. One thing's for sure, he's hiding something."

"Just like Hudson."

Connor took a sip from the bottle of water. "There seems to be a lot of that going around." He sat down across from Dylan. "See what you can find out about Mia and Ryan. Especially Ryan. I'm going to see if I can get into Dr. Brown's computer."

Like the previous night, they worked in silence. While Dylan explored the dark web, Connor set about finding his way into the doctor's computer. His best chance would be through an unsecured port. It took the better part of an hour. Once he was in, he navigated through the doctor's folders with ease. Dr. Brown took organization to the extreme. Even a novice could have found his way to Hudson's file.

His client files were stored in a folder that was predictably called CLIENTS and sorted further into ACTIVE and INACTIVE folders. Connor clicked the ACTIVE folder and found still another layer of folders—these designated by the clients' names and ordered with the last name first.

He had no interest in prying into the lives of anyone other Hudson Davis. He didn't even want to know who the other clients were. As such, he scrolled to the Ds without reading any more of the names than he had to. Once he found DAVIS, HUDSON, he clicked the folder and was presented with a series of files. Here, Dr. Brown had stored admission documents, billing statements, and, most importantly, client notes.

Connor scanned the client notes for anything that stood out. Although the doctor labeled his files and folders clearly, his notes were all but arcane, written in a sort of shorthand that only the doctor himself could easily read. The process was slow in the extreme. Most sentences had to be parsed over and over until they transformed into something meaningful.

After a while, Connor began to learn some of the doctor's phrases: "pt" was patient, "ar" was anger, "drm" was dream. (Apparently, he was a Freudian.)

"You know," Dylan said, without taking her eyes off her work, "if Chris was poisoned, it could have happened earlier in the day."

"We should talk to the whole cast and crew when we're done here," Connor replied.

Then they worked in silence some more.

The doctor's notes did indeed indicate Hudson was working through anger issues, most of which seemed to be directed at his wife. She had been distant for years. Hudson suspected she might have had an affair—maybe more than one—although he hadn't been able to prove it. And he wasn't going to divorce her because he didn't want to give her half of everything and pay alimony on top of that. She wasn't entitled to it.

As interesting as that was, it was not a reason to kill Chris.

However, seventeen pages in, Connor found something that might be. It was a particularly cryptic passage. When Connor was done trying to decipher it, all he could say for sure was that it had something to do with Chris and an email Hudson had received. The contents of that email were not detailed, but Connor got the impression blackmail might have been involved.

"That's interesting," he said.

Dylan looked up from her screen. "What?"

"I think Hudson might have just jumped to the top of our list of suspects."

"What makes you think that?"

"Come here," Connor said, beckoning her over.

Dylan walked around the small table and leaned in so she could read the text Connor was pointing at.

"This section here."

"How can you make sense of any of that?"

"Read enough of it, and you'll get used to it. Anyway, I think somebody might have been blackmailing Hudson. Maybe that's why he changed his mind about putting Chris in the movie."

Dylan straightened up. She crossed her arms over her chest. "You think it was Chris who blackmailed him? He's a big star. Why would he care about getting on any one movie? Even if he did want to end his career on a high note, it didn't have to be this film."

"I don't know," Connor said. "Maybe it wasn't. Either way, we need to find out what was in that email."

"If you're right, I guess it would be a motive for murder. But let's also not forget that Hudson was in Atlanta when it happened. So if he had something to do with Chris's death, he wasn't working alone."

"I agree."

"And let's not get tunnel vision. He's not the only person we need to find out more about."

Connor spun around in his chair. "You ran across something in your research?"

"Not on Mia. She's a wannabe socialite. She comes from a middle-income family, used to be big into punk rock. Likely went into theater for the attention. Now she plans on marrying rich, and probably expects to get the attention from that. As far as I can tell, she doesn't have much of a personality of her own. She'll be whatever she needs to be to get what she wants. It's like she's putting on an act."

Connor frowned, doubtful. People changed, sure. But just because people changed didn't mean they were putting on an act. He had been big into punk rock as a teenager, too. His favorite band had been the Sex Pistols. These days, he rarely listened to them, preferring instead the relatively smooth sound of classic rock. He wasn't putting on an act.

"You saw her," Dylan said. "Remember that picture of her online from a few years ago? She's completely transformed. That's not normal."

Connor frowned again.

"Well, whatever the reason for her transformation, she doesn't have any deep, dark secrets that I could find. Ryan, on the other hand, is an enigma."

"What you do you mean? You found something on him?"

"No. That's the problem. I didn't find anything on him."

"I don't get it."

"I mean nothing." She touched her thumb to her fingers, making an O. "Zero. A big nada. Not an address or a social media page or one shred of anything that would suggest he even exists. He's practically a ghost. Even his phone seems to be one of those prepaid deals. That makes him worth another look, don't you think?"

Connor had to agree. It was nearly impossible to go through life without leaving a digital trail these days, whether you knew it or not.

"I mean, who doesn't have a Facebook page?" she continued.

"Hopefully, we'll find out more at the club," Connor said.

"Hopefully."

"In the meantime . . ." Connor turned back to his computer. He sent a quick email to Hudson:

> The police think Chris was poisoned. Looking into a suspect.
> Would you like us to call later with an update?

"What are you doing?" Dylan asked, as she read the message over his shoulder. "You'll tip our hand."

"He probably already knows about the poison. And we do have a suspect we can tell him about. Ryan. But that's not the point of the email. When he answers, we can use his IP to hack into his computer, just like we did Dr. Brown's. Then, hopefully, we can find the email

Hudson mentioned and figure out what's going on. Fingers crossed he answers quickly."

"What do you want to do while we wait?"

"Exactly what we said we should do. Let's talk to the cast and crew."

CHAPTER 22

MARIA SAID SHE WOULD gather everyone in the lobby, then told Connor and Dylan to meet her there in ten minutes.

When Connor and Dylan stepped off the elevator, there were some sixty to seventy people crowded into the small space between the bar and the front desk. It was a much larger group than Connor expected.

"You think they all work on the movie?" Dylan whispered.

"They have to. Maria said there wasn't anybody else staying in the hotel."

"This is going to take forever." She looked around. "Do you see her?"

Connor caught a glimpse of Maria standing on the far side of the room. "She's over there." He weaved through the crowd with Dylan behind him.

When they reached Maria, she gave them a quick hello before turning to the group and holding up her hand to get their attention. "Ladies and gentlemen," she called, raising her voice over the hubbub of conversations. "Ladies and gentlemen, could I have your attention, please?"

The crowd settled down.

"I know this has been a difficult time. I want to assure you that I have been in talks with the producer, and we will all be getting back to work very soon. In the meantime, this is Connor Callahan and Dylan . . ." She looked questioningly at Dylan.

"Naese," Dylan said.

"Dylan Naese," Maria said. "They're looking into Chris's death. Hopefully they can get us some answers faster than the police can. They would like to talk to all of you. Please make yourselves available to them." She looked again at Dylan, this time also catching Connor in her gaze. "How did you want to do this?" she said softly.

Connor had been thinking about that since he had seen the size of the crowd. They couldn't possibly conduct in-depth interviews of all these people efficiently. Even if they did manage to talk to everyone, when would they have time to verify all of their stories? The police had the manpower for something like that. Connor and Dylan did not. If they wanted to get an answer to Chris's death quickly, they would need to be surgical in their approach.

But they still needed to talk to each person, even briefly, if only so they could match names with faces and look for any obvious holes in their stories. Depending on where the investigation led, they could always follow up with anyone here later.

Then Connor realized there might be one more reason to talk to everyone. He studied the crowd, looking for the man with curly black hair who had been standing outside his hotel room last night. It wasn't much to go on, but even with the little he had, he didn't see anybody who resembled their spy.

"Maria, are you sure everybody's here?"

"I think so."

"Nobody's checked out since last night?"

Now Maria was studying the crowd as well. "I don't think so. You'd have to check with the front desk to be sure."

"On it," Dylan said, who seemed to get where Connor was going with his last question.

After she walked away, Maria said, "I can email you a list of everyone working on the film, if that helps."

"Thank you," Connor said. Then he addressed the cast and crew: "We're just going to get some preliminary information from each of you for now. It shouldn't take too long."

"What if we already met you at breakfast?" a woman said. It was Meg, from wardrobe.

"We want to speak to everyone," Connor responded. "No exceptions."

Dylan returned from the front desk. "No one's checked out since last night."

Good, Connor thought. At least there was that. It didn't mean their spy hadn't skipped town, but if he worked on the movie the odds seemed fair he was still around here somewhere.

"We're going to meet with you one at a time," Connor said, addressing the crowd again. The question was where. The plush leather chairs behind them—the ones where they'd sat when they first spoke with Maria—did not offer Connor the privacy he was after. Then he noticed Meg again, fidgeting with annoyance, and thought about the dining room where they had eaten breakfast. He remembered seeing a small table in the corner near the restrooms. A two-seater against the wall. That would be perfect. "There's a little table in the corner behind the bar. Please stay here until we've talked to you."

Connor selected someone from the front row at random and led them to the table. Before he walked away, he said to Maria, "Please get us that list as soon as possible."

"I'll go back up to my room and send it right now," she assured him.

CHAPTER 23

A S IT TURNED OUT, not everyone had come down to the lobby when Maria had asked them to. Laura had seen the group text, but was in no mood to speak to Connor or Dylan again anytime soon.

Laura had begun her career on *Days of our Lives*. Her parents—both real estate agents and Los Angeles natives—couldn't have been prouder. All three of them were sure it marked the beginning of an exciting film career. But for the next decade, she had languished in that three p.m. slot, unable to make the jump to primetime or film. Her chance had finally come when a supporting actress on a major motion picture had dropped out and the director was short on time to replace her.

Laura had walked onto the set, both excited and terrified. That feeling, however, had lasted only minutes before the director had approached her and said dismissively, "You're good enough. At least you won't ruin the movie."

Those words had left her feeling like a fraud, like she'd never amount to anything in this industry, like maybe she should just go back and get her real estate license like her parents had done (and who, incidentally, had wanted to be actors, too). But the longer she stewed on that comment, the angrier it had made her, and that anger had motivated her to prove how good she really was. In the end, the role had got her nominated for an Oscar, and the nomination had opened up doors on other productions.

It had been a long, hard road to get to where she was. What right did Connor and Dylan have to come into her world, talking to her the way they did?

No, thank you. She would not spend any more time around them than she had to. Besides, she had someone more important on the phone, someone she *wanted* to talk to.

"I should be touching down late tonight," the person on the other end of the line said.

Laura walked to the window of her hotel room. She pulled the curtain back and looked out, as if she could see the caller approaching. Of course, that was impossible. He was calling from the plane. Nonetheless, she absently stared out into the distance without registering either the bank or the film trailers that were directly within her line of sight.

She was still wearing the black dress she'd had on at breakfast. "I can't wait to see you. I thought Hudson was going to take much longer to make this decision."

"I think the money got to him. He wants everyone back to work as soon as possible. From what I gather, it will make him feel better. He's already spent a lot on this movie. I think he's decided he's going to finish it, no matter what Connor or the police find."

There was that name. *Connor.* Her upper lip curled with distaste. Then, as quickly as he'd entered her mind, she pushed him out again. "I'm just glad you're coming. If Chris had to die to make that happen, that's okay with me."

CHAPTER 24

THE FIRST PERSON CONNOR and Dylan spoke to was a woman named Marilyn Astrot. With the table still pushed to the wall, each of them sat on one of the three remaining sides. Marilyn worked with Meg in wardrobe, claimed she had not met Chris before the film, and had spent the day of the murder putting the finishing details on a complex outfit for a later scene before having drinks in her room with several coworkers.

Connor had his cell on the table so that, with Marilyn's consent, he could record the conversation.

When they were done, he checked to see if he had received an email from Hudson or Maria. He was pleased to see he had emails from both.

The one from Maria contained an attached Word document with a list naming everyone on the cast and crew who was checked into the hotel. He forwarded that email to Dylan, and she went to the front desk to see if they could print it for her.

While he waited for her to return, he opened the email from Hudson. It read:

> Yes, I want to know about any leads you have. Call as soon as you can with an update.

Connor had seen Hudson's name pop up on his phone while they were talking to Marilyn, announcing an incoming call. He hadn't answered, first of all because he thought it was important to finish the conversation uninterrupted, and, second, because he suspected Hudson might have skipped straight from getting Connor's email to placing the call. That would not have gotten Connor what he needed.

Unfortunately, the email Connor had received wasn't what he needed, either. Hudson had sent it from his cell. There was no doubt about that, since it ended with Apple's trademark signoff: "Sent from my iPhone."

"Shit," Dylan said when he told her. "What are we going to do?"

"I have an idea. I'll fill you in when we're done here."

Dylan handed Connor two loose pieces of paper with a list of names on them. He found Marilyn's and scratched it off. "We might not know if everyone's telling the truth when we're finished, but at least we'll know if anyone's missing."

They worked through the rest of the list methodically, asking everyone they spoke to how they felt about Chris, what they were doing the day he died, and the names of anybody who could verify their whereabouts.

Hannah Wells, the PA, was still mourning Chris's loss—"It's not fair that this should happen to him"—and of course Meg Gardner, from wardrobe, seemed put out that she should have to answer any questions at all—"Couldn't you tell from the way I reacted at breakfast that I didn't kill Chris?"

Luke Cross, the actor, continued to proclaim that he was glad Chris was gone—"But that doesn't make me a killer"—and Marty Campbell, head of FX, continued to insist he wasn't—"Just because I didn't want him on the movie didn't mean I wanted him dead."

Connor suspected Marty's comment harkened back to their discussion about the future of the franchise and asked him about it. Marty reluctantly told them that was not all there was to it. "I didn't want to say it in front of everybody, but the day Chris died, he had threatened to get me fired."

Out of the corner of his eye, Connor saw Dylan prick up her ears. The interviews had clearly begun to bore her. Marty's comment had her back in the game.

"Really? Why?" Connor probed.

"There was an incident on the set. One of my guys wired up some extra squibs to his costume. It ruined the whole scene. They had to reshoot. He blamed me because it's my department."

"What's a squib?" Connor asked.

"It's like a tiny explosive hooked into a sack of fake blood. We use them to simulate gunshots."

Connor nodded contemplatively.

"I know what you're thinking," Marty continued. "You've probably heard about what a great guy Chris is. You probably think he'd never do anything like that, right?"

Connor did not respond because he was not thinking anything of the sort; he'd never met Chris personally, and no one they'd talked to so far had commented on Chris's personality.

"Well, he wasn't always that way. When he got mad, he could really lay into you."

"Why are you telling us this now?" Dylan said.

"Because maybe he told somebody else on the set he wanted me fired, and I thought you'd better hear it from me first." He seemed to study Connor's and Dylan's expressions, then blurted out, "Look, I've got debts, okay? I can't afford to lose this job."

After Connor and Dylan sent him away, Connor whispered, "Do you think that's enough of a motive for murder?"

"It might be," Dylan said. "It certainly might explain why Chris was upset."

It certainly might, Connor thought. Either way, it was as close as they got to answering that question during the interviews. Nobody else seemed to have any idea what might have been bothering him.

When they were done, there was only one name they had not been able to scratch off the list: Laura Hackett.

"Maybe she got tired of waiting," Dylan said. "She's kind of a prima donna."

"Then we'll go to her." Connor called Maria to get Laura's room number.

On their way to the elevator, Dylan said, "I guess our spy isn't staying in the hotel."

Which also meant he wasn't working on the movie, Connor thought, and wondered again about Ryan.

The actress did not try to hide her annoyance when she answered the door. With one arm propped against the frame and the other hand holding the door handle, she glared at them. "What do you want?"

"Why didn't you stay downstairs?" Connor asked.

"I didn't come downstairs."

"You didn't get Maria's text?"

"I got it."

"So you're just too precious to talk to us, is that it?" Dylan said.

Laura shifted her gaze, aiming all of her annoyance at Dylan. Connor saw her take a small step back, like she might be getting ready to close the door, and instinctively readied himself to stop her if he needed to.

"Can we come in?" he said. "It's not going to take long."

Laura seemed to think it over. Then, just when Connor was certain she was going to tell them to fuck off, she sighed and begrudgingly swung the door open. "Fine. You'd *better* make it quick."

As Connor stepped into the room, he realized it was no larger or grander than his own. He expected an actress of Laura's stature to have something special. He assumed Laura, in particular, would have insisted on it. She seemed like the kind of star who would want someone to separate her M&Ms by color for her and perhaps that same someone to sprinkle rose petals across every inch of her massive suite whenever she left. Maybe this boutique hotel simply didn't offer the kind of accommodations she would normally expect. Maybe that was part of the reason she was in such a bad mood.

"We're just trying to get a handle on everyone's actions the day Chris died."

Laura took a seat at a table that looked identical to the one in Connor's room. "I was on the set, and then I came back here."

"Alone?" Dylan asked.

"Yes, *alone*. What are you trying to imply?"

"She's not trying to imply anything," Connor said, although he wasn't sure if that was true. "We're just wondering if you have anybody who can verify your whereabouts."

"I was tired," Laura continued, "so I came back up here, ordered room service, and watched some TV."

"What did you order?" Dylan asked.

"A hamburger and fries."

Dylan raised an eyebrow. "Really?"

"Check with the kitchen."

"What did you watch on TV?"

"I don't remember. A movie. Something with Bruce Willis. I hadn't seen it before. I'll be honest, I wasn't paying that much attention. I was just trying to kill some time before I went to sleep."

Dylan didn't seem to like this answer any more than she did the last one.

"If you don't believe me, why don't you get the hotel footage?" Laura snapped. "And get the day's footage while you're at it, if you want to see me on set. In fact, why don't you go collect everyone's cell phones, too? Everyone here's always snapping pictures and taking little videos for social media. You could probably piece together the whole day with all the footage you could get."

Laura's cell phone was sitting on the table in front of her. She grabbed it and thrust it toward Dylan. "Here. You can start with mine."

CHAPTER 25

"**Y**OU SHOULD HAVE LET me see what was on her phone," Dylan said once they were back in the hall. She had reached for the phone when Laura offered it, but Connor had pushed her hand away, insisting it wasn't necessary.

"She's not a suspect," Connor said. "Besides, even if she was, what do you think you're going to find? A picture of rat poison? A checklist for murder?"

"Maybe we'd have found an email to Hudson that we could link to the blackmail."

"I don't think she's our blackmailer."

"We don't know, do we? Because we didn't look."

They headed toward the elevator. "I get it," Connor said. "You don't like her. She's kind of an entitled bitch. That doesn't make her our killer. Or our blackmailer. We have to get onto Hudson's computer if we want to find out who that is. Like I told you, I have a plan for that."

"What is it?"

Connor almost smiled. "You're going to like this."

Olin, however, was not going to like Connor's plan. But after what he had done at Hudson's office, Connor was confident his friend would see the mission through. Over the years, he had moved one slow inch at a time away from his black-and-white view of the world. Connor still remembered the first clue he had gotten that Olin was beginning to see life in more subtle shades. They had been searching for a missing woman when Olin had all but outright suggested they break into her sister's house to see what they could find.

So getting him to sneak into Hudson's house shouldn't be a problem. Not morally, anyway.

"Are you at the office now?" Connor asked. He and Dylan were back in his hotel room. The phone had been placed on the antique table between them and switched to speaker.

"Not right now," Olin said from the other end of the line.

"Make sure you go back there first. I have a USB stick in my desk. Take it with you. Hudson's computer will probably be locked, so you'll need it."

"What's it do?"

"There's a program on it that will self-install when you plug it in," Connor said. "It will take about twenty seconds. I'll be able to use that to get on the computer myself, and Hudson will never be the wiser."

"You sure I shouldn't do this at the office?" Olin said. "It would probably be easier to get in."

"How are you going to get him out of the room again?" Dylan asked. "It's not like you can spill Coke on his rug a second time. Hell, he probably won't even let you in there with a Coke now. If he lets you in at all."

"Yeah, well, that was your grand plan," Olin said. "If we hadn't wasted it already—"

"*Wasted* it? Do I need to remind you it was my grand plan that got us the information about the blackmail to begin with?"

Connor held out a hand, signaling Dylan to calm down. Then, to

Olin, he said, "If you can think of another way to get him out of the office, I'm all for it."

Olin sighed. "No, I guess I can't."

"All right, then," Dylan said. "When you're at the office, take my lock pick kit also, in case you need it."

"I don't know how to use that."

"Well, let's hope you don't have to. Maybe you'll find an open window or something."

"Fine," Olin said.

"Call us when you're done." Connor hung up. He grabbed the phone off the table and slid it back into his pocket.

"Do you think he'll do it?" Dylan asked.

"He'll do it."

"So now what? Do we just wait?"

Connor got up, paced once to the window and back. He didn't like the idea of sitting on his hands, even if it was getting late. Then he remembered something Laura had said. "The footage."

"What?"

"We can't go collecting everyone's cell phones. But we can watch the footage they shot that day and see if there's anything on it that might give us a clue."

"You think there could be?"

He shrugged. "We should find out."

CHAPTER 26

MARIA LED CONNOR AND Dylan to a trailer outside the bank and unlocked the door. "You'll find everything you need in here." She swung the door open and held out her hand, palm up. "After you."

Connor stepped into the dark trailer first.

"Light switch is on the right," Maria said.

Connor found it and flipped it on. An overhead light flickered as it came to life. Along one wall there was a built-in desk with a monitor and keyboard on top. A locked cabinet of some sort sat beside it. A sofa had been pushed up to the wall opposite the desk and a chair had been squeezed in between them.

"This is it?" Connor asked.

Maria closed the door behind her. "What were you expecting?"

"I don't know. Where's all the footage?"

She slid past Connor and unlocked the cabinet, then opened the doors to reveal a series of shelves partitioned in such a way that they might best be described as a DVD rack. "This is what you're looking for."

"There's no film?" Dylan said.

"Film started falling out of fashion a long time ago," Maria said. "Some people still use it. In my opinion, digital gets you the same quality, and it's easier to work with."

Connor nodded. "All right. How do we see it?"

Maria unlocked another cabinet, this one underneath the desk, to reveal a computer that was more powerful than anything Connor had ever owned. She turned the machine on, slid a disk in, and sat down in the desk chair. Moments later they were looking at a digital editing bay on the monitor.

Maria showed them how to work the controls, then pointed to the cabinet containing the disks. "The newest are on bottom. Each disk is labeled with a date." She handed the keys to Connor. "Lock up when you're done."

"Will do." Connor took Maria's place at the controls when she got up.

Without another word, Maria let herself out of the trailer.

Connor followed her to the door, locked it behind her. Then he returned to his seat. On the screen in front of him was a closeup of Laura, her face frozen in a look of contempt. The disk Maria had selected came from the top of the stack. Connor ejected it and replaced it with one from the bottom.

"Let's see what we can see," he said.

Dylan sat down on the sofa behind him. The monitor had been strategically positioned so that they both had a good view of it.

The editing bay on the monitor was complex, and even though Maria had shown them how to use it, Connor fumbled with the keyboard as he tried to work the digital controls.

"Do you want me to do it?" Dylan said.

"This isn't as easy as it looks."

"Let me give it a shot."

They switched places. Dylan put her hands on the keyboard and paused. She spun around in the chair. "Weren't you supposed to call Hudson back?"

"Oh. Right."

Connor did not want to give him a reason to be annoyed, to stay up late checking his phone for updates when he should be asleep. That would only make Olin's task harder.

He dialed Hudson's number, and Hudson answered immediately. "You know someone from your office came here accusing me of being involved in Chris's murder," he said without preamble. "I think his name was Owen. What the hell was that about?"

Olin, Connor thought, but did not bother to correct him. Even a person with a mild temper might not react well to such a correction. Hudson could very well explode. "I'm sorry. I don't think that was his intention."

"It sure sounded like it to me."

Then Connor heard the man take several deep breaths—something his psychiatrist had encouraged him to do when his emotion was getting the better of him.

"What did you find out?"

"He met with some friends the night he died—"

"I know that."

"One of them seems to be avoiding us."

What are you doing? Dylan mouthed. *Don't tell him that.*

Connor shifted his gaze to his feet. "His name is Ryan. He DJs at a club part-time. We're going to catch up with him there tomorrow."

"That's it? That's all you've found out? You're basing your whole theory on the fact that some guy is avoiding you?"

"Not just that," Connor said. Then he told Hudson about the man's online presence—or lack thereof—and played it up in a way that made it seem as important as Connor suspected it was.

Dylan stamped her foot on the floor to get Connor's attention. He reluctantly looked up. Her lips were pressed together so tightly they had turned white. Her eyes had narrowed to slits. She pointed at him and mouthed, *Don't tell him anything else.*

That was fine with Connor. He was done with he wanted to accomplish. "I'll get back to you when we know more," he said by way of ending the call.

"What did you tell him all that for?" Dylan snapped.

"You knew I was going to tell him about Ryan."

"I thought you were going to keep it vague."

"If he's involved, I didn't tell Hudson anything he wouldn't expect us to know already. Think about it. If we find out Ryan was his man in the UK, then certainly he knows Ryan does not have an online presence. And Ryan would have told him someone came by the house looking for him. It wouldn't be much of a leap for Hudson to assume that was us, especially if Ryan saw us through the window. Frankly, if he's involved and we didn't tell Hudson all that, he might think we were holding out on him."

Dylan stared at Connor for a while, processing what he had said and doing some deep breathing of her own. "Okay. Maybe you're right." She spun the chair back around. "Now let's see what's on these tapes."

CHAPTER 27

A T FIRST, DYLAN TOO had fumbled with the controls on the digital editing bay.

"Not so easy, is it?" Connor had joked, to which she had replied, "Shut it."

Now they were cruising through the footage with ease.

Somebody held a clapboard in front of the camera, indicating this was Scene 27, Take 4, and snapped it shut. Then Chris charged through the bank doors wearing diamond-shaped sunglasses and a red overcoat long enough to sweep the floor.

Maria yelled "Cut!" from offscreen.

There was a momentary flash, then, faster than Connor could snap his fingers, the scene started over: another clapboard (indicating they were on Take 5) and Chris once again came charging through the door, this time carrying a Glock in each hand.

He fired one of the guns at the ceiling. "This is a robbery!"

"Cut!" Maria shouted. "Punchier next time."

The scene reset again. Chris came back in, fired his gun at the ceiling, and declared, "This is a robbery!" with more drama than before.

"Cut! Is that really the best we can do?"

This time, the camera did not stop rolling. Connor and Dylan watched Maria step into view, where she huddled with Chris and a man wearing a plaid button-down. Connor knew from his interviews that third person was the cinematographer.

"I don't know why anyone would want to be an actor," Dylan said. "Reshooting the same scene over and over. It seems incredibly tedious."

Connor didn't respond. He was focusing all his attention on the conversation happening on the screen. Most of it was hard to understand, but he got the impression they were brainstorming alternatives to Chris's line. Eventually, Maria threw up her hands and said, "Fine. We'll make it work as is."

Then another reset, another clapboard, and they began again.

This time, the scene continued uninterrupted. Chris charged in, fired his gun at the ceiling, and declared this was a robbery. Extras screamed and ducked. Chris fired at the tellers on the far ends of the counter. Blood exploded from their chests as they fell to the ground.

"Those must be the squibs Marty was telling us about," Connor said.

Chris removed a garbage bag from his back pocket and placed it in front of the only teller still standing. "Fill it up." When the teller did not move, he repeated the command: "Fill it up, Brittany!"

After she sprang into action, Chris turned his attention back to the extras. "We don't need any heroes here, you got it? This is all going to be over in seconds. Nobody needs to get hurt."

The teller placed the garbage bag, now full, back on the counter.

Chris tipped an imaginary hat. "Thank you, ma'am." Then he grabbed his bag and, as he made his way out the door, a voice from off-camera said, "You know I'm not letting you leave with the money."

The camera panned out to reveal Luke Cross on the opposite side of the bank, dressed in a pinstriped suit. He, too, had a gun.

"Try it," Chris said. "I dare you."

Then Luke looked straight at the camera. "He dared me."

Connor had learned from Maria that when an actor spoke directly to the audience it was referred to as "breaking the fourth wall." He'd seen it done from time to time in movies that dated as far back as *Ferris Bueller's Day Off.* He had always thought it was a little bit cheesy, but funny and effective, nonetheless.

More gunshots followed. The extras screamed and ducked. From the crowd, two men wearing white suits joined the firefight. Chris charged for the exit. Blood burst forth from his shoulder just as he reached the door, and in the center of his back two more squibs went off in rapid succession.

He staggered outside.

"Dammit!" Maria shouted. "Cut! What the hell was that?" She looked around. "Marty? Where's Marty?"

The screen flashed and the scene had again reset. The clapboard indicated they were on Take 8.

Dylan paused the video. "You think that was the issue with the squibs Marty told us about?"

"Probably," Connor said.

Dylan pressed Play.

This time, the scene went off without a hitch. When Chris stumbled out the door after only one squib had exploded, Maria yelled, "Cut! That's a wrap!" and everyone broke into applause. The two men in white gave each other a high five. The extras smiled and shook each other's hands. Luke Cross threw a fist in the air and exclaimed, "That's what I'm talking about!"

Chris was the only one who still didn't seem happy. He came back through the door, his expression sullen— so much so that if Connor had to judge the success of the scene only by looking at him, he would have assumed the take hadn't gone well. Obviously, that wasn't the case. "We're done for the day?" he said toward the camera, before the screen went black.

No additional footage followed.

"That must have been the last thing they shot before Chris died," Dylan said.

"Something was really bothering him, wasn't it?"

"Looked like that to me."

"I wish we could figure out what it was."

Dylan ejected the disk. "Maybe if we go back through the other footage, we'll see something."

"Maybe," Connor said. As far as he could tell, the camera hadn't caught much other than the scenes themselves. But the footage was still probably worth looking at, if only so they might be able to pinpoint when Chris's mood had changed. Had he been happy the day before? What about the day before that? Everyone they'd talked to had spoken only to his mood the day he died. Nobody could say for certain when it had taken a turn for the worse.

Dylan grabbed the next disk nearest the bottom. "We'll work our way up."

Then a knock on the door drew Connor's attention. His head whipped toward the sound, and for a brief moment, he wondered: Was he right to be worried last night? Had their spy come back, after all?

CHAPTER 28

OLIN ARRIVED AT HUDSON'S close to four p.m. The house was surprisingly understated for a man who—based on his office—seemed to prize excess and elegance above all things. The two-story brick structure sat deep in a neighborhood of modest houses just outside the city's perimeter.

Olin parked along the curb two streets over. He dialed Hudson's office and, using an assumed name, asked to speak to the producer.

"I'm sorry. Mr. Davis is in a meeting," the receptionist informed him.

The three people Olin had seen in Hudson's waiting room came to mind. However, that had been hours ago. Almost certainly they had already left. Not that it mattered who he was meeting with. All Olin wanted to know was that Hudson was not at home.

The receptionist asked if Olin would like to leave a message, and Olin said he would call back later. Then he cautiously walked toward the house. He tried to play it cool, but everything he did felt unnatural. He put his hands in his pockets. He took them out. He made a point of looking at the houses he passed, then made a point of not looking. He tried to imagine how he might walk if he wasn't planning a break-in, and nothing came to mind.

He could feel a person behind every window watching him suspiciously, even though there was likely nobody there. He did not understand how Connor or Dylan could be so comfortable doing some of the things they did. They made it look easy, natural even. Olin felt like he was trying to juggle a group of basketballs that had been set on fire.

When he got to the house, he finally gave in to the urge to look over his shoulder and was relieved to see the neighborhood residents were not chasing him with pitchforks. He was still alone.

Like Connor had done at Lance's apartment, Olin knocked on the door to see if anyone was home. No one answered. He tried to turn the knob. The door was locked. He circled around the house, passed through a gate that led to the backyard, and tried the rear door, only to find it locked as well.

None of that was a surprise. Nor was the ADT alarm panel he saw through the window.

"If he has an alarm, there's a fifty-fifty chance it won't be armed," Connor had said.

A little red light at the top of the touchscreen indicated it was.

"And if it is armed, you're still going to have to go in. Just be quick about it."

Olin clenched his fists and ground his teeth together. If Connor and Dylan weren't on the other side of the Atlantic, he would tell them to come do this. Olin might have a PI license, but he was still an accountant at heart. None of this came naturally to him.

He pulled the lock pick set out of his right pocket and popped open the leather case. Inside was a collection of strange metal tools he had no idea how to use. He was going to have to call Dylan.

The person at the trailer door knocked again.

"Who do you think it is?" Connor whispered.

Before Dylan could answer, a voice outside called his name. He recognized it as Hannah's.

"Can I help you?" he asked her, after he opened the door.

"Can I come in?"

Connor looked over at Dylan, and Dylan shrugged. "Yeah, I guess so," he said. Then he stepped back, let Hannah climb on board, and locked the door behind her.

Hannah took two steps forward, putting her halfway between Connor and Dylan. "Maria told me you were going through the footage to see if you could find something."

"Maybe," Dylan said, even though the statement did not seem to invite a response.

"Do you mind if I help?"

"I thought you wanted us to leave," Dylan said.

Hannah had her hands clasped nervously in front of her. She looked down at them. "It's just . . . that guy who was spying on you . . . and now the articles online saying Chris was poisoned. Maybe it wouldn't hurt to have somebody other than the police looking into his death, too."

Connor could hear the pain in Hannah's voice. He thought about the five stages of grief: denial, anger, bargaining, depression, and acceptance. Hannah seemed to have been squarely in the second stage when they arrived. Now she seemed to be teetering somewhere between bargaining and depression. Not bargaining for Chris's return, of course. That was impossible. But perhaps bargaining for justice.

"Sure," he said. "You can stay."

"Hold on—"

"It's fine, Dylan." Connor returned to the sofa and sat down. "Look at her." Then to Hannah: "Come have a seat."

Hannah did.

"Start the next disk," Connor told Dylan.

Dylan stared angrily at Connor for a couple of seconds. "Fine." She spun around in the chair. Before she could click the PLAY button on the virtual editing bay, her phone rang. She looked at the screen. "It's Olin."

Connor knew it was too early for him to have gotten what he was after at Hudson's, which had to mean he had run into a problem. And since he was calling Dylan, it was likely a problem getting inside.

Dylan stood up and headed for the exit. "I won't be long."

Tall trees and a six-foot privacy fence hid most of Hudson's backyard from his neighbors. Nonetheless, Olin watched the closest houses for prying eyes. When Dylan answered, he shifted his attention back to the leather case he had in his hand.

"Everything's locked up tight. How do I use these?"

"You mean the lock picks?" Dylan asked.

"Yes, of course the lock picks."

"All right, calm down, Tex. What kind of lock are you dealing with?"

"How am I supposed to know that?"

"Is it a deadbolt?"

Olin looked at the lock. "Yes, it's a deadbolt."

"Okay. What about the handle? Is it locked, too?"

He turned the knob. "I don't think so."

"Good. Go into the kit. You're looking for one L-shaped pick and another one that's sort of jagged along one side."

Olin squeezed the phone between his shoulder and his ear so he could use both hands to sort through the picks. He pulled out the two that seemed to match Dylan's description. "Got 'em."

"All right. When you look at the keyhole, can you tell which way you would put the key in?"

"Yes."

"Take the one that's L-shaped and slide it into the lock along the edge where the flat side of the key would go. You're going to want to apply a little bit of pressure to the long end of the pick, just not so much that it bends. Got it?"

Olin looked over his shoulder, once again scanning the tall trees along the edge of Hudson's property and the houses on the other side of them. For the second time, he assured himself it would be difficult for anyone to see what he was up to.

Focus. The sooner you get inside, the sooner you can put this behind you.

He slid the L-shaped pick into the lock and applied pressure. "Done."

"Now, take the other pick and kind of work it around inside the lock. You're trying to push all of the pins into place."

"How will I know when I've got it?"

"You'll know."

Olin inserted the second pick and wiggled it around. After a minute or so, he suddenly felt the L-shaped pick begin to move, followed by a small rush of adrenaline. "I think I got it."

"See? Easy, right?"

He continued to apply pressure to the pick until the lock had turned as far as it could. "I'll call you back if I need any more help." Then he hung up, returned the picks to the leather case, and slid the case back into his pocket.

Olin knew once he opened the door, he'd have about thirty seconds until the alarm went off and likely several more minutes until the police arrived. It would be enough. When he had spoken with Connor and Dylan earlier, they had made it clear there was only one way he was going to be able to make this work. And it was not searching the house for a second computer that likely wasn't even there.

Olin turned the knob, took a deep breath, and pulled. The door opened. He stepped through and closed it behind him. The alarm began to beep, indicating that a countdown had begun.

Now that he was inside, he wished he had told Connor and Dylan to go to hell when they had suggested this plan. Unfortunately, it was too late for that. He had passed the point of no return.

Olin went in search of the stairs.

The house was cozy, with a lot of soft colors and floral prints. Again, not what he expected from a man like Hudson Davis. Perhaps his wife was responsible for the decor.

He made his way to the second floor. Then he quickly scanned the ceiling until he located a set of pulldown stairs that would take him to the attic. As soon as he grabbed the drawstring, the alarm began to sound. It was loud and intimidating. Every cell in Olin's body screamed for him to run.

He refused to give in to his instinct, and not just because he had passed some imaginary point of no return. The way he saw it, running out of the house now would be even more risky than following through with Connor's plan. There may not have been people watching when he had entered the house, but there sure would be if he went bolting out of there with a siren screaming in the background.

He pulled the drawstring, unfolded the stairs, and climbed into the attic. Then he awkwardly reached down and pulled the stairs closed.

With that, he was done. At least for now.

Olin stayed still, quiet. There was enough light to see, thanks to the gables, and he quickly assessed his surrounds. Plywood covered the floor at the top of the stairs, and he knelt carefully on a piece of it. Along most of the floor, however, there was only insulation between the wooden beams to stop him from falling straight through the drywall that divided the attic from the second story.

The alarm wailed on. One long minute stretched into another. Finally, he heard police sirens coming toward the house. They got closer and closer until they stopped. The officers must be right outside, Olin told himself, probably searching for a way in. It wouldn't take them long to find the door Olin had left unlocked.

Another minute passed.

The hot air in the attic and the stress made it hard to breathe.

The alarm was too loud for him to hear anything that might be happening on the floors below. Olin imagined the officers going room by room, guns drawn, in search of an intruder. He did not think they would pull down the stairs to the attic. Neither had Connor or Dylan when they'd discussed the strategy. It was an unlikely place for an intruder to hide.

Then Olin thought about all of the insulation around him, how sometimes a small piece of it would fall the floor when you climbed into an attic like this. He could picture Inspector Poirot or Sherlock Holmes picking it up between his thumb and first finger, studying it, then turning their attention to the pulldown stairs. That was, of course, absurd. There would be nobody like Inspector Poirot or Sherlock Holmes searching the house for a burglar. But an overzealous cop might do the same thing. And what would happen if a cop did come into the attic? Where would Olin go then?

There was only one answer to that: jail. There would be nowhere for him to hide.

The hot air seemed grow increasingly thick as he strained to hear any sound other than the alarm. Then, quite suddenly, it stopped, and in its place, a voice: "—no one here, sir."

The man had been shouting to be heard over the alarm and, based on his inflection, was as surprised when it stopped as Olin was.

The man continued talking, although not as loudly. Olin could no longer make out what he was saying.

He assumed the speaker was a cop and the man he was speaking to was likely Hudson. It seemed reasonable to think the producer would have rushed home after getting notified his alarm had gone off.

Or maybe he had already been on his way, Olin thought. Hudson's house was too far away from his office for him to have gotten here that quickly. His secretary had said he was in a meeting, but perhaps he was taking that meeting from the car.

Had Olin beaten him inside by mere minutes? What would have happened if he'd gotten stuck at another light or two? What would have happened if he had stopped for a soda? Would Hudson have found him at the back door, trying to break in?

The possibilities chilled him and, despite the small rush of adrenaline he had felt when he'd managed to get the lock open, he reminded himself that this sort of thing was not for him.

He pushed the thoughts out of his mind. In the end, they were questions that would never be answered and, as far as Olin was concerned, didn't need to be.

He strained to hear the conversation below him. He thought he might have heard someone use the phrase "false alarm," but he could not swear to it. All he could say for certain was that there were several men involved.

Olin had been on his knees until now. They were starting to hurt.

Slowly, carefully, he moved into a seated position, crossing his legs in front of him. The floor squeaked a little, but not enough to draw attention.

A moment later, there was the sound of a door slamming shut, and after that, only silence.

Olin began to wonder if everyone had left. Then he heard the muffled sounds of a man and a woman talking, which he thought might be Hudson and his wife. Had she been close, as well? Right down the street, maybe, or at a neighbor's?

That question could not be answered, either.

What mattered was that the police were gone. Only the two of them were left in the house.

Well, the three of them.

CHAPTER 29

DYLAN HUNG UP AND looked around the dark parking lot. The empty film trailers crowding the lot loomed large and ominous. Streetlights threw long, dark shadows in every direction. A cool breeze cut through the chilly night air, blowing a plastic bag from one end of nowhere to another.

She had the uneasy feeling she was being watched. She spun around a full three-hundred-and-sixty degrees, looking for any subtle movement, any glint of light that might suggest she was not alone, and finding neither.

"You're being stupid," she said to herself. She had seen the way Connor looked at the trailer door when Hannah knocked. She knew he must be thinking about the spy that had been outside his bedroom the night before. He was worried. That worry must have found its way into her without her realizing it.

There was nobody out there, she told herself, nobody watching them.

They were alone.

Strangely, that was somehow just as frightening. Perhaps because the parking lot—dark and deserted as it was—looked like the sort of dystopian set Hudson might feature in one of his movies.

She climbed back into the trailer, moving faster than she normally would, and locked the door behind her. She hated herself for that. She was a no-nonsense, kick-ass kind of woman who had grown up as a no-nonsense, kick-ass kind of girl. Fear had no place in her life.

She returned to her seat.

"Everything all right?" Connor asked, by which he meant: *Were you able to help him get into Hudson's house?*

"It's fine," she said, by which she meant: *Yes*. Then she spun back around to face the computer and started the next disk.

They watched hours of footage. The same scenes were shot over and over again, often from different angles. Hannah explained that was typical for a movie. "Ever notice how the perspective in a movie shifts every few seconds or so? Sometimes faster if it's an action sequence? Most movies are shot with a single camera. So for every new perspective, we have to move the camera, reset, and shoot again. When it's all said and done, we usually only get about three minutes of usable footage a day."

"You know a lot for someone who doesn't care for movies," Dylan said, while on the screen in front of her, Luke, dressed in a tuxedo, held up a drink as he proposed a toast.

"The first day, I asked Chris why we kept moving the camera around. He's the one who explained it to me."

The subtle melancholy in Hannah's voice reminded Dylan of the pain the woman must be feeling. She should try to be more sympathetic, she told herself. Hannah might have been rude when they arrived, but she seemed to be coming around.

The disk came to an end. Dylan ejected it and started another one.

CHAPTER 30

OLIN SAT QUIET AND still in the attic, moving only enough to check the clock on his phone once in a while. Large blocks of time passed where he heard nothing at all. Perhaps Hudson and his wife were reading or working or making or dinner. Perhaps they had moved to a part of the house where their voices would not carry to the attic. Whatever it was they were doing, Olin never heard a door open or close, so even in the longest blocks of silence, he was certain they were still in the house.

As the sun set, the attic grew dark. Eventually, Olin could not even see his hand in front of his face—which he tried to do. The only thing he could see was the thin ray of light that peeked through the crack around the attic door. Then that was gone, too.

Olin was certain that meant Hudson and his wife were going to bed. He decided he should stay where he was for another hour. It would take Hudson and his wife time to fall asleep, and he did not want to risk coming down from the attic prematurely.

Then something crawled onto his arm. In his mind's eye, he pictured the creepy crawler as a roach, big and black and disgusting. He immediately shook the bug away and felt his pants legs for others. He found none. However, that didn't mean they weren't out there in the dark, coming his way. He looked at the time on his phone. It had been fifty-three minutes since the light coming through the crack around the attic door had gone out. Long enough, he decided, and gently pushed the foldup stairs open.

The floor in the hallway was solid oak, so he had to be careful not to make too much noise when he unfolded the stairs. There was no changing his mind at this point, Olin told himself. If Hudson or his wife came out of the bedroom, he would not have time to retract the attic stairs before they saw him.

He climbed down, careful to be as quiet as possible, and folded the stairs up behind him. The house was dark, but not as dark as the attic, and he had no trouble making out even the smallest of details. He noticed the drawstring was swinging a little, and reached up to stop it. Then he tiptoed down to the first floor.

All he knew for certain was that he was looking for Hudson's laptop.

He found a computer bag leaning against an island in the kitchen. Since there were two people living in the house, there was a fifty-fifty chance that this was the machine he was looking for.

Olin placed the bag on the countertop, unzipped it, and looked through its pockets for anything that might tell him who the machine belonged to. He found a stack of papers with Hudson's name on them and decided he had struck gold.

He had the lock picks and his phone in his right pocket, his keys and Connor's USB stick in his left. Or so he thought. When he reached into his left pocket to remove the USB stick, he could not find it.

He cursed, began to panic, pulled the keys out to be certain the USB stick was not tangled up in them. It wasn't.

Olin tried to remember the last time he had been into that pocket. It had not been since he'd left their office, he realized, which meant the USB stick could have been anywhere. Perhaps he had lost it when he pulled out his keys to lock the door to their suite. Or perhaps it had fallen out when he'd pulled out the keys again to unlock the car. Or maybe it had slid out of his pocket when he was getting in or out of the driver's seat. There was simply no way to know.

He called Connor to tell him what had happened.

By the time his phone rang, Connor had grown numb and tired from scrutinizing all the footage. He checked the screen, said he would be right back, and exited the trailer. There was no need for further explanation. Dylan would know who it was.

Eyes on the monitor, she and Hannah barely acknowledged Connor as he stepped outside.

He looked around the dark parking lot.

"What's up?"

"I've lost the USB stick," Olin whispered. "What do I do?"

Connor tried to think. This wasn't good. He didn't have a backup plan, and teaching Olin how to hack into the computer with only his wits would be impossible over the phone.

"Are you sure?"

"Yes, I'm sure," Olin snapped. Instinctively, his eyes cut toward the doorway that led to the hall. His voice dropped back to a whisper. "I've checked both pockets. It's gone." Then he thought of one more place the USB stick might be: the attic. "Actually . . ."

"What?"

"I might know where it is. Let me check something."

"All right. If you can't find it—"

"I'll call you back." Olin hung up.

He crept back up to the second floor and pulled down the attic stairs. From where he was, he could see the door that led to the master bedroom. There was no light coming from behind it, which probably meant Hudson and his wife were still asleep.

Olin hated being here. His nerves were frayed beyond any reasonable limit. But if he thought he had come too far to abandon the plan when he'd first entered the house, he had definitely come too far now. If this didn't work, he dared not imagine what Connor and Dylan might ask him to do next.

He climbed halfway up the stairs and used one hand to feel the plywood around the area he had been sitting. His stomach turned at the thought that he might press his hand down on top of a roach or, worse, a whole swarm of them. He told himself that was unlikely. There would not be a swarm of roaches in the attic. But he couldn't shake the thought, and he couldn't find the USB stick, so he reluctantly used the flashlight app on his phone to examine the space.

Just as his common sense had told him, there was not a swarm of roaches within sight. But—look at that!—there was the USB stick. It must have fallen out of his pocket when he was shifting from one position to another.

He grabbed the stick and turned off the flashlight app. The plan was back on track—for a whole thirty seconds. As he was folding the stairs back up into the attic, he felt something under his thumb he could not identify. It did not feel like a roach, but it did not feel like the wooden stairs, either. His stomach began to turn again as he shifted his hand away from it and, in doing so, he lost his grip on the stairs.

They unfolded fast, clattering loudly as they hit the floor. Olin gritted his teeth, tensed up, looked again at the bedroom door. He hoped against hope Hudson and his wife were sound sleepers.

But it was obvious they were not when a bedroom light came on.

Olin remembered breaking into a house with Connor years ago and getting chased out of it by a man with a shotgun. That was not a moment he wanted to repeat.

He hurried down the stairs to the first floor as quietly as he could. Before he got to the bottom of them, he heard the bedroom door open. Nobody spoke, but Olin had no doubt Hudson was coming, armed with a weapon of some sort.

The adrenaline rushing through his system pushed away almost all rational thought. For less than a second, he stood in the foyer trying to remember where he had left the computer. Then he hurried to the kitchen and grabbed the laptop bag.

Connor had said it would take about twenty seconds to install the software. Olin would not have to log in, but the computer would have to be on. That could take another thirty seconds or more. He needed to find someplace he could hide for a full minute, if not longer.

Olin looked around. There did not seem to be anywhere. He couldn't very well hunker down behind the sofa or tuck himself into a closet. Hudson would check all of those places. So what was left?

Nothing.

If Olin was going to get Connor onto Hudson's computer, he was going to have to take the machine with him.

Normally, Olin would not consider stealing somebody's computer. Even if he could justify it, he would have agonized about the decision. But Olin wasn't thinking straight and didn't have time to analyze the pros and cons of his choice. All he knew for sure was he would be damned before he came back to try something like this again.

He grabbed the computer out of the bag and ran back out the same door he had come in.

Olin was back on the street before the alarm started to sound, and he did not stop running until he reached his car. Sprinting, actually. Pumping his legs faster than he ever had before, gripping the computer in one hand, he might have been able to keep up with Usain Bolt.

He fished his keys out of his pocket while he was still on the move and tapped the unlock button. Then he tossed the laptop into the passenger seat, kicked his BMW into gear, and drove off as fast as he felt like he could without drawing attention.

The neighborhood dumped him onto a two-lane road that dumped him onto a four-lane. As he navigated the streets, he repeatedly checked the rearview mirror to make sure he wasn't being followed.

On the four-lane road, the traffic was thick. He was just one driver among many. The stress of being in Hudson's house eased a little.

When he hit a stoplight, he reached over, opened the laptop, and pressed the power button. The screen immediately came to life. Hudson must have put the computer to sleep when he'd left the office instead of turning it off entirely. But it wouldn't have made any difference to Olin when he was standing in the kitchen, even if he had known. He still would have needed at least twenty seconds to install the software. He still would have needed a place to hide. And, at that moment, it had seemed neither had been available to him.

He plugged the USB stick into the computer. As far as he could tell, nothing was happening.

He looked up at the traffic light. When it turned green, he pressed down on the gas and called Connor.

"I found the stick. I got it into the computer. It doesn't seem like it's doing anything."

"That's okay. You wouldn't be able to tell," Connor said. "After twenty seconds or so, just pull it out and get out of there."

"I'm already out."

"What do you mean?"

"I had to take the computer with me."

"What? Why?"

"Hudson woke up," Olin said. He did not feel like telling Connor any more than that.

"You should have left it. We could have found another way."

"We need to find out what's in his email, right? I wasn't going back in that house again later. It was now or never. I can send the computer back to him when we're done."

Connor paused, then said, "Okay. Find somewhere private, like a park or a deserted shopping center. I'll call you when I'm ready for you to tether it to your phone."

"Why don't I just take it home?"

"The same reason you shouldn't have taken it with you to begin with. Some laptops are equipped with GPS tracking. Whenever they connect to the internet, the computer will reach out to a monitoring center to report its location. Hudson seems like the kind of guy who might have something like that, and we don't want the location it reports to be your apartment."

"Oh my God. Do I have to worry—"

"Relax. As long as you're not connected to the internet, you'll be fine."

CHAPTER 31

WHEN OLIN HAD CUT Connor off during their previous call, Connor was just about to tell him that he should simply leave if he could not find the USB stick for exactly the reasons he'd just explained to him now. But what was done was done. Frankly, if he had been in Olin's position, he likely would have taken the computer as well. Regardless of how good a hacker Connor might be, without the computer or a way to access it, he wasn't getting in, no matter what he did.

Back in his room, Connor turned on his own computer and launched the application that would connect it to Hudson's. Dylan sat in a chair beside him, watching him work. Hannah—who had not been invited to join them—had said she had to go to bed and would return the trailer's keys to Maria on the way.

Connor had his phone open on the table beside the computer and Olin on speaker.

"Ready when you are," Connor said.

Olin had found a shuttered CVS and parked next to the dumpster in back. "Connecting the laptop to my phone now," he said. Then, after a couple of seconds, he added, "All right. Done."

"Great." Connor clicked a button so that the two computers could talk. Then, behind the scenes, the software implemented a series of procedures that would bypass the login, and a moment later Hudson's desktop appeared on the screen before him.

"Just remember," Olin said, "I'm on battery over here, so I don't know how long you've got."

Dylan rolled her eyes as if to say, *Duh*. But she didn't actually speak. After Olin had warned Connor about the battery, he didn't either. They were both waiting anxiously to see what Connor would find.

Connor opened Hudson's Outlook, filtered the emails based on Chris's name, and scanned through them, starting with the newest ones first. Most were about the production or involved negotiations with Chris's agent.

"There," Olin said, who could see on the laptop's monitor what Connor was doing. "At the bottom of the screen. What's that?"

"What?" Connor asked.

"An email. The subject line reads 'Make sure you hire the right actor.'"

Connor clicked the email.

Good day, Mr. Davis.

I know you are considering several actors for the role of Habersham. I suggest you see to it that Chris Miller comes out on top. I would hate for these pictures to find their way to someone they shouldn't.

Sincerely,
A Friend

Connor clicked on the first picture. It showed a man and a woman standing on the sidewalk in front of a Mexican restaurant called El

Taqueria Del Ray. It was a candid photo, similar to those Dylan had taken the one time they had been hired by a woman who wanted to find out if her husband was cheating on her.

Both subjects' faces were clearly visible.

"That's Hudson," Dylan said, referring to the man.

"Who's that with him?" Olin asked. "Is that his wife?"

None of them had seen Hudson's wife, and if Connor didn't already know who the woman was, they might have had to do some digging to answer that question. "No," he said, still wrestling with the implications of the picture. "That's Jax's."

For a beat—maybe two—nobody responded.

"Well . . . maybe they were meeting to talk about a part," Olin said. Like Connor, he knew Jax's wife, Melissa, wanted to be in film and had thus far been unsuccessful.

The picture looked innocent enough. In another context, Connor might have thought Olin was right. But you wouldn't attach the picture to an email like this if it was as innocent as it seemed.

Olin knew that. Connor could hear it in his voice.

Instead of responding, he clicked on the next picture. This one showed them holding hands. The one after that showed them kissing.

There were ten pictures in all, each one more graphic than the last.

"That's a hell of a way to get a part," Dylan said.

Connor turned toward her. "If the sender forwarded these pictures to Hudson's wife, she would divorce him, for sure." He was thinking about the notes they had found in the psychiatrist's file.

Dylan must have been operating on the same wavelength, because she responded by adding, "If there was a judge out there who wouldn't have given her half before, they sure would once they saw these."

She stood up. "I guess we know why he hired Chris now."

"But who wanted him to hire Chris?" Connor asked. "It still seems like a stretch that Chris would be behind the blackmail."

"Probably," Dylan said. "But it's as good a reason for murder as you can get if he was."

"You think there are any other emails?" Olin said.

Connor changed his search to filter on hudsonseyesonly@gmail.com, the sender's email address. No other results came back. "We need to figure out who sent this."

Easier said than done, though, perhaps. Connor had no doubt that this account had been created specifically to blackmail Hudson. Since Gmail accounts were free, anyone could have been behind it.

There might be another way, though. Like he had done with the psychiatrist's email, Connor retrieved the sender's IP from the header and hacked his way into the associated computer. He expected that, somewhere in the files and folders on that computer, he would find a name. If he was lucky, it would be one he already knew. They had met a lot of people since they'd started their investigation. There was a fair chance the blackmailer was among them.

What he found instead were records that indicated the computer was owned by PS Printing.

"Who's that?" Dylan asked, looking over his shoulder.

"I don't know," Connor said. He had never heard of PS Printing.

A quick search online indicated the company provided printing services (obviously) as well as computers you could rent by the minute.

"So they're kind of like a FedEx," Olin said.

"Yeah," Connor agreed, "but it looks like they only have a couple of locations. Both in the Atlanta area."

"Whoever it is was smart enough not to use their home computer," Dylan said.

Connor nodded.

"Any chance you can find out which location it was?"

"What are you thinking?"

"We know what time the email was sent. If we know where it was sent from, somebody at the store might be able to tell us who sent it."

Connor leaned in close to the phone. "Olin, how do you feel about going by PS Printing and asking them if they have a way of telling who was using their computer at that time?"

"As long as you don't ask me to break into someone's house again, I'm fine with it."

Connor dug around the machine some more but was unable to determine which of the two locations the blackmailer had used. "Looks like you're going to have to visit them both. Fingers crossed they can tell you something."

CHAPTER 32

LANCE STOOD IN FRONT of a painting on the top floor of the Garder Museum, staring at it. The piece was by renowned impressionist Andrew Thompson and was one of his favorites. It was titled "April Rain."

A field of unidentifiable yellow flowers extended from the bottom of the canvas to the top. Subtle touches in the work suggested they were being tossed about by a hard wind.

Lance blurred his vision and watched the painting come to life. The flowers began to sway the way they might have on the day Andrew had painted them.

He let his mind wander. It landed on the Facebook message he had received—CHRIS IS DEAD—and the phone call that had followed.

The yellow flowers began to sway more feverishly. Lance could almost see the wind pushing them around.

"A storm was coming," he said to himself.

He made the statement only within the context of the painting. After he said it, however, he realized it might indeed mean more than that. Because a storm *was* coming. Jax had ruined his life. He had broken Lance's arm. Lance couldn't let that stand. What might the actor do next if he did?

He needed to take Jax down a peg. A lot of pegs, actually. He needed to put him all the way into the ground.

In his mind only, lightning flashed. Rain began to fall. The yellow flowers were now being battered relentlessly.

Then he blinked, and the painting was once again a painting. The flowers no longer swayed. The rain no longer fell. But the memory of that storm—the emotion it had created, the statement it had inspired—stayed with him. And now he said something else out loud, something he had only thought before: "I need to put him all the way in the ground."

It needed to be done soon, too. He did not think he would find a moment's peace as long as Jax was out there walking around.

He headed to the stairs and took them down to the lobby, forgoing his rounds on the top floor.

"That was even longer than usual," Ned said as Lance approached the desk. He had a microwavable meal in one hand—Swedish meatballs, it looked like—and a plastic fork in the other.

Lance had not thought he'd been gone long enough for Ned to notice, especially since he had cut his rounds short. How long had he been staring at that painting? Three minutes? Four? It couldn't have been longer than that, could it? Then he remembered that he had once stood in front of a painting for more than ten minutes, during which it felt like only seconds had passed. He knew this only because he had happened to look at the clock on the wall before and after.

Could it have been longer than ten minutes?

He shook his head, decided it didn't matter.

"You really like those paintings, don't you?" Ned said.

Lance glanced at his partner. "I have to go," he said, and began to move quickly towards the door.

Surprised, Ned tossed his meal onto the desk and scurried around it. Actually, Lance thought, "waddled" might be more accurate.

Regardless, he was moving faster than Lance had ever seen him go.

"Wait, wait, wait," Ned said, holding his hands up.

Lance could have barreled straight past him if he wanted to, but since Ned was the closest thing he had to a friend, he stopped. "What is it?"

"Stuart's going to be mad if you leave me here alone."

Stuart Winkle was their boss, and he was about as much of douchebag as anyone could be.

"So what?"

"He might fire you."

Lance hesitated. He needed a job, and—as far as jobs went—this one wasn't too bad. What would he do if Stuart fired him? Serve ice cream at the mall? Pack boxes at a warehouse? Get a truck driving license and start running long-haul trips across the country?

He looked at the plush desk chair where he sat whittling away the hours from dusk until dawn. He thought about the decades of artwork that hung on these walls. It was a hard gig to walk away from.

But, he reminded himself, he wouldn't need a job at all if it weren't for Jax. He needed to settle the score now. If he was right—if Chris's death meant what he thought it might—waiting until tomorrow could be too late.

"Let him," Lance said and pushed his way past Ned. Then, before he left, he turned around. "But, if he says anything like that, remind him I've been here for five years. *Five years*, got it? Except for that little vacation I took"—he used his one good hand to put air quotes around the word vacation—"I have not missed a single day."

Ned nodded, and all three of his chins jiggled. "Okay. I got it. I'll tell him."

Lance pointed at him. "Don't forget."

Now Ned was shaking his head. "I won't."

Lance turned the lock on the door and stepped out into the night air.

The museum was located on Peachtree Street, a thoroughfare that cut straight through the heart of Midtown. During the day, it was besieged by six lanes of bumper-to-bumper traffic. Right now, there wasn't a car within sight.

For the first time in years, Lance did not bother to cross the street to the twenty-four-hour gas station and get a newspaper. It did not even cross his mind. Nor did the fact that he had taken a bus here—not until he got to the staff parking lot and realized his car wasn't in it.

Dammit!

The buses wouldn't start running for another hour, which only made him angrier. He wished Jax had never come into his life. If Jax had never come into his life, his arm wouldn't be broken. He'd be able to drive his car right now. Actually, strike that. He wished Jax had never been born. If Jax hadn't been born, he wouldn't need to drive his car right now, because he wouldn't be working here. Lance would be a movie star. There were no two ways about it. He had, after all, been the only other actor besides Jax to be called back for the part in *Descendant.*

Lance felt his rage deepen to the point that he had to scream. He had to relieve some of the pressure. Then he charged back around the building and pounded on the glass door to get Ned's attention.

"I need a fucking taxi," he said when Ned opened up.

CHAPTER 33

HANNAH AWOKE TO A text message from Maria on her phone. Everyone was to meet in the lobby at eight a.m. She wondered what Maria wanted this time. It couldn't have anything to do with Connor and Dylan. Hannah had stayed with them until they called it quits, and they had found nothing unusual on any of the tapes.

Maybe Maria just wanted to give them another pep talk, assure them everything would be all right. A little rah-rah, team cheer bullshit. But everything wasn't going to be all right. Chris was dead.

She dragged herself out of bed and made it downstairs early enough to pour a cup of tea before the meeting started. Yesterday, she had noticed Connor and Dylan drinking coffee. Them and all of the Americans on the shoot. Disgusting black muck. She didn't understand how anyone consumed it. It was probably the worst thing to drink any time of day, but first thing in the morning—that had to be the absolute worst. It was just so . . . bitter.

She took a seat on a leather sofa in the lobby and waited for the meeting to start. She sipped from her cup of tea.

If she was being fair, it wasn't just the Americans who drank coffee, she thought. Chris and a handful of other Brits working the film had picked up the habit while they were living in the States, so they drank it, too.

Not that it mattered. It was still disgusting black muck.

The inane conversation she was having with herself on the merits of coffee versus tea rattled around in her head until Marty sat down beside her. Today, instead of a Grateful Dead tee shirt, he was wearing one with the band Phish on it. Hannah had listened to neither group, but she gathered they were legends of a sort in the hippie community.

"What do you think it's about this time?" he asked.

"Guess we'll see," Hannah said.

"I heard Connor and Dylan were going through all the footage last night."

Hannah wasn't surprised he already knew about that. Being on a film set was like being back in high school—especially when there wasn't any action. Everybody gossiped.

"Do you know if they found anything?" Marty asked.

Hannah shook her head, took another sip of her tea. "I was with them the whole time."

Marty sighed, turned his attention toward the lift. Enough of the cast and crew had gathered by now that all he could see were the bodies in front of him. "I guess we'll find out," he said, echoing Hannah's statement at the start of their conversation.

They didn't have to wait long.

The crowd was too thick to see Maria step off the lift, but Hannah heard her call them to attention. "Everyone! Eyes up front!"

Marty stood up and crossed his arms over his chest as the cast and crew settled down. Hannah looked around to see she was the only one still sitting and reluctantly stood as well.

"This better be good," Marty grumbled.

Hannah did not have high hopes. She braced herself for another feel-good speech.

"I have news you're going to want to hear. Please, everyone, be quiet." Maria waited another thirty seconds for the last of the chatter to die down before continuing. "You have all been very patient the last several days. The support you've provided to me and each other during this tough time has been heartwarming."

Rah-rah, Hannah thought.

"I know some of you were close to Chris, and there is still a lot of healing to do. But we're here to do a job, and we're going to get back to it starting today. To that end, I would like to make several introductions."

Maria gestured toward the hall that led from the lift to the toilets, and out stepped two men Hannah did not recognize. They both looked to be in their forties and were wearing tailored suits she suspected were expensive.

"They must be from the studio," Marty said, and he was right.

Maria rattled off their names, said they were from Nightbird and that they would be overseeing the rest of the production.

The chatter resumed, this time with an uneasy edge to it, and Hannah understood why. While she did not care whether the studio wanted to oversee the movie, she knew a lot of the people working on it would. She had learned from Chris there was often a degree of tension that existed between the studio and those working on the film. In some cases, it bordered on quiet animosity, and in the worst cases, outright hostility. That was, quite simply, because each side did not fully trust the other to do what was in the best interest of the film. The cast and crew wanted to make art. The studio wanted to put butts in seats.

Hannah just wanted a paycheck.

"What do we need them for?" someone in the crowd shouted. "We can't do anything without someone to play Habersham."

That was also true. Without an actor for Habersham, there was nothing for the execs to oversee.

Maria ignored the comment and made her next pair of introductions. This time, a man and a woman appeared from the hallway. They were the writers, Maria said, and would be reworking the film in light of the tragedy.

So far, the whole series of introductions struck Hannah as a tad dramatic. These were people you would not recognize if you were standing right in front of them. You would not even know them by name. There was no need to "bring them to the stage," as it were, with such flair. Not unless Maria was building to something bigger, which Hannah suspected she was.

We can't do anything without someone to play Habersham.

"And finally, everyone, please welcome the newest member of our cast, Jax Hart."

Jax stepped out wearing a red blazer, a white tee shirt, and blue jeans. He waved to everyone. "Thanks, Maria. I'm glad to be here."

Maria nodded and smiled in response before once again addressing the crowd. "The writers have already identified several scenes we can move forward with. We're going to begin re-shoots today where we need them, starting with scene twenty-seven."

Hannah knew that was the last scene Chris had shot before he died.

"Now, if some of you need more time, I totally understand. Please come see me after we're done here, and we will see what we can do to move you off the film. I do not want any of you to feel like you need to go back to work before you're ready. Any questions?"

There was more chatter. None of it was directed at Maria.

"All right, then. I want everyone in position at nine o'clock. See you on the set."

Maria returned the way she had come. The cast and crew gathered around the newcomers. There were a few cool handshakes and lukewarm welcomes shared with the studio execs. Most of the attention was directed toward Jax and the writers.

Hannah wasn't in a mood to speak to any of them. She tried to slink away in all the commotion and had almost made it to the stairwell when Jax shouted her name. "Come over here, will you?"

She did as he requested.

"Maria told me you were friends with Chris. I don't want this to be weird. Are you okay?"

"Why would it be weird?" Hannah said. She could feel everyone's eyes on her. She didn't like being the center of attention. She wanted to wrap this conversation up as quickly as possible and get back to her room.

"Look, someone has to play Habersham, all right? I promise I'll do the role justice."

"I said it wasn't weird."

"You're sure?"

"I'm sure."

"Then why were you sneaking off without saying hello?"

"It's just . . ." She pointed toward the stairs. "I have something I have to do in my room."

"All right, all right. Well, it was nice to meet you. I'll see you on the set."

Hannah smiled awkwardly. "You, too," she said, and moved away from the crowd.

CHAPTER 34

THE TAXI TOOK FOREVER to get to the Garder Museum. Lance hung around by the door and Ned peppered him with questions about where he was going and what he was going to do. At first, those questions were general. As the minutes wore on, they became more specific, and even though Lance had answered none of them, Ned finally worked his way around to the matter at hand. "If this has something to do with Jax—"

"It's something I have to do," Lance snapped, finally turning around so that he was looking at his partner instead of the street. He could hear the fury in his own voice, the intensity with which he clipped his words.

Ned could hear it, too, Lance realized. The man looked wounded, almost as if he had been physically struck.

"I was only trying to help."

Lance did not feel like apologizing, even though he knew he should not have snapped at his friend like that, so he said, "I'll wait outside," and then did just that. He hoped Ned would not follow him onto the sidewalk and continue asking questions.

Ned seemed to have gotten the message. Without further comment, he locked the door and went back to the desk.

The taxi moved slowly, taking a route Lance would not have recommended and stopping at all the yellow lights. The driver's primary interest seemed to be in letting the meter run up as large a tab as possible. It annoyed Lance (right now, everything annoyed Lance), but he did not say as much. He did not want the driver to remember him later. After Jax turned up dead, he didn't want the man phoning the police, telling them about a belligerent customer he'd picked up late at night and driven to Jax's neighborhood.

Not to Jax's house, mind you. Lance had intentionally given him the wrong address. But if an aggressive conversation triggered the driver's memory, even the neighborhood might be enough to cause problems for Lance.

When the driver pulled over to the curb, Lance handed him enough cash to cover the bill with a modest tip. (He didn't want to be remembered as being too generous any more than he wanted to be remembered for being too difficult.) Then he said, "Thank you," and got out.

The driver barely acknowledged him. Good. That was exactly what he wanted.

Once the driver was gone, he walked up to Jax's house. He already knew Jax had a gate controlled by a callbox, so he did not waste time trying to find a way through it. There was no need, anyway. The thing about a lot of gates—and the fences they were attached to—was that they did more to keep out cars than people. Lance could easily pull himself over the brick wall surrounding Jax's property, even with one good arm—so easily, in fact, he did not bother to seek out a patch of shadows that would conceal him from the street. He hopped, pulled, swung. One minute he was on the sidewalk; the next, he was gone. If you blinked, you would have missed it.

Lance landed in a bed of hollies that pricked and scratched him through his uniform. He gritted his teeth and repeatedly curled his hands into fists to distract himself from the pain as he made his way free of them.

In his book, this was just another cruelty he had to suffer because Jax was in his life, another reason to kill him.

He walked to the driveway and then straight up the middle of it. From there, he was in plain view of the security cameras. He looked directly at one of them and smiled. "I'm ready for my closeup, Mr. President."

Just as it was too late for anyone to see him jump over the wall, it was too late for Jax to see him coming now. He and his wife would be in bed.

That's right—his wife. Enraged as he was, Lance had forgotten about her. Well, she was no innocent. Jax would just have to kill them both. It should be easy. Kill them, wipe down his prints, take the security tapes. He might still be home by dawn.

Lance pounded on the large steel door, armed with only his one good fist. Eventually a woman's voice came from the callbox beside it. "I've called the police, Lance. You'd better get out of here before they come."

For a moment, Lance was surprised she knew who he was. Then again, why should he be? The man who had taken his picture had probably told them both about him. Hell, maybe even *Jax* had told her about him—how he had stolen the part in *Descendant* and ruined Lance's chances of stardom just for the fun of it. They'd probably had a good laugh at his expense.

"You'll let me in, Melissa, if you know what's good for you."

"Get out of here!"

Lance stepped off the porch and circled the house, looking for a window and a rock he could use to break it. He found the window first. With the curtains drawn, he could not tell where it led. But it was big enough to crawl through, and that was all that mattered.

The rock he found only seconds later. It was roughly the size of his fist. *Perfect.* He was not going to get through the glass by throwing it, though, so he scooped the rock up with his left hand and began to pound.

The glass cracked and then shattered. Melissa began screaming from inside.

Lance reached in, turned the security latch, and lifted the frame.

The window opened onto a bathroom. Lance awkwardly climbed through, using the toilet as if it were a stepstool to reach the floor.

He stepped into the hall, looked left, then right. There were doors everywhere. "Come out, come out, wherever you are."

By now, Melissa had stopped screaming. She and Jax must have found a place to hide, he thought. Not that they would be able to hide for long. Lance intended to turn this place upside down if that was what it took to find them.

On the way here, he had worried about getting caught. Now, he no longer cared. He had come to do a job, and he was not going to leave until he was finished. His life was already ruined. How much worse could it get? But Jax—things could get a whole lot worse for him, and they were about to.

"Come out, come out, wherever you are!" Lance repeated as he started down the hall, throwing open every door he passed and searching the spaces behind them.

The house was like a maze. Hallways connected to rooms in unexpected ways. Or maybe it only seemed that way because the place was so large.

Jax and Melissa were not hiding in this bedroom, or that one, or the closet. They were not in this bathroom, or the next one he entered, or the living room. They were not in the office, or the billiard room (*he has a damn billiard room!*), or the library.

"You're only going to make this worse for yourself!"

Then he came to a door that was locked. He turned the knob several times in each direction to make sure. He pressed his ear to the jamb, thought he heard the creak of a floorboard or maybe a soft whimpering. He slammed his palm against the door. "I know you're in there, Jax! Get the hell out!"

Someone on the other side of the door squeaked out a sound like they were trying to suppress a scream.

If Lance had had use of both of his hands, he would have grabbed a piece of heavy furniture and slammed it into the door like a battering ram. But his legs would do just as well. They knew how to take the abuse of a long run—the constant pounding on the soles of his feet, the burning in his calves and thighs. He kicked the door beside the knob and kept kicking until the wood splintered.

The person on the other side no longer tried to suppress her screams—and he could hear her well enough now to know it was indeed a "her." Which almost certainly meant he had found Melissa. And if he had found Melissa, he had found Jax, too.

Once he had kicked a hole wide enough to get his hand through, he peeked inside. He wanted to know what he was getting himself into before reaching in to unlock the door. Last thing he needed was Jax, armed with a knife, taking off a finger.

He felt like Jack Nicholson in *The Shining.*

"Heeeeeeeere's Johnny," he called, playing into the moment.

The door opened onto another bedroom. Melissa was cowering in the corner and had begun screaming again, even louder this time. Jax was nowhere to be seen.

Lance unlocked the door and stepped in. "Tell me where he is, Melissa."

The wannabe actress was not just screaming. She was also crying. A real blubbering mess. "He's not here!"

"Tell me where he is!"

"He's not here, I swear! He went to London for a movie. He isn't here! Please, please—leave me alone. Please!"

Lance knew immediately she was telling the truth. She was not a good enough actress to summon that level of authenticity at will. If she was, she'd be a bigger star than Jax.

A previous conversation flashed through his mind—the one that had started with a Facebook message and ended with a phone call:

CHRIS IS DEAD.

What do you think it means?

I don't know.

Lance had said he didn't either, but he'd had a suspicion the studio might bring Jax in to replace the dead actor, and it looked like he was right.

Melissa continued to plead for her life. Underneath that tiresome drone, Lance realized he could hear a siren getting louder.

Police cars were approaching.

Lance was going to jail, for certain. He could imagine some of the charges the DA would throw at him: breaking and entering, criminal trespass, destruction of property. No doubt there were others. Probably a lot of them. That would have been okay if he had managed to kill Jax. He had already prepared himself for the possibility. But going to jail now—with Jax still walking around alive and well—would be nothing less than another serving of injustice heaped onto a plate that was already overflowing with it.

So he turned to run. He went out the back door and disappeared into the night.

CHAPTER 35

CONNOR AND DYLAN DID not want to risk another awkward breakfast and were unaware of the meeting Maria had called to introduce Jax and the other newcomers. As such, they thought it best to order room service and stay right where they were. Besides, they had work to do.

After room service came, Connor poured a cup of coffee for himself and another for Dylan while she spread the food out on the table in his room. They had ordered eggs—both omelets and scrambled—plus bacon, sausage, and whole grain toast.

Connor selected items from the various dishes and piled them onto a smaller plate while Dylan did the same.

"I've been thinking about that email," he said. "The one Hudson got. I don't think it suggests he was involved in the murder, no matter who sent it."

"You don't?"

"Mia told us Hudson was considering Jax for the role. Remember?"

"Yeah," Dylan said as she unfolded her napkin and put it in her lap.

"I think he wanted to ship Jax off to London so he could spend more time with Jax's wife without looking over his shoulder so much. Then someone came along threatening to expose him if he didn't hire Chris instead."

"You don't think that's enough to kill for?"

"I don't think he knows who sent it. Even if he suspects Chris was behind the blackmail, he wouldn't kill him while Chris was working on his movie. Look at all the attention that has drawn to the production." Connor was referring to the hundreds of articles he had seen online since the news broke, most of which referenced Hudson's production company by name. "Hudson is a smart guy. He doesn't strike me as someone who acts rashly. If he'd wanted to kill Chris, he would at least have had the good sense to wait until after the movie had finished shooting.

"But I do think Hudson was afraid of being blamed for the murder if this email ever got out. And I think that also answers the question of why he hired us. He didn't want to get taken by surprise if the police zeroed in on him as a suspect. Maybe it also made him feel better having someone other than the police looking for the killer in case that happened."

"I guess you could be right," Dylan said. "But if Chris sent it, I still say it's a hell of a motive."

"Which is exactly what the police will think if they ever see that email."

Dylan shrugged as she slathered a piece of toast with butter.

"Anyway, I suppose we'll find out who sent it soon enough."

"Hopefully," Dylan said.

"Hopefully," Connor agreed, and slid the plates around to make room for his laptop. "In the meantime, I think we need to take a closer look at our other suspects—Marty and Luke, in particular. At the very least, it will give us something to do until we can talk to Ryan."

CHAPTER 36

OLIN DID NOT SLEEP well with Hudson's laptop in his apartment. He stared at the walls, imagining all sorts of scenarios that might bring the police to his door. They ranged from the obvious—Hudson had seen him—to the absurd—that the tracking device (if there was one) was still broadcasting the computer's location, even though the machine was not connected to the internet and the battery had died.

He did not call Connor with these theories because he knew how paranoid he would sound. If Hudson had seen Olin steal the computer, Connor would have already heard about it and called him. As for the tracking device, Connor had already explained how it worked. And as for the theories in between, a little reason was all he needed to take them off the table.

Olin was as safe as he could possibly be. Still, he made a point of visiting the FedEx outlet close to his house as soon as it opened so he could mail the laptop back. Actually, he was there ten minutes before it opened. He did not want that computer in his possession one second longer than it had to be.

He also did not want to mail it from PS Printing, even though their website claimed they offered the exact same service. It was best, he thought, to keep that conversation focused on the blackmailer.

The first PS Printing location he visited was in a suburb north of

Atlanta, nestled right in the middle of a strip mall filled with boutique shops, like Bella's Jewels, which featured a large photo of a diamond tennis bracelet in the window, and Pet-a-Doos, a pet groomer with a sleek black-and-white waiting room reminiscent of the sort of thing you might see at an upscale salon.

PS Printing was modest by comparison, with an assortment of office equipment scattered throughout the store. Copiers and large paper trimmers were to the left. Packing supplies and a pair of small workstations were to the right. Each workstation had a computer you could rent by the minute. If the blackmailer had sent the email from this location, he must have done so using one of those machines.

Olin glanced at the man behind the counter. He was busy assembling a stack of papers into a binder, perhaps filling a customer's order. Olin went to the nearest of the two computers, entered his credit card into a reader, and waited for the computer to grant him access.

Once it had, he followed the instructions Connor had given him to check the computer's IP address. Then he pulled out his phone, located the digital note where he had written down the IP address the hacker had used, and compared them. They were not a match.

He repeated the same steps at the next computer. It was not a match either.

He looked back at the man behind the counter.

This time, the man looked at him as well. "Can I help you?"

"Maybe," Olin said, realizing that the email might not have been sent by a customer at all. He approached the counter and asked the man if he had been working there on the date the email had been sent.

The man considered the question. "No, I don't think so. Why do you ask?"

"Do you know who was?"

"Sorry, man. You lose something?" He reached under the counter and pulled out a plain cardboard box about the size of a shoebox. "We got a little lost-and-found here. Maybe somebody turned it in."

"It's not that."

"What is it, then?"

Olin took a step back. "You know what? Never mind." Before he started accusing employees of blackmail, he figured he had better check out the computers at the second store. An accusation like that would turn into gossip as soon as Olin left. The man behind the counter would call someone who would call someone else, and it wouldn't be long before everyone who worked for PS Printing would be talking about the crime.

If Olin's theory was right, the blackmailer would inevitably hear about it before they knew who he was and would just as likely disappear before they ever got a chance to talk to him.

The man looked at Olin with a mix of suspicion and confusion as he backed toward the door.

"Really," Olin said, "it's not important." Then, if for no other reason than to break eye contact, he turned around and left.

He had parked in a row directly in front of PS Printing. The walk from the store to his car kept him within the man's line of sight the whole time, and, while he didn't know if it was true, he could feel the man watching him every step of the way. He urged himself to stay calm, to avoid drawing any additional attention by moving too fast.

Once he had pulled out of the lot, he chastised himself for approaching the man without thinking through the implications. It was the kind of thing Connor might have done. However, Connor was quick on his feet in a way Olin was not. Acting on instinct, Connor could navigate through the consequences of even the hastiest decisions as if he was already prepared for them. Olin should have known better than to try such a thing. He could charm most women he met with a smile and a bit of small talk, but he needed a plan for a conversation like the one he had just had.

Well, you'll get another chance, he told himself, by which he meant another chance to talk to a PS Printing employee, not another chance to accuse one of them of blackmail.

Olin followed the directions to the second PS Printing location. Unlike the first one, which served Atlanta's wealthy, this store had been opened in a part of town populated by strip clubs and frequented by people who looked like they might use PS Printing to mail someone a severed hand.

Both stores shared an identical floorplan and, like at the last location, the only person in the store besides Olin was a man working the counter. He was a brunette instead of a blond, had glasses instead of a beard, and was restocking a display of postcards instead of filling a binder with papers, but was otherwise interchangeable.

Olin made his way over to the workstations and, this time, got a hit with the first computer. He compared the IPs twice to make sure he wasn't mistaken. No doubt about it. This was the computer the blackmailer had used.

He took a deep breath, rehearsed what he wanted to say, then cautiously approached the man behind the counter.

"Hi, Joe," Olin said, reading the name off the man's nametag.

Joe looked from the display to Olin and put the small stack of postcards he was holding on the counter. They featured a variety of Atlanta landmarks: the High Museum of Art, the Georgia Aquarium, the World of Coca-Cola.

"What can I do for you?" he asked.

"I work with Red Sky Investigators," Olin said. Based on the man's reaction—the subtle shift in his expression, the way he straightened up a little—this conversation was starting better than his last one had. "My name is Olin. I need to get some information about a person who was using one of these computers."

"What for?"

"You heard about what happened to Chris Miller?"

"The actor?"

Olin nodded.

"Of course. I mean—I heard he died. Doesn't seem like anybody knows much more than that yet."

"We've been asked by the studio to look into it."

"Didn't Chris die in London?" Joe said.

"He did."

"So what would it matter who was using the computers here?"

"We think it might be related."

"How—"

"I can't go into how," Olin interrupted. "Will you help me?"

Joe glanced at the pair of public computers, then nodded. "Yes. Sure, if I can."

"Thank you. I noticed you've got credit card readers on the computers. Is that the only way to pay for time on them?"

"No. You can also buy a prepaid card from us."

That was not the answer Olin was hoping for. Prepaid cards could often be purchased with cash. If that was the case here, it could turn this lead into a dead end. Olin asked to confirm his suspicion.

"Sure, we take cash. Don't most people? Why? Are you trying to find out the name of somebody who used it?"

"That's exactly what I'm trying to find out. But if they paid with cash . . ."

Joe was already shaking his head. "It wouldn't matter. I couldn't tell you who might have been using that machine when, no matter how they paid. We don't keep those sorts of records."

Olin sighed. Then he had another idea and looked around the store for security cameras. There were two mounted to the ceiling. "What about those?" he said, pointing to the cameras.

"What about them?"

"Are they recording?"

"All the time." Suddenly, Joe seemed to understand what Olin was after. "You're thinking maybe you can see who was on the computer?"

"Hopefully," Olin said. Dylan had once shown him how he could use an image of a person to look them up online. Maybe, if the camera had caught a good view of the blackmailer's face, Olin could download the image and do a similar search again.

That was, assuming Joe let him see the footage at all. Olin wasn't the police, and a lot of places had privacy policies that would prevent an employee from sharing such footage without a warrant.

Joe, however, did not hesitate when he said, "All right. We can do that. I mean—why not? We're talking about Chris Miller."

Apparently, even after they died, celebrities could open doors that would otherwise remain closed.

"Just don't tell anyone," Joe added. "You know when he was here?"

Olin had included the date and time the email was sent in the same digital note where he had recorded the IP. He referred to it quickly and relayed the information to Joe.

Joe gestured for Olin to follow him to a back room. "Come this way."

Olin moved toward the edge of the counter.

"Actually," Joe said, now looking at the cameras himself, "stay there.

Let me see if we have anything. Call out if anyone comes in."

All right, so it wasn't the unfettered access Olin thought he was going to get. At least Joe was being helpful. "Sure."

Joe pushed open a door. Just before he disappeared behind it, Olin added, "If you find the person using the computer, can you print off an image of him?"

"Let me see what I can do," Joe said. Then he was gone.

Ten minutes or more passed before he returned, during which no other customer entered. Olin watched the door and the cameras and began to feel like he was being watched in return. He was being paranoid. He knew that. There was nobody outside the door and only a digital recorder on the other side of the camera. And so what if there was somebody watching him? It wasn't as if he was doing anything wrong.

"Hey," Joe said.

Olin turned around.

Joe was standing in the doorway that led to the back room. "I can't print anything off, but I found who you're looking for. Come here."

Olin stepped around the counter and made his way to the door.

"Just a quick look, all right? I've got the guy up on the screen already."

"Sure," Olin said, disappointed he would not be able to run an image search for the guy online. But they knew it was a guy. That was a step forward. In seconds, Olin would also know what he looked like. That was worth something, too.

Turned out, though, once he saw the image, he would know even more than that.

He followed Joe past metal racks stacked high with paper of all sizes to a small desk tucked into one corner. On it sat a monitor, and on the monitor was the image of a man.

"That's your guy," Joe said.

Olin recognized him right away. *Oh, shit.*

CHAPTER 37

WHEN CONNOR AND DYLAN found nothing new on Marty or Luke, they expanded their search to the rest of the cast and crew. It was that or watch TV, and at least this way they were doing something.

By the time Olin called, they still hadn't uncovered any useful information. Not that these people were saints. Far from it. But they had not yet found a reason to suspect any of them of murder.

Connor barely managed to say hello before Olin blurted out: "I know who sent the email to Hudson."

Connor felt a sudden rush of excitement. "Hold on. Let me put you on speaker." After he did, he said, "Okay, go ahead."

"Dylan's there?"

"I'm here."

"Lance sent the email."

Connor wasn't sure he had heard Olin correctly, so he clarified: "Lance Casey?"

"Yes. Jax's stalker. He could have had something against both of them," Olin said.

"Doesn't seem like helping him get a job would fall under that category," Dylan said. Then she paused and added, "Unless the whole point was to get Chris here where someone would kill him."

Connor looked across the table at her. "Does that feel right to you?"

"Why not? You can't have a better alibi than being on the other side of the Atlantic. Maybe he hired somebody over here to kill Chris and then sent him to spy on us once we arrived."

"You're thinking about Ryan, aren't you?"

"Everything you said to Hudson was right. We've got a lot of reasons not to trust him, and nothing else has panned out so far."

"How do you suppose they knew each other?" Connor asked.

"Maybe when we talk to Ryan tonight, he can tell us."

"How would Lance know we were coming?"

Dylan threw up her hands. "I don't have all the answers, but if we're going to rule out Hudson, it seems like the best theory going so far. If you want someone crazy enough to plan a murder, seems like he fits the bill. And if he's our blackmailer, he has to have something to do with it, doesn't he?"

Connor took a deep breath. "Maybe. Let's see if we can link him to anybody working on the movie. If he actually sent someone to spy on us—even Ryan—then somehow he had to know we were here."

CHAPTER 38

THE POLICE WOULD NEED time to question Melissa and search the grounds to make sure Lance was gone before requesting an arrest warrant, and they would need an arrest warrant before coming to his apartment.

However, Lance worried about beating them there, anyway. The buses still weren't running yet, and it took even longer to get a taxi to come pick him up in the suburbs than it did in Midtown.

He surreptitiously cased the exterior of his apartment building from the back seat of the taxi before going inside. The only activity he saw was the shadows dancing underneath the flickering porch light. Once he decided the coast was clear, he asked the driver to stay where he was. Then he raced through the door, charged up the stairs, and immediately headed for his closet.

First things first: He needed to change his clothes. He grabbed a pair of jeans, a maroon tee shirt, and an Army jacket he had gotten at Old Navy. He had picked the clothes with no more consideration than his proximity to them. He did not care that the jeans were wrinkled or the shirt was stained. His only goal was to blend in.

Then he scoured the shelf above the hangers in search of his passport. He had gotten it years ago when he'd imagined one day soon he would be a famous actor, regularly traveling the world, but he had never used it.

He shifted around a whole manner of junk—old mail, crumpled receipts, empty beer bottles he had no memory of putting up there—and dumped everything he removed from the shelf onto the floor.

By the time he found his passport, the room looked only marginally worse than it had before he started looking.

Then he ran through a quick mental checklist to make sure he had everything he needed: keys, wallet, phone, passport.

He was good.

Almost.

He wanted to do one last thing before he left.

Lance pulled out his phone and called his London contact. "Jax is there."

"I know. I was going to call you."

"I'll be there soon."

He hung up before his contact could respond and returned to the taxi. "Take me to the airport."

CHAPTER 39

TRYING TO MAKE A connection between Lance and anybody working on the film was no more fruitful than anything else Connor and Dylan had done that day. And it was only further complicated by the possibility that, if Ryan was involved, he might be the link between the two.

Connor closed his laptop. He stood up and stretched his arms over his head.

He and Dylan had eaten breakfast and lunch in this room. All of their dishes were stacked up on the dresser so they had enough space on the table for their laptops. If they didn't get out of here soon, they'd have to put their dinner plates on the crowded dresser as well.

"This is pointless," he said. "Even when we narrow down the cast and crew to those who live in Atlanta, we're not getting anywhere."

"We haven't finished looking yet."

"No, but it's late. We need to head down to the Circle to talk to Ryan soon. It kind of seems like if we're going to get any answers, that's where they're going to come from. However, before we do that, we should probably call Steve, see if he's got a picture of our mystery man."

"He's the DJ," Dylan said. "He can't be hard to find."

Connor got her point. It was usually pretty easy to spot the DJ booth. They were often on raised platforms and almost always drew attention to themselves with one lighting effect or another. That might not be the case at the Circle, though. Even if it was, Ryan might be on a break or away from the booth for some other reason.

Connor explained all of this to Dylan and then added, "We need to go into this assuming Ryan is involved. I'm not saying he is, mind you. But if he is—*if* he was the person spying on us the other night—then he already knows what we look like. If we don't know what he looks like, too, he might slip away before we get a chance to confront him."

"We saw the guy outside our room."

"Not well enough to identify in a dark club."

Dylan nodded. "All right. Call him."

Connor pulled out his phone and dialed the number Steve had given him. After three rings the call rolled over to voicemail.

"No answer?" Dylan asked as Connor slipped the phone back into his pocket.

"Afraid not." Connor needed only a second to consider his options. "Let's stop by his house. Maybe he turned off his phone so it won't wake the baby."

"Or maybe he's avoiding us."

"Either way, we should stop by his house."

Dylan gestured toward the door. "Lead the way."

As they headed to the elevator, Connor requested an Uber and the app notified him the nearest driver was thirty minutes away. That felt like a long time right now.

"Maybe we should call Dean," Dylan said.

"Who?"

"The driver who took us to Steve's last time. We're going to need somebody to wait for us while we talk to him again, and the next driver might not be so accommodating."

"You're right." No matter how far away Dean was, it probably wouldn't take him more than thirty minutes to get to the hotel.

Connor fished around in his front pocket for the slip of paper Dean had given him. It was creased and crumpled in ways it hadn't been yesterday. He carefully unfolded it. The slip of paper had come from a science book, Connor remembered, when he saw the letters "OLOGY" on the left and the number "232" on the right. Between them was Dean's phone number.

Connor dialed, and Dean picked up right away. Once Dean realized who was calling, he was more than willing to help. He was enthusiastic, even. He said he could be at the hotel in ten minutes.

Connor and Dylan went outside to wait.

Dylan tapped Connor's arm and pointed across the street. "Hey, what's going on over there?"

Connor followed her finger toward the bank. The sun had started to set along the horizon in front of them. Through the glare, he could see people milling about the trailers and climbing up and down the stairs that led to the bank doors.

"I don't know," he said. "We've got a few minutes. Let's go find out."

As they got closer to the bank, Connor recognized everyone he could see as crew members from the movie.

"Do you think they've restarted production?" Dylan asked.

Connor felt a twinge of annoyance.

They stepped into the parking lot. "Excuse me," he said to a man carrying a tripod between the trailers. "Where's Maria?" Like everyone else within sight, Connor recognized him as one of the people he and Dylan had interviewed yesterday. However, he could not remember the man's name.

"She's in the bank," he answered. "Why? You got something?"

"No, I . . ." He trailed off, then added a quick "Thank you" and started moving again. Wouldn't Maria have told them if they had started filming? And if they had, who had they gotten to replace Chris?

They stepped into the bank. Maria was standing just inside the doors talking to two men in suits, neither of whom Connor recognized. He picked up just enough of what they were saying to suspect the conversation revolved around the film's budget before Maria turned toward him. "Oh, Connor," she said as if she was surprised to see him. Then, without waiting for him to respond, she introduced the two men she had been talking to as executives from Nightbird Studios.

One reached out to shake Connor's hand, and Connor responded with barely a glance and a wave in his direction. Dylan did not give the executive even that much.

"Why didn't you tell us you had resumed production?" Connor asked.

"I didn't think it mattered," Maria said, answering Connor's first question. "It's not like it has any bearing on your investigation."

"You still should have told us."

"Why?"

"Because," Dylan said, "until we're done, we need to know everything that's happening around here."

When Dylan had initially observed the action on the set, her tone had suggested mere curiosity. Connor wasn't sure if she was backing him up now because she was as annoyed as he was that Maria had kept them in the dark or simply because she would always take Connor's side, no matter who was right. Which—if he thought about it—he was not. The film's production status had nothing to do with their investigation. Still, he thought he had the right to know.

"Okay, okay," Maria said. "I won't do anything else without telling you first. Are we good now?"

Before Connor could respond, he saw a man approach from his peripheral vision. As soon as he spoke, Connor knew it was Jax and turned to face him.

Jax was wearing the same dramatic red overcoat and diamond-shaped sunglasses Chris had been wearing in the footage they had reviewed, which answered Connor's second question.

"I was thinking," Jax said. "I'm not a fan of the line 'This is a robbery.' Feels kind of contrived to me. What if, when I fire the gun at the ceiling, I say something like, 'You all know why I'm here. Let's get this party started'"?

Maria smiled. "I love it! I hated that line from the beginning, but nobody could come up with anything better."

Jax shrugged with one shoulder. "It's what I do." Then he finally looked at Connor and Dylan. "Hi, you two. Good to see you."

"You were expecting us?"

"Hudson told me you would be here. How's the investigation going?"

"Fine," Connor said.

"Good," Jax replied. "I'm glad he hired you." Then he turned his attention back to Maria. "I'm ready whenever you are," he said and walked away.

Connor watched him go, unsure what he should make of that exchange. He was surprised Jax had not had any follow-up questions. Most people would have.

"Are we good?" Maria asked again.

Connor's phone rang. He recognized the number as Dean's. He was probably calling to tell Connor he was at the hotel. "Yes, we're good," he said to Maria. Then he pressed the phone to his ear long enough to tell Dean, "We're coming."

On the way out, he glanced back at Jax just in time to see Hannah approach him with a cup of coffee, which the actor gladly accepted.

"There's something strange about this."

"What do you mean?" Dylan said.

"I don't know. I can't put my finger on it. Something about Jax being here doesn't seem right."

"Mia said he was their first choice, and we know Hudson wanted him out of Atlanta so he could spend more time with Jax's wife. I guess now that Chris is dead, Hudson didn't see any reason not to hire him."

"Yeah, but he didn't ask any questions about our investigation," Connor said, following her down the steps outside.

"He's a narcissist. Which, come to think of it, is probably why his wife is cheating on him."

"I guess," Connor said, but he couldn't shake the feeling he was missing something.

CHAPTER 40

D EAN DRILLED CONNOR AND Dylan with questions all
the way to Steve's house. Connor was starting to wish they
had waited the extra twenty minutes for a different driver.

When they arrived at the two-story yellow house with the thatch
roof, Dean pulled over to the side of the road and asked, "Are we here
because you think Steve killed Chris?"

"No," Connor said.

"But you think he knows something."

"We'll be right back," Connor said as he and Dylan climbed out of
the back seat. They made their way through the gate in the picket fence,
strode up to the front door, and knocked.

The baby started to scream from inside and Steve's exasperated wife
yelled, "Dammit! I just got her down. Go see who it is!"

Steve opened the door, looking even worse than he had the last time
they were here. Once he saw Connor and Dylan on his doorstep, he
immediately stepped outside and closed the door behind him. "This is
not great timing."

"I don't think that's what matters here," Dylan said. "We're trying
to find out what happened to Chris, or don't you remember?"

"Of course. I'm sorry. It's just . . . You should have called."

"We tried," Connor said.

"You should have answered," Dylan said.

Steve ran a hand through his hair, shook his head like he had just remembered something. "I put my phone on silent. We were trying to get the baby to sleep." Another wail from inside the house. "I guess that's over for now. What can I do for you? Did you find anything out?"

"We're still working on it," Connor said.

"Were you able to reach Mia? What about Ryan?"

"We talked to Mia. Ryan . . . Ryan has presented some challenges."

"More like he's being a pain in the ass," Dylan said.

"What do you mean? What did he say?"

"We haven't been able to talk to him yet."

Steve stepped off the porch and led them away from the door. "Yeah, it's like I said: You'll probably have to go see him at the club if you want to talk to him."

"It's not just that," Dylan clarified. "We can't seem to find anything out about him at all online."

"That's not a surprise. Ryan was never big into the whole social media thing."

Dylan raised an eyebrow, doubtful. "An actor who isn't big into social media?"

"Ryan wasn't an actor."

"You said you met him at the Waterton Theatre."

"We did. Ryan's a playwright and says he doesn't need an online presence. He doesn't even want one. I keep telling him that some sort of social media account will help him raise his profile and maybe get him more work. He says he already knows everyone he needs to know in the London theater community and just doesn't want to have anything to do with it."

"That's how he makes his living, writing plays?" Connor asked.

"He makes some money doing that. Not enough, though. That's why he supplements his income with the whole DJ thing. I think if he did a better job networking, he wouldn't have to DJ at all. But he doesn't listen to me."

Suddenly the door flew open, and Steve's wife came charging out. She was wearing a button-down the same color as the house, blue jeans, and a pair of slippers. Without the door to muffle the sound, the crying was no longer limited to the occasional wail.

She pushed Steve out of her way as she headed toward the street. "I've had enough. I need a fucking break. I'm going to my mum's. You take care of her."

Steve let her go without comment.

She threw open the gate with the same force she had the door and went straight for the driveway along the side of the house. Once she was gone, tooling away in her VW, Steve sighed and went back inside. Connor and Dylan followed him.

Steve scooped up the baby, who was lying in the pack-and-play on the living room floor, and carried her into the kitchen. "There, there," he said to the child, rocking her as he went.

"She just . . . left?" Dylan said.

Steve grabbed a bottle off the table and began feeding the baby, which seemed to be enough to quiet her down. At least for now. "She does that sometimes," he said. "I've kind of been expecting it. We've had reporters up here at all hours since the story broke trying to get a quote. Neither of us have gotten any sleep."

"I can't believe—"

Connor grabbed Dylan's arm and shook his head. He could tell where that was going and didn't want Dylan playing judge and jury with Steve's homelife. They were here for information. That was all.

Steve looked at Dylan like he was waiting for the accusation she no doubt intended to level. He was a bad parent. His wife was a bad parent. They shouldn't have had a child. He seemed like he might be ready for any of those things. And since this wasn't the first time his wife had left, he had likely heard all of them before.

"We can't believe there wasn't anything else about Ryan online, though," Connor said, redirecting the conversation. "We didn't limit our search to his social media presence."

"What do you mean?"

"There's nothing about him online at all. Not anywhere. It's like he doesn't exist." Connor stopped short of saying they had looked him up on the dark web, since that might not play well. Hopefully, he had said enough to elicit a more substantive response.

Steve looked confused as he continued to gently rock the baby. Then his eyes widened. "Oh, well, I guess you wouldn't, would you? I'm sorry—Ryan's a nickname. We've been calling him that ever since we knew him, but his real name is Nolan. Nolan Clarke. Sorry. I should have told you that from the beginning. Frankly, I'm kind of surprised you didn't figure it out on your own, though."

"How were we supposed to figure that out on our own?" Dylan asked.

"It's a pretty common nickname."

"It's also a pretty common first name," Dylan said.

Steve placed the baby's bottle back on the table, then hoisted her up onto his shoulder and began patting her back. "Anyway, sorry. I don't see why it should matter. Ryan didn't have anything to do with Chris's death."

"We still need to talk to him," Connor said.

"Right. Sure you do."

"The club's going to be crowded. It would be helpful if we knew what he looked like," Connor said. "Do you have a picture of him?"

Steve shrugged and carried the baby into a nearby bedroom, where he placed her in a wooden crib; Connor and Dylan stayed out in the hall by the door. A mobile made of stuffed teddy bears and unicorns hung above the crib. Steve tucked a blanket around the baby, watched her for a moment to make sure she would not start to cry again, and came back out into the hall, closing the door gently behind him. He removed his phone from his pocket, clicked and scrolled. Then he turned the phone toward Connor when he found what he was looking for.

It was a picture of two men with their arms draped over each other's shoulders and the Waterton Theatre in the background (which Connor only recognized because the theater's name was displayed in big red letters above the doors). One of the men was Steve. The other Connor didn't recognize.

"That's him," Steve said.

"Can you send that to me?" Connor asked. He did not bother to provide a phone number since Steve would have it in his list of missed calls, and Steve did not ask for it for the same reason.

"Done," Steve said and Connor's phone dinged.

On instinct, Connor checked the phone to make sure the message Steve sent did indeed include the photo. "Thank you," he said as both men slid their phones back into their pockets.

"Anything else I can do for you?" Steve said.

Connor shook his head.

"All right, if you don't mind, I'd like to get you out of here before you wake the baby again."

Steve opened the front door, and Dean, who was now leaning

against the side of his car waiting for Connor and Dylan to return, waved in a way that struck Connor as a little too enthusiastic.

Steve awkwardly waved back.

"Thank you again," Connor said as he and Dylan stepped outside.

Steve closed the door without responding.

CHAPTER 41

"**D**ID YOU GET WHAT you were after?" Dean asked once they were all back in the car.

Connor, who had his phone in his lap with the photo Steve had sent him on the screen, did not answer. Instead, he turned to Dylan and said, "Did you know Ryan was a nickname for Nolan?"

Dylan shook her head. "That's why I asked him how he thought we would figure it out on our own."

The car was running, but still sitting on the side of the road in front of Steve's house. Dean spun around in his seat so he could look at Connor and Dylan without having to use the rearview mirror. "Come on, mates. I'm driving you all over London. The least you can do is tell me what's going on."

Connor sighed and decided he didn't see the harm in telling him about Ryan. He raised an eyebrow in Dylan's direction to make sure she was okay with it, and she shrugged to indicate she was.

"Chris was with three friends the night he died. We've spoken with two of them. We haven't been able to get in touch with the third. Steve told us he should be DJing at the Circle tonight. So we stopped by here to get a picture of him to make sure we knew what he looked like before we went there."

"You think *he* had something to do with the murder?" Dean said.

"We just want to talk to him. But that's why we're here. Do you mind taking us to the Circle and waiting outside again?"

"Mind?" Dean spun back around in his seat, satisfied with the little bit of information Connor had shared. "Try to stop me." He pulled back out onto the road—a country lane, really—and initiated a three-point turn.

"Do you know where you're going?"

"Sure I do. That's one of the hottest places in London right now. It's still early for the clubs, but I bet you there's already a line around the block to get in."

And so there was.

The line was at least forty people deep. Two bouncers at the door were checking IDs. Both were wearing black tee shirts tucked into black slacks and were of a height and girth that would intimidate any sane person. One of them, who perhaps thought he was too cool for school, was also wearing a pair of sunglasses, even though the sun had set and the only light to block out came from the streetlamps that dotted both sides of the road and the surrounding storefronts.

Dean pulled into an alley between the club and a convenience store. A sign noted the narrow road was meant for "Deliveries Only."

"There won't be any deliveries this time of night," Dean said. He flipped on his hazards.

Connor and Dylan approached the bouncers from the side opposite the line. "Excuse me," Connor said, already reaching for his wallet so he could flash his PI license.

Too Cool for School barely glanced at him before he said, "Back of the queue."

Connor tried again, this time with his PI license already held up for the bouncer to see.

"We're not here for the music," Dylan added when the man looked in their direction.

Connor expected some wise-ass remark like he had gotten from Crew Cut at the bar. *You're a good long way out of your district, aren't you?* But the bouncer hardly even glanced at the ID before he tilted his head toward the door and said, "Go on."

Connor was certain the man hadn't had time to read his license. He must have seen enough of it to get the gist. Then it occurred to him—there had probably been other people around here flashing IDs lately. Police and reporters, in particular. If the bouncer thought it was just more of the same (which he seemed to), what else would he have done?

An assortment of complaints rose up from the line as Connor and Dylan slipped inside.

"Hey," the bouncer said, "take it down a notch or you're not getting in at all."

Then the door closed behind Connor, and he heard nothing else that happened outside. One or two steps farther and they probably wouldn't have heard anything, anyway. Some sort of monotonous techno hip-hop was blasting from speakers along the ceiling.

A man inside a ticketing booth held up a hand to indicate the entrance fee was five pounds. Connor tried to explain they were there to talk to Ryan, but he could barely hear himself, so he wasn't surprised when, after turning his left ear toward Connor, the man in the booth pointed firmly to a sign taped to the glass that likewise indicated the price.

Connor paid for himself and Dylan simply to put an end to the discussion.

The man stamped both of their hands with the name of the club, then directed them to another door.

There, the music got even louder. An assortment of colored lights shone down on a dancefloor that occupied most of the space. People were packed in tight. As the crowd shifted, Connor noticed a bar on the far side of the room that did not seem as crowded. He scanned the rest of the space for a DJ booth and didn't see one.

"Any idea where Ryan might be?" he shouted at Dylan.

She was scanning the room as well. She leaned in close to hear him, and he repeated the question only an inch from her ear. She pointed toward a dark corner near the bar. When Connor's eyes had drifted across that part of the room before, he had not been able to see anything. Now, with some of the overhead spotlights off and others on, he could make out the shape of a raised, partially enclosed platform.

He couldn't see enough to say for certain that it was the DJ booth, but it looked promising.

He gestured for Dylan to follow him.

They circled around the dancefloor instead of trying to fight their way through the crowd and climbed the four steps to the back of the booth. From there, all they could see was a black door with a gold doorknob. No telling what was on the other side.

Connor grabbed the knob, wondering for less than a second if it would turn, if Dylan would have to pick the lock to get them inside, if she could do it fast enough to avoid drawing attention, and what they would face if that was the route they had to go.

But the knob did indeed turn, the door did indeed open, and, from the assortment of electronics inside, they had indeed found the DJ both. Only problem: It was empty. Apparently, Ryan had cued up a song—maybe several—and stepped away.

"Perhaps he's in the bathroom," Dylan shouted.

"Stay here," Connor said. "I'll check."

Connor went into the bathroom. None of the people inside looked like the man in the photo Steve had sent him. "Not there," he said to Dylan when he returned.

"I have an idea." She pointed to the bartender.

"You think he'd know?"

She shrugged, and they approached the man. As packed as the club was, he was not as busy as the bartender at the Crown had been, perhaps because there was another bar to their left—this one closer to the dancefloor and fielding most of the drink requests.

The bartender was working a stainless-steel cocktail shaker up and down.

"You know where we can find the DJ?" Dylan asked.

He nodded toward the DJ booth and poured the drink he was mixing into a martini glass.

"He's not there."

Then the bartender gestured with his thumb toward an "Exit" sign and mimed smoking a cigarette. Or perhaps he meant vaping. Either way, the meaning was clear enough.

"Thank you," Dylan said. She and Connor made their way toward the emergency exit.

Normally, Connor would have been reluctant to open such a door since it might set off an alarm. But somebody had wedged a wooden block between the door and the jamb, so that was not a concern here.

Dylan pushed through the door first.

It led them to a narrow cement platform and a set of stairs that exited onto an alley. To their right, Connor saw a dumpster and a dead end. To their left, he saw Dean's car. And at the bottom of the stairs, he found the man he was looking for.

Ryan was wearing a black hoodie and matching jeans. He was not alone. The man opposite him was wearing neon everything and had his back to Connor. They couldn't have looked like a more mismatched pair if they had tried.

Neither one of them was smoking . . . or vaping. They were engaged in something far more nefarious.

Connor and Dylan had stepped through the emergency exit just in time to see Ryan grab a wad of cash from the other man's hand while at the same time producing a small plastic bag with a white powder inside.

He looked at Connor and Dylan, his eyes wide with alarm, and it took him less than a second to turn and run. The man in neon also turned toward Connor and Dylan but froze instead.

Connor raced down the steps after Ryan, pushing the guy in neon out of his way as he went. He did not look back to see if Dylan was behind him, did not even wonder if she might be. The only thing he was concerned about was catching up with Ryan before he slipped away.

That would not be easy. Ryan was fast. Connor could see the distance he was putting between the two of them expanding rapidly. Then Ryan swerved around the driver's side of Dean's car, and everything changed.

Dean threw open his door—too late for Ryan to stop or change course. He slammed into it and fell to the ground. Dean hopped out, did a little fist pump into the air. "How do you like that?" he shouted at Ryan, who was already scrambling back to his feet.

Before he could start to run again, Connor grabbed him from behind. Spewing a string of expletives, Ryan struggled to get free. He was as strong as he was fast, and Connor wasn't sure how long he'd be able to contain the man on his own.

"Help me hold him!" he said to Dean, who likewise wrapped his arms around Ryan.

From the corner of his eye, Connor could see Dylan standing beside him now. "Calm down," he said to Ryan. "We don't care what you were doing back there. We're here about Chris."

"Sod off, you fuckin' coppers!"

Connor had no idea what that meant, but it clearly did not suggest a willingness to cooperate. "We were hired by the studio to look into his death, okay? We just want to talk to you."

Ryan either wasn't listening or didn't believe him. He continued to struggle until he wore himself out, during which time Connor repeatedly insisted they were just there about Chris and that if he would calm down, they would let him ago.

The fight went out of him slowly. Once he was still, Dean let go first. Connor, more reluctantly, let go a moment later.

Breathing heavily, Ryan looked from Dean to Connor to Dylan. "You're not going to arrest me?" he finally said.

"I told you," Connor replied, "we're not cops."

"Well, you're not British cops, at least. I'll give you that much."

Connor assumed he must be referring to his accent. Before, Ryan had been so wrapped up in his attempt to break free that he probably hadn't paid any attention to what Connor said, let alone how he said it.

"Will you please talk to us? We just need to ask you some questions about Chris."

Ryan moved his head from side to side like he was popping his neck, then rolled his shoulders around. He leaned against Dean's car. "Yeah.

All right. If it's about Chris. What do you want to know?"

"The night he died—you were with him, right?"

"Yeah, sure. Me and Steve and Mia. The old gang, back together again."

Connor was about to ask if Ryan had seen anything unusual when Dylan slipped in a question of her own first. "Why didn't you answer the door when we stopped by Steve's place a couple of nights ago?"

"That was you?"

"Why? Who did you think it was?"

"The police. Or . . ."

Dylan crossed her arms over her chest. "Or?"

"There's a guy I owe some money to, okay? I thought you might be him."

"So that's why you were staying there? You were hiding out?"

"Yeah."

"You weren't evicted?" Connor said.

"I guess you heard that from Steve, huh?" Ryan looked down, as if ashamed. "No. I just told him that. He doesn't know anything about . . . *this*," he said in a way that made it clear he was referring to the drugs.

Connor had a feeling he had lied to Steve about more than just that. Connor had a feeling he lied about a lot of things. Like the reason he didn't want an online presence. Maybe it really would help him network with other professionals in the London theater scene, but it also would make him easier to identify if the police took an interest in him.

Could the man looking for Ryan have anything to do with Chris's death? Although it seemed unlikely, Connor decided he'd better probe a little further to be sure. "Why do you owe him money?"

Ryan crossed his arms, perhaps unconsciously mirroring Dylan, and looked off into the distance while he weighed whether he should answer.

Dylan snapped her fingers in front of his face. "Hey! Don't be difficult. We're trying to find out what happened to your friend, or don't you care about that?"

He rolled his eyes. "Fine. It's a guy I buy from. Normally, he advances me the stuff, and I pay him back when I sell it. But after Chris died, he didn't want to have anything to do with me anymore. But he wouldn't take the stuff back, either. He wanted cash money. So I had to hide out until I could sell the rest of the supply."

Connor considered that and decided it was probably true. Any murder Ryan had been close to would bring unwanted attention in his direction. But when the victim was someone like Chris, it would bring a whole lot more than usual, and Ryan's dealer probably wanted to put as much daylight as he could between the two of them so he didn't draw that unwanted attention to his own criminal activities.

"I'll be able to pay him back soon, but I can't do it yet," Ryan said.

"He hasn't been here looking for you?"

"He doesn't know I work here."

Connor nodded. That seemed reasonable, also. The two men were business associates, not friends. His dealer probably hadn't cared how Ryan unloaded his drugs, as long as he got paid.

Connor decided he had explored this line of questioning as far as he needed to for now and would be best served redirecting his questions back to the night of Chris's murder. "So nobody seems to know why Chris was upset the day he died. Did he say anything to you?"

"I wish he had. Maybe he'd still be alive if he did."

"Do you know of any reason someone might have wanted to hurt Chris?" Dylan said.

"No." He hesitated, then pointed thoughtfully at Connor. "You know who might know something? Hannah Wells. Chris got her a job on the film set. She's been friends with him as long as I have."

"You know Hannah?"

"Sure. From way back. Her brother went to school with Chris, and we all hung out together for a while there. Have you tried talking to her?"

"We have."

"Well, she probably knows as much as anyone would about why he was upset."

CHAPTER 42

JAX'S RELATIONSHIP WITH HUDSON was complicated. Almost as complicated as the one with his wife Melissa. He knew they were sleeping together. It had been happening on and off for about a year. At first, he had been unsure how to handle it. He worried confronting Hudson could mean the end of his career; Hudson was a powerful man within the industry. And he worried divorcing Melissa might result in a scandal that could have the same effect. Not because of the divorce itself. That happened all the time. But because if it wasn't amicable, Hudson's name would almost certainly come out in court, and that would be at least as bad as confronting the man directly. Maybe worse. Hudson cared a lot about his reputation and had ruined careers for much less.

Which was why he had started sleeping with Laura Hackett. They had met at a party and—as the saying goes—one thing had led to another. The relationship had started as something casual, a way for Jax to feel a little better about what Melissa was doing behind his back, but over the last eight months it had grown into more. Jax would have married Laura if he could have. For now, the safest thing to do was to keep their relationship a secret. Laura, God bless her, understood that.

Here, though, they were so far away from the people who knew them that the prying eyes and wagging tongues of their many friends and neighbors were not a concern. The paparazzi might catch a picture of them together at dinner—which was where they were going now—but so what? No matter what the headline might read, Jax and Laura could claim they were just two colleagues getting a meal together.

Jax had booked a reservation at Ava's, the swankiest restaurant he could find. The food started at one hundred pounds a plate. As such, it was the kind of place where no one would cast an eye in their direction. That was the thing about being famous that a lot of people didn't understand—even celebrities wanted to be treated like everyone else from time to time. It could be exhausting being in the spotlight. And, when you were that famous, being treated like everyone else came at a premium.

They took a taxi to the restaurant and held hands only while they were in the cab (no sense in being reckless). The hostess seated them at a private, candlelit table near the back. Then, after a quiet meal of fish and wine, where they lingered longer than any two colleagues might, they took another taxi back to the hotel. They both knew the next stop would be Jax's bedroom.

At least, it would have been, if they had been alone.

Lance had taken the first flight out of Atlanta he could get. He didn't care that he couldn't afford it. He had a credit card, and with the lingering home invasion charges plus what he'd rack up in the UK, there was little chance he'd be a free man when the bill came due.

He knew which hotel Jax was staying at from his contact in the UK and the room he was in for the same reason. However, he had not counted on Jax stepping out of his room at the same time he was getting off the elevator.

If Lance had been able to get his hands on a gun, he would have.

But he had stopped in a pawn shop on the way over and learned those were hard to come by in the UK. A knife, he had decided, would have to do. He could still handle that weapon with one arm in a sling, and he just might enjoy getting up close and personal. He could almost imagine standing only inches from Jax, watching his beautiful face contort into an ugly expression of pain and regret as Lance drove the blade over and over into his torso.

To get that close, though, he would have to take Jax by surprise. Meeting him in the hall between the elevator and his room wouldn't cut it. Fortunately, the hallway had been constructed with one branch leading straight off the elevator and another one heading to the right.

Lance stepped off the elevator and turned right before he was seen. He had bought himself seconds to find a place to hide. Once Jax reached the elevator, he would almost certainly see Lance if Lance did nothing more than make that turn. He hurried down the hallway, grabbing the knob of every door he passed, hoping one of them might open. None of them did.

As he closed in on the end of the hallway, he realized it was not the dead end he thought it was. Here, the hallway turned left, and Lance did the same.

Finally, he was safe. There was no way Jax would see him now when he reached the elevator. Lance could have stayed where he was until Jax was off the floor. But curiosity got the better of him, so he kept moving.

The hallway turned twice more. The second time, Lance found himself facing the elevator from the opposite end of the hall. Jax was gone. Apparently, the floor had been constructed as one giant loop.

It was an interesting piece of trivia, Lance thought, although not particularly useful. . . . Or was it? As soon as Jax left his room, Lance had been faced with a choice—although he had not recognized it until now. He could either follow Jax to wherever he was going, hope that Jax didn't spot him, hope that he would have a chance to take the actor by surprise, or he could hang out here and wait, kill him in the privacy of his room like he had imagined doing on the plane.

As soon as Lance realized what his options were, the right decision was obvious. Jax's room was close to this end of the hall. That had been a detriment when Lance stepped off the elevator. Even if he had wanted to bum-rush Jax, push him back into his room, there would have been too much ground to cover. There was no way Lance could have gotten from the elevator to Jax before Jax was back inside his room, door barred and on the phone with the police.

At this end of the hall, that detriment became an attribute. Because no matter how Jax closed his door—whether by hand or by letting the pneumatic device that was undoubtedly attached to the door close it for him—Lance would be able to get into the room before the latch clicked into place.

All he had to do to make that work was stay right where he was.

Just as Lance knew which hotel Jax was in and which floor he was on, he also knew the floor was otherwise unoccupied. Maria had booked the cast and crew into the first three floors when she had reserved the hotel. The only empty rooms on those floors at the time were now occupied by Connor and Dylan. And the only empty room on those floors now had previously been occupied by Chris.

Jax had been offered Chris's room so he could be closer to his colleagues, but he did not want to stay in a place that had been so recently used by a man who was now dead. Regardless of how it had come about, though, it meant Lance would not have to explain his presence to anyone, which was all that mattered.

Jax and Laura maintained an air of professionalism for the benefit of the staff as they passed through the hotel lobby. They maintained it on the elevator for the benefit of the camera in case some bottom-feeding journalist got hold of the security footage looking for dirt. But once they were at Jax's door, once Jax had slid his keycard into the slot and the little light on the reader had turned green, Laura grabbed hold of Jax's free hand and smiled up at him in a way that betrayed the truth of their relationship.

He smiled back. "Get inside," he whispered into her ear.

She did.

Then Jax felt someone push him from behind. He slammed into Laura, and they both went tumbling to the floor.

"What the hell?" she said as she rolled over.

Jax grunted and pushed himself back up to his knees, before likewise turning to see what had happened. A flurry of possibilities ran through his mind. None of them made any sense. Was this a crazed fan? Somebody from the hotel staff? A coworker playing a joke? He could not think of anybody who would want to hurt him. Nobody but Lance, and after the beating he had given Lance in Atlanta, even he would probably keep his distance now. Besides, Lance was *in Atlanta*.

Once he saw the man towering over him, he realized he was mistaken, which only introduced another flurry of unanswerable questions. Most notably: *How did Lance find me?* and *Why is he here?*

Then, as Lance produced a knife from inside his jacket, Jax asked himself the one question he could answer: *Is he going to kill me?*

Lance turned the knife around so that the blade was facing away from his thumb. He swung at Jax, and Jax rolled out of the way. Laura screamed.

Jax looked around in a panic. There was no getting around Lance, no escaping into the hall. That left only the bathroom. He grabbed Laura's wrist—"Come on!"—and hurried across the room as she rolled to her feet and scrambled to keep up.

He heard a *woosh* of air from behind him. Lance had again tried to stab him and missed. He pulled Laura into the bathroom, slammed the door, and turned the lock.

"What's going on out there? Who is he?" Laura whimpered, as she backed up to the wall between the toilet and the tub.

Lance banged hard on the door. Jax had no idea what he was using, but it wasn't his fist. The sound was too loud for that.

"He's crazy," Jax said. "He's been stalking me for a while. I thought I was done with him. I have no idea what his problem is."

"Call the police!"

Jax pulled his phone out of his pocket and froze, staring dumbfounded at the keypad. If he was in the US, he would have dialed 911. He didn't know what the emergency number was here. Nor did he know how to access the emergency call button built into his cell phone.

He quickly ran through his other options. He could call the front desk, have them call the police. But that would take time—he would have to look up the number for the hotel, navigate his way through a series of touch-tone menus to get to the receptionist, explain the situation—and with Lance banging on the door, he wasn't calm enough to do all that.

Then he remembered that there was somebody else who might be able to help. Connor. He knew from Maria that the PI was staying in the hotel. He had to be close by. He quickly found Connor's number in his call log and clicked on it.

When Connor answered, Jax immediately began talking over him.

"I need your help! Lance is here! He's here! He's trying to kill me!"

"Is that the police?" Laura said.

"Where are you?" Connor said.

"It's Connor," Jax told Laura. Then, back to the phone, he said, "I'm in my bathroom with Laura. We've locked the door."

Another bang.

"What are you doing?" Laura screamed, as she tried to grab the phone from him. "We need to call the police."

"I don't know how long we're going to be able to keep him out," Jax said to Connor, fighting to keep hold of the phone.

"You can't—"

"Just get here! I'm right upstairs. Room four-ten."

"Okay, we're coming," he heard Connor say as Laura wrenched the phone out of his hand and fumbled with it until it fell into the toilet.

"Shit!" Jax said as they both looked down into the bowl and Lance continued to pound on the door. "What did you have to do that for?"

"We needed to call the police, not Connor!"

He reached into the bowl and grabbed his phone. "I don't know the number for the police! Do you?"

"It's nine-nine-nine. You should know that if you're going to be working over here."

Jax turned over the phone so that the screen was facing up. He was still glad he'd called Connor because Connor was close. But since Laura knew the emergency number, there was no reason not to call the police as well. Unfortunately, when he clicked the screen, nothing happened. The device was dead. He cursed again. "Do you have your phone on you?"

"It's out there," Laura said, pointing toward the door.

Suddenly the banging stopped, and it remained quiet long enough for Jax to ask, "Do you think he went away?"

Then the blade of Lance's knife sliced through the door and there was another bang as the hilt connected with the wood.

CHAPTER 43

CONNOR AND DYLAN WERE on their way back to the hotel when Jax called. At Connor's urging, Dean raced the last several blocks, speeding through red lights and swerving around traffic, while Connor called the police from the back seat. Not more than a minute had passed between the time he had received Jax's call and the time they reached the hotel, but it felt like it was much longer.

There were no police cars parked in front of the lobby doors, Connor noticed, as he and Dylan jumped out of the car. That came as no surprise. They were certainly on their way, but they couldn't have gotten here any faster than Connor and Dylan had.

"Wait!" Dean shouted. "What are you doing? You've already called the police! Let them handle this!"

That wasn't going to happen. Connor would take the police's help where he could get it, but he wasn't going to sit around and wait for it.

He went for the elevator as Dylan headed toward the stairs. "This way," she said. "It'll be faster."

Jax and Laura stepped backwards into the tub so they could get as far from the door as possible. He wrapped his arms around her, held her close. Every time Lance slammed into the door or stabbed his knife through it, he could feel her shudder.

There had to be something he could use a weapon, he told himself. It was a thought driven by desperation, unmoored from reality. He had already checked under the sink and found nothing. There was no linen closet. Unless he wanted to throw a roll of toilet paper at Lance or try to defend himself with the shower curtain, he was out of options.

"What are we going to do?" Laura whispered.

"Connor will be here soon."

"What is *he* going to do?"

Jax wasn't sure. At least Connor had the element of surprise on his side, and that had to be worth something.

Lance used the knife to put another hole in the door and then hit it again. For a while, his assault on the door had seemed devoid of calculation. He was running on emotion, Jax thought, like an animal trying to escape a trap. As desperate to get in as they were to keep him out.

That wasn't it at all.

Lance was using the knife to compromise the integrity of the door and then hitting those weak spots with the hope of breaking through.

When Jax realized this, he said, "It will hold," with a confidence he did not feel.

Then Lance changed his approach. He stabbed through the door close to the knob. Once, twice, three times. He was still trying to compromise the door's integrity, but now he was doing it where it mattered most. While Jax might have been right before—the door might have held until Connor arrived—he knew that was no longer the case.

Lance hit the door hard. There was an audible crack. The knife came through the wood again.

"He's going to get in," Laura said, her voice trembling.

So, as far as weapons went, maybe the shower curtain would have to do, after all. At the very least, Jax could throw it over Lance when he broke through the door, disorienting him and buying them enough time to get away.

Maybe.

Lance might also bump into them when they tried to get past and start stabbing blindly, determined to kill whoever he could.

Don't think about that. This is the only chance you've got.

Jax looked up at the top of the shower curtain to see how it was attached to the rod and realized there had been a better weapon at hand the entire time. "The rod," he whispered, as he let go of Laura so he could pry it free from the wall.

At first, the brass rod refused to move. Jax pushed and pulled, straining the screws that held it in place. He was fueled by adrenaline and had ten times his strength because of it. Once he could feel it starting to give, he pushed harder.

The knife sliced through the door again.

Laura, who must have seen the rod begin to shift slightly against the wall, reached up to help. With one final push, screws tore through drywall. The rod came free of the fasteners holding it in place. The curtain slid off onto the floor. Jax gathered it up just as another blow to the door sent it careening open.

Lance, who Jax now knew had been delivering those blows with his foot, stepped in fast, his knife at the ready.

Jax felt like a knight—his sword the rod and his shield the shower curtain—and he knew he had to time his attack just right if he and Laura were going to get out of that bathroom alive. But "just right" meant "right now," since Lance had not stopped moving from the time he'd stepped through the door.

Jax threw the shower curtain, hoping it would land on top of Lance, which it did, momentarily blinding him. Then Jax shoved the rod into Lance's gut as hard as he could.

Lance doubled over, stumbled backward.

This was it. Now or never. "Let's go!" he said to Laura, and once again grabbed hold of her arm to lead her from one room to another.

They had barely made it out of the bathroom before Lance pulled the shower curtain from over his head and began coming after them. "You think you're going to get away from me?" he shouted.

Jax yanked open the door to the hotel room. "This way," he said as he stepped through the door, turned toward the elevator, and found himself face-to-face with Connor and Dylan.

"You're okay?" Connor said, as surprised to see Jax as he was to see them.

Jax did not stop running. "Move!" he shouted, just as Lance came through the door after them.

Neither Connor nor Dylan needed any more instruction. They raced down the hallway behind Jax, followed him into the stairwell. In the seconds it took them to get to the landing between the fourth floor and the third, Connor realized Jax intended to take the stairs all the way to the lobby. That would be a terrible idea. If the police had not yet arrived, there would be nowhere to go but out onto the street, where there only chance of getting away from Lance would be outrunning him.

Lance was fast—faster than even Ryan had been. Connor had experienced that firsthand when the man chased him down in the parking lot of Gianna's. It was no surprise, considering his history as a runner. It also meant that outside, where speed would be the only thing separating them, they would have little chance of getting away.

They needed to put a door between them. Even if Connor had known Lance had broken through the one that led to Jax's bathroom, he would still have said that was their best option. At least it would buy them some time—probably enough for the police to get there and stop him.

"Third floor!" he shouted.

"Are you crazy?" Jax said, halfway between the landing Connor was on and the door that would take him into the third-floor hallway.

"Trust me!"

As Jax descended the steps to the third-floor landing, he looked from the door to the stairs like he was trying to decide where he wanted to go. Then, at the last possible moment, he jerked open the door and shouted, "You'd better be right!"

Connor, who was at the tail end of the foursome, risked a look back up the stairs as he passed through the door.

Lance was moving more slowly than Connor would have expected, although not much. Maybe his broken arm was slowing him down, or maybe there was some other injury Connor couldn't see. Either way, he was certain getting everyone into his own room was still the right choice.

"Room three-twenty-seven!" he shouted, running again and fishing in his pocket for his keycard.

When Dylan, Laura, and Jax reached the door, they made room for Connor as he came barreling down the hallway. He slid the keycard into the lock, jerked it out. The reader flashed red. Shit! He was in a panic, moving too fast. He needed to slow down, give the reader a chance to work. But he couldn't slow down. Lance was in the hallway now, too, and coming their way.

"Hurry!" Laura shouted.

Connor slid the card in again, and again pulled it out too fast.

"What the fuck, Connor?" Dylan shouted.

Farther down the hall, another door opened. Hannah looked out. "What's—"

Connor whipped his head around, saw her. "Come on!" he said before Hannah could finish her question. He bolted toward her door with Jax, Laura, and Dylan behind him. Then he pushed his way into the room—not that Hannah was trying to stop him—and stood by the door, ready to close it once everyone was inside.

"What's going on?" Hannah asked.

Connor wasn't listening. He watched the three people with him come through the door one at a time and swung the door shut. But the attached pneumatic device made it hard to close fast. Before the latch could click into place, Lance slammed into the other side, pushing Connor back.

Connor lost his footing, stumbled away from the door. He knew immediately there was no stopping Lance now. The only thing he could do was retreat farther into the room and hope that Lance, when faced with so many people, would not launch into a rampage, trying to kill all of them.

Because Lance had clearly come to kill Jax—that much was obvious. His stalking had devolved into its worst possible shape, no doubt helped along by Jax's late-night visit to Lance's apartment. Connor had told Jax not to confront his stalker. He had not listened. This was the consequence.

Wait. No. That wasn't right. Not entirely. Lance was more than Jax's stalker. He was somehow connected to every part of the mystery Connor had come here to solve. He had blackmailed Hudson, which meant he knew Chris had been working on the movie. And once Jax had replaced Chris, he had come here to kill Jax, which meant he knew where the movie was being filmed.

And if he could kill Jax, he could have killed Chris. Connor just didn't know how yet (or why), because Lance had been in Atlanta when Chris died.

None of that was important right now, though. The only thing that mattered now was getting out of this room alive.

CHAPTER 44

LANCE ENTERED THE ROOM slowly, which Connor took as a good sign that he didn't want to take on five people at once. Actually, six. There was a man standing by the curtains who was not Jax. He must have been in the room when they entered.

Connor was reluctant to take his eyes off Lance and could not get a good look at that sixth person. From what he could see, the man did not appear to be from among the cast and crew.

Connor saw a beer bottle on the nightstand and remembered Hannah had been carrying two through the lobby the other night. He had assumed at the time both were for her. Perhaps one had been for this stranger. Perhaps he was Hannah's boyfriend. She wouldn't be the first person to bring her significant other on a work trip. Which begged the question: Were there other people staying in the hotel as well?

Maria had told him that the hotel had been reserved only for those working on the movie. If people had brought their husband and wives, boyfriends and girlfriends, there could be dozens of guests here who had thus far been unaccounted for.

Like so many other thoughts Connor had spinning around in his head, that also did not matter at that moment.

You just need to focus on staying alive.

Since they weren't going to be able to hide behind a locked door until the police came, they needed to stall.

Lance slowly took a step forward.

"What do you want with Jax?" Connor blurted out. "Why are you doing this?" He did not expect much of an answer, but any answer he got meant Lance was talking instead of killing, and he could not think of any better way to stall right now.

"Jax knows what he did," Lance said without taking his eyes off the actor.

Jax had his hands raised as if Lance were aiming a gun at him and demanding his wallet. "I really don't."

"Yes, you do. How could you forget?" Another step forward.

Jax stepped back, bumped into a nightstand. "I promise. If I remembered you, I would tell you. Especially right now. If I did something to put all this in motion, then I need to apologize. Give me a chance to make it right."

Lance's gaze shifted around the room before returning to Jax. "I don't look the same, I guess. My hair was shorter then. Maybe you don't remember me. I bet you remember a little film called *Descendant*, don't you?"

"Of course."

"You remember auditioning for it?"

"Yeah. What about it?"

"You remember the callback? It was you and one other actor. Do you remember that?"

Jax's expression changed, and he looked at Lance in a new way. "You were the other actor at that callback."

"Now we're getting somewhere."

"That's what this is all about? That's why you started stalking me? That's why you . . . Hell, you followed me to Atlanta, didn't you? I mean—you must have. Why? Because I beat you out for a role? What's the matter with you? That happens all the time!"

"You didn't beat me," Lance said. "You stole it. You know that. You and the casting agents—you were all just there making fun of me the whole time. And as if that wasn't enough, you had to get my agent to drop me. You know nobody else would take me on after that? Nobody. You probably planned that too. What was the matter? Were you afraid I was a better actor than you?"

Jax lowered his hands. "Hold on. That's not what happened."

"You were over there improvising lines just to throw me off my game."

"I didn't improvise anything."

"Don't lie to me!" Lance took another step forward.

"You were drunk. You must remember that. You were babbling and incoherent. After I was hired, one of the casting agents came up to me and said he felt sorry for you. He said you were so good before. If your agent dropped you, that's why. It didn't have anything to do with me."

"Stop lying! You ruined my life!" Lance screamed, spittle flying from his lips.

He looked like he was about to charge straight at Jax. Connor knew that if he tried to stop him—even if *everyone* in the room tried to stop him—Lance would slash his way free. Connor had to defuse the situation, stall a little longer. The police had to be only seconds away. Maybe they were already here, going floor by floor looking for Lance.

Then Connor realized he might be able to do more than merely stall. Lance was in a talkative mood. Maybe he could find out why the man had wanted Chris dead. If he was really lucky, he might even be able to find out who Lance was working with.

"I understand why you're mad at Jax," Connor said, feigning sympathy. "But what did you have against Chris? Why did you kill him?"

Did he blame Chris for his failed career the same way he blamed Jax?

When Lance turned his attention from Jax to Connor, Dylan fell out of his line of sight. Unlike Connor, who had been trying to control the situation through conversation, Dylan seized this opportunity to take a more active approach.

"What are you talking about?" Lance said to Connor, as Dylan quietly grabbed the beer bottle off the nightstand. "I didn't kill Chris. I helped him get the damn job so Jax wouldn't get it. At first, I just wanted to ruin him. Then he came and did this." Lance gestured toward his broken arm. "It occurred to me that he was never going to stop fucking up my life until I put an end to him for good. Why would you think I killed Chris?" Then, just before Dylan swung the bottle at Lance's head, he said to Hannah, "What is he talking about?"

The bottle made a loud crack as it connected with Lance's skull. Shattered glass rained down around him as he stumbled forward. "What the fuck?" he screamed, even more enraged than he was before.

Dylan must have thought the blow would be enough to knock him out. It was not, and worse than that, he now seemed to have all of his anger trained on her. He slashed at her with the knife, and she dodged the blow. Laura screamed and grabbed Jax's hand.

Connor looked around for anything else he could use as a weapon and found nothing. But he had to do something. Dylan might not be able to dodge the knife a second time. Desperate times called for desperate measures. He launched himself onto Lance's back. Lance fell to the ground, screaming in pain as he landed on his broken arm and dropping the knife. Dylan stomped on his hand when he tried to grab it, kicked it away.

And that was all they needed to do, since the police—using a master key provided by the hotel clerk—had finally found them.

CHAPTER 45

FTER LANCE WAS DRAGGED away, Hannah explained that the man in her room was her brother Jami. He had come into town after Chris died to comfort her and, just as importantly, so she could comfort him. He had been Chris's friend since childhood and, after Chris's career had started to take off, his business manager. As such, he had moved with Chris to Hollywood and later Atlanta, where he and Hannah, who had tagged along with Jami, lived now.

But that wasn't all he was. He was also the man who had been sneaking around outside Connor's hotel room the night they arrived. Now that Connor had a chance to look at him straight on, he had no doubt about that.

Jami did not try to hide it, either. In fact, he was the one who brought it up first. "I'm sorry for spying on you that one night. You probably know how Hannah felt about you guys coming here. She wanted my opinion on you, and that seemed like the best way I could think of to find out what sort of investigators you were." He looked toward the door, as if he could see through it and beyond to wherever Lance had been taken. "I guess you were better than either of us could have imagined."

Connor had taken the statement at face value. Just like he had taken it at face value that Jax and Laura were nothing more than coworkers.

Now, back in his room and packing his suitcase, he remembered the way Laura had grabbed Jax's hand and knew they were more. Like Jax's wife was cheating on him, he was cheating on her. That seemed like the most reasonable explanation for what Laura had been doing in Jax's room when Lance showed up.

Not that any of it mattered.

An article published online hours earlier said previous reports of poison in Chris's death were unfounded. The lab was doing a toxicology screening, sure. It was standard procedure in a case like this, and it determined Chris had died from an overdose of ketamine. Developed as a horse tranquilizer, ketamine had made its way into an ever-growing class of street drugs, where it was best known as "Special K" or simply "K."

Nolan Clarke had been arrested for selling him the drugs and, even though Nolan refuted the charges, ketamine had been found in his possession.

That report officially ended their investigation and tied neatly into everything they knew about Lance so far. Lance had been confused when Connor had accused him of killing Chris because he hadn't. He had truly believed he could derail Jax's career by keeping him off the movie. He was just that crazy.

But Lance did have a contact with knowledge of the film. It was the only way he could have known everything he did. And it was still hard for Connor to believe Lance's obsession with Jax and Chris's death were unrelated. That was just too many big problems for one movie to have.

Add to that the fact that nobody thought Chris had used drugs, and Connor was certain they had not uncovered the entire story behind Chris's death.

But what could he do about it? The case was over. People were moving on with their lives. He might get a little cooperation from Maria for a day or two if he wanted to keep investigating on his own. However, like everyone else, she was ready to put the whole thing behind her. Celebrities died from drug overdoses often enough that it was almost routine. If Connor was in a cynical mood, he might even say she believed it would be good for the film (and thus her career). People would talk about Chris and the movie he'd died while making and they would come see it for that alone. Ticket sales would skyrocket.

And Hudson, who no longer had to worry that the blackmailer's email might be seen by the police as a motive to kill, certainly didn't have any interest in continuing to pay for the investigation.

Dylan rolled her suitcase through the adjoining door and into Connor's room. "What do you want to do until it's time to go?" They still had eight hours until their plane was scheduled to depart.

Connor zipped his suitcase shut, sat down on the bed. "I don't know." He sighed. "It just doesn't feel right, does it?"

She sat down beside him. "No, it doesn't. But we're out of time. We've done the job Hudson hired us to do. Lance is in jail. The police are satisfied. I think we're going to have to chalk this up as a win, no matter what really happened."

"I'd still like to know who told Lance Jax would be working on the movie. At least we could close out one mystery, even if it was just for us."

"Yeah, I'd like that, too. However, I don't think that's going to happen."

Then Connor thought about Jami's reason for spying on them. He had been wrong to take Jax's explanation of his relationship with Laura at face value. Maybe he was wrong to take Jami's at face value as well. After all, if Jami had nothing to hide, why wouldn't he have come to talk to Connor?

Especially after Hannah had come around to Connor's side.

Perhaps Jami was the link to Lance he had been looking for. Because of his relationship to Chris, Jami would know everything Lance knew. And perhaps—Connor could feel himself getting excited—he was also the link that would explain Chris's death.

Connor thought again about the probability of a movie being impacted by two unrelated events that were both so horrible. Could Jami *really* be the connection? Was Connor so close to unraveling not one mystery, but both? He decided he'd better run it past Dylan to make sure emotion wasn't getting the better of him. The last thing he wanted to do was talk himself into a faulty conclusion.

"What about Jami? Do you think he could have been Lance's man on the inside?"

Dylan shook her head. "What would his motive be?"

That was indeed a problem. Although, it didn't mean there wasn't a connection. Or—he remembered something else—maybe it wasn't Jami at all. Maybe it was Hannah. Maybe Jami had stayed quiet not because he was involved but because he was protecting his sister.

When Connor had accused Lance of killing Chris, Lance had first asked Connor what he was talking about. When Connor didn't answer, he had turned the question to Hannah. Out of all the people in the room, he had directed the question to her, as if she, above all others, might answer him.

It wasn't just that, either. It was how he had asked the question. There was something in his voice that, in retrospect, sounded to Connor like he knew her.

He tried the new theory on Dylan and was met with the same problem: Motive.

"We can't even connect the two," Dylan added this time.

But that wasn't true. Connor shifted in his seat to face her as his theory gained clarity. The excitement must have shown on his face, because before he could explain, Dylan said, "What is it? You have a way to draw a line from one to the other?"

"I might. What do we know about Lance already?"

"He was a nutcase?"

"Seriously. What do we know?"

"He was a runner. He wanted to be an actor."

Connor was shaking his head. "No. That's not what I'm after."

"Just tell me, all right?"

"Lance was in rehab recently. Remember? We found that when we dug into his past."

"So what?"

"Who else do we know was in rehab recently?"

Dylan thought for a moment, and then Connor could see that she, too, had started to put the pieces together. "Hannah."

"Bingo," Connor said. She had told them about it in the car on the way from the airport.

Dylan removed her laptop from her suitcase and sat down at the table. "Do you remember the name of the facility he was staying in?"

"Was it Midtown Place?"

"Midtown Recovery Palace," Dylan said as she powered up her computer and started typing. It didn't take her long to find what she was looking for. Dylan had proven time and again she could find anything she wanted on the dark web. She pointed to the screen. "There. See that?"

Connor had been standing behind her for the last ten minutes, watching her work. He leaned in close. "She was there at the same time he was."

"That has to be how they met."

"Why would she help him blackmail Hudson?"

Dylan did not have an answer to that.

Connor began to slowly pace the room while she turned back to her computer in search of additional information. He stopped. "Maybe . . . maybe she wanted this job more than she let on. Maybe she needed it, and getting Chris cast as Habersham was the only way to get it."

"So they both got something out of the arrangement," Dylan said.

Connor shrugged.

"Why would she need the money? Her brother probably made a pretty good living as Chris's business manager."

There was a knock on the door. For a brief, foolish moment, Connor worried Lance might be out there, that somehow he had escaped custody and come back seeking revenge.

"What are you doing?" Dylan said. "Answer it." She was not suffering from the same misplaced fear he was.

Connor pushed the thought out of his mind, opened the door, and was met by Marty Campbell, the bearded man in charge of special effects. He was back in his favorite Grateful Dead tee shirt. "It probably doesn't matter now, but the cameraman found some additional footage from the day Chris died. The last disk they used was still loaded into the recording device on the set. I just thought . . . I don't know. Anyway, if you want to see it—"

"Yes, we want to see it," Connor said, while at the same time Dylan replied with a "You bet."

CHAPTER 46

HUDDLED TOGETHER IN THE trailer that housed the video equipment, now with Marty instead of Hannah, Dylan once again took control of the editing bay. Marty was sitting on the sofa next to Connor, elbows on his knees and leaning forward with a look of anticipation as Dylan queued up the latest disk.

"It's strange," Marty said, watching the black screen.

"What is?" Connor asked.

"The whole overdose thing. That's not like Chris at all. Some people are good at hiding it, but . . . I don't know."

Connor had been wondering why Marty had brought the disk to their attention. Now it looked like he had his answer. "You don't think it was an overdose?"

"I don't want to be one to second-guess the police, but . . ." He held out his hands, palms up, and frowned as he shrugged his shoulders.

Dylan pressed PLAY.

An image appeared on the screen—a closeup of Chris. A makeup woman was fussing about, dabbing his forehead with a small sponge, turning his head one way and then another to get a better look at her work. "That'll do." She stepped away.

Somebody snapped a clapper in front of the camera. Maria yelled, "Action!" from offscreen. Chris's expression changed. He suddenly looked somehow serious and broken at the same time. "That's not happening again," he said. "Not after what you did to her."

"Great!" Maria shouted. "Cut!"

The image was replaced by one of Laura, who read off a line of her own.

This went on for a while, with one actor or another, and finally ended when Chris said, "She was my mother."

Connor was sure it would all have been appropriately dramatic when the film was done. However, isolated as the lines were, they came across as overacted and nonsensical.

Sometimes the clips cut directly from one closeup to another. Other times, the camera would keep rolling for several seconds after the line had been read. Such was the case with Chris's final line. He stepped away from the camera, moving deeper into the bank. Connor, Dylan, and Marty watched as Hannah ran up to him with a mug in her hand.

"It's been a long day," she said. "Thought you might like some coffee before—"

The camera cut again, this time to Jax entering the bank in the red overcoat and diamond-shaped sunglasses.

Dylan paused the disk, spun the chair around. Connor could see her wheels turning. "That must have been the last take of the day. Looks like everything from here on out would be after Jax arrived."

"Do you think . . . ?" Connor began.

Dylan nodded. "Maybe."

Marty had a puzzled look on his face as he watched them converse in a shorthand it seemed only they could understand. "What is it?"

"Chris wasn't the only one who knew Ryan," Connor said, directing his response to Marty. "Hannah did, too."

"And she brought Chris that cup of coffee even though he hadn't asked for it," Dylan added.

"You don't think she was just being nice?" Marty said.

Instead of answering, Connor asked a question of his own. "What do you think she was going to say?"

Dylan glanced at the screen thoughtfully, then turned back to Connor. "My guess: 'Thought you might like some coffee before you go out tonight.' Probably something like that, anyway."

"You think she poisoned Chris," Marty said, finally getting the gist of the conversation.

"Do you think we could still test the mug?" Connor asked Dylan.

"I don't know. It's probably been washed by now, if Hannah didn't just throw it away."

Dylan was probably right, and without the mug, he wasn't sure they would be able to prove anything. But that shouldn't stop them from trying. First, though, he needed to get his head around both what they knew and what they thought, so he restated it all for Dylan's benefit as well as his own.

"All right, here's what we've got: Lance was obsessed with Jax. He believed—*really believed*—Jax sabotaged his audition and ruined his chances of becoming an actor. He was so obsessed, he followed Jax to Atlanta. He had probably been stalking him online and in person for years—he was definitely doing it in Atlanta, which was how he knew Jax's wife was having an affair with Hudson."

"Yes, I know that," Dylan said.

"I don't," Marty said, who was sitting even farther forward in his seat, hanging on every word Connor said.

"Please bear with me," Connor continued. "There's a lot to unpack, and I want to make sure it's all clear."

Dylan gestured for him to carry on.

Connor took a beat to clear his head. "Something in Atlanta triggered him to stop quietly stalking Jax and start interacting with him."

"It started about the time he came out of rehab," Dylan said.

"Right. So that was probably it. Maybe he saw the world differently once he was sober and was finally ready to get the revenge he thought he deserved. Or maybe it had something to do with meeting Hannah. Maybe they bonded over their shared Hollywood connections. Either way, he set out to ruin Jax's career just like he thought Jax had ruined his. This was likely where Hannah came into play. Thanks to her brother, she would likely have known Jax had beaten Chris out for the part of Habersham and would have been able to provide Lance with Hudson's email address to initiate the blackmail."

"That all sounds correct to me," Dylan said.

"She's probably also the one who told Lance Jax was here. I don't think she did it because she thought Lance would come here to try to kill him. She seemed as surprised to see Lance in the hotel as we were. She might have just told him because they were friends."

Marty nodded along, as if he agreed with every point.

"But she clearly had something to gain by helping Chris, since she wouldn't have gotten the job on this film without him. So why would she kill him?"

"That's where we get stuck."

Connor tapped the tips of his fingers together several times. "Maybe not. Hannah really wanted us to leave when we first got here, and she kept singing that tune until we made our way into this trailer. Then, suddenly, she showed up with a whole new attitude. And even though going through all those disks was tedious, she stayed the entire time. It was like she was afraid we might see something she had overlooked. Maybe something like her handing Chris a cup of coffee he didn't ask for."

"But, like you said, she showed up with a whole new attitude. She told us she was there because she wanted to help, so I'm not sure how much that gets us."

"She also acted like she didn't know who was spying on us the first night we were here. If she'd really wanted to help, she would have introduced us to her brother. And let's not forget—she said she didn't know who Chris was meeting the night he died. That doesn't make sense because Ryan said they all used to hang out together. Seems like Chris would have told her who he was meeting."

"I think he would have invited her," Marty said.

"Exactly," Connor said. "Unless he was mad at her."

"Mad enough for her to kill him?" Dylan asked.

"Or maybe she didn't go because she didn't want to be close to Chris when he died. Either way, there's an awful lot of evidence pointing at her and none pointing anywhere else. Maybe we don't know why she poisoned him yet, but she's definitely the one who did it, and that right there has to be the moment she did it," Connor said, pointing to the screen.

Dylan had paused the video just after Jax had entered the bank, but everyone knew which moment Connor was referring to.

"We still need proof," she said.

"We could go by the jail and talk to Ryan. If he sold the drugs to Hannah, he might tell us."

"That wouldn't be enough."

"It would be a start. Who knows what else he might say? Let's stay. Just a couple more days. On our own. If I'm right, we probably don't need Maria's cooperation to get the evidence we're after."

Dylan slowly nodded. "All right. I'm on board. Let's do it."

The last time Connor had been in this trailer, he had kept the door locked—an unnecessary precaution, it seemed, since all indications were the one person they should have kept out was the one they let in. But it was a precaution Connor should have taken this time. Unfortunately, he did not realize that until he heard the door click shut and turned to see Hannah standing at the end of the trailer with a gun pointed at them.

CHAPTER 47

CONNOR SLOWLY STOOD UP and took a step toward the back of the trailer. Marty and Dylan stayed where they were. "You couldn't leave well enough alone, could you?" Hannah said. "You had done your job, gotten paid. The case was closed. Why couldn't you just go home like you were supposed to?"

Nobody answered. Connor did not think Hannah expected them to.

"I heard everything you said from outside the trailer."

Dylan began to ask how, and Hannah gestured with the tip of her gun to the tinted window behind the sofa. "You gave me the keys, remember? I came back and opened it just a little in case you two returned to go over the footage another time."

Connor looked over his shoulder. The window was indeed opened a crack.

He should not have been surprised, but he was, and Hannah must have picked up on it because the next thing she said was, "You didn't think that one night outside your room was the only time Jami or I had eyes on you?"

It was another rhetorical question and, again, nobody answered.

"You were right about everything you said. Mostly. I'm sure you know that. That's why I can't let you go talk to Ryan. I was good. I was careful. But you're good, too, and if you stick around long enough, you might just be able to make the police believe you."

She turned the gun toward Marty. "And you—why did you have to get messed up in this? Those two would have been easy to get rid of. Everyone thinks they're leaving, anyway. Now I have to deal with you also, and that sucks."

Connor's mind was racing. He did not think Hannah would shoot them inside the trailer. That meant staying here was the best thing they could do until he could figure out how they were going to get away from her. He decided to employ the same tactic he had with Lance: He would stall. And, like with Lance, there was still a question he wanted answered, so he decided this was as good a time as any to ask.

"You heard everything we said."

"Every single word."

"Why did you kill Chris?"

Hannah smiled mischievously. "Who said I did?"

With that, Connor realized he was not going to get the same sort of easy answer out of her he had gotten out of Lance. He also realized he was not going to be able to stall for as long as he had hoped. Hannah was not as much of a conversationalist as Lance had been.

As if to prove Connor correct, Hannah said, "First things first. I want all of your cell phones over here. Toss them this way."

Connor, Dylan, and Marty did as instructed. The phones landed by Hannah's feet. With one hand keeping the gun trained on Connor, she gathered them up and slid them into the various pockets of her jeans. "Now, all of you, out of the trailer."

Then Dylan got up and, instead of moving toward the door, took a step behind the chair. "No."

Surprise plastered itself across Hannah's face. She leveled the gun at Dylan. "Excuse me?"

"Guns are hard to buy in England," Dylan said. "Where did you get that?"

"From the set. Why does that matter?"

"It's a prop gun, then. It won't fire."

"This is not a prop."

Dylan turned to Connor. "She's trying to bluff us."

Marty started to speak when Hannah said, "Shut up! All of you, shut the fuck up! Get out of the goddamn trailer right now!"

Dylan had not taken her eyes off Connor. She had not seen Hannah wrap one hand over the other like she was preparing to pull the trigger. If she had, Connor thought she might have second-guessed what she was about to do next.

She nodded at Connor, and he nodded back.

Suddenly, Dylan spun around, shoved the chair at Hannah. The chair was neither heavy enough nor moving fast enough to cause any real harm. But Connor knew that wasn't Dylan's intention. She was merely looking for a distraction. In that capacity, the chair seemed to do exactly what it was intended to do.

As the chair moved toward Hannah, so did Dylan. Hannah reached out a hand to grab it. Dylan ducked as the woman simultaneously swung the gun toward her and pulled the trigger. Perhaps that was no more than instinct, Connor would think later. There was no way Dylan would have pushed the chair into Hannah if she believed the gun was real.

But it was an instinct that may have saved her life.

The gun fired, and the bullet tore a hole through the stack of disks and the wall behind them. The shot surprised everyone, including—it seemed—Hannah. But where Connor and Dylan were surprised the gun was real, Hannah was surprised by the power of the blast. Perhaps this was the first gun she had fired because she did not seem prepared for the weapon to recoil. As it did, her hands jerked wildly up and away, no longer trained on any target.

Marty was on his feet, too. He had stepped back toward Connor and looked equally alarmed about what might happen next.

Dylan kept charging, if only because she was too close to Hannah to stop. It was a good thing she did, too. This would be their one and only chance to get out of the trailer alive. Now that Hannah had fired one shot, she had no reason not to fire more. Any hope Connor had had of engaging Hannah in dialogue was gone.

Dylan grabbed the chair and shoved it hard into Hannah, knocking her to the ground. The gun slid under the built-in desk.

"Let's go!" Dylan shouted, already hopping over Hannah so she could get to the exit.

Connor and Marty did not need to be told twice. Trying to stop her from getting to the gun was not an option. Hannah was already reaching under the desk for it. If she got her hands on the weapon before they could immobilize her, one of them might end up dead.

Once they were outside of the trailer, they all looked wildly around for where to go next. The overcast sky meant the little light they had came from streetlamps nearby. On the opposite side of those streetlamps, the trailers cast dark shadows. Dark enough to swallow them up entirely, Connor thought. If they could get there without being seen, Hannah would have no idea where to find them.

He led Dylan and Marty around the back of the nearest trailer. "We should be safe here for a minute," he said.

Dylan caught her breath. "I thought the guns on the set were props," she said to Marty.

"I tried to warn you."

Connor remembered Marty had indeed tried to tell them something when Hannah had shouted for everyone to shut up. "You mean they're not props?" he asked.

"It's a misnomer. Some sets do use replicas. But, up close, replicas don't look like the real thing. Anyone who has ever fired a gun can spot a fake, so a lot of movies use real firearms."

"With real bullets?"

"Sometimes. It depends on the shot. Either way, they're called props, because that's what they are. When they're handed to the actors, they're designated as 'hot' or 'cold' so everyone on the set knows what kind of ammo has been loaded. Does that really matter right now?"

No, it doesn't, Connor thought. The only thing they needed to be thinking about at this moment was what they were going to do next. He considered their options. They did not have their phones, so calling the police was not among them.

If they could get back to the hotel, they would probably be safe. Lance might have been willing to chase them through the hotel, witnesses be damned, but Connor couldn't picture Hannah shooting up the place like some wannabe Terminator.

However, the hotel seemed particularly far away right now. They could dart from the shadows of one trailer to another for a while, but they would have to make most of the trip without cover. Although Hannah would not come into the hotel shooting, she might fire at them while they were crossing the street. Her aim was not good, but it didn't have to be. One lucky shot, and Connor's and Dylan's lives would be changed forever.

That left only one other option: the bank.

"It's locked," Marty said.

"Not a problem," Dylan replied.

Connor knew she was telling the truth. She might not have her lock pick set with her, but she had gotten through a deadbolt before without it and could probably do so again.

Perhaps Hannah had made a mistake coming after Connor and Dylan. She had no way of being certain they would find any evidence that would sway the police's position.

Regardless, she had to kill them now for certain. Marty, too. Although the police might never have arrested her for killing Chris, they sure as shit would arrest her for attempted murder if any of them survived.

Hannah had arrived at the trailer with a plan. Marty's presence had thrown a wrench into it. But as she fished the gun out from under the desk, she was already revising that plan into something that would work for all three of them, as well as explain the shot she had fired.

She straightened up and looked out the window just in time to see Marty duck behind a trailer nearby. That was good. They would be easy to pick off back there. Three quick shots, and this time, she would be prepared for the recoil. Up close between the trailers, she was confident she could hit her targets.

She grabbed her phone and called Jami. He had rented a car when he arrived. She would need it to get Connor's and Dylan's bodies out to the countryside. She would also need his strength to help her get the bodies into the car and to dig their graves.

Marty, she intended to leave stretched out in the trailer by the editing bay. A scene like that would raise more questions than it would answer, but any conclusion the police might draw would not put Hannah in their crosshairs.

"Hi," Jami said. He did not know what Hannah was up to at that moment, just like he hadn't known she had killed Chris until after it was done. But she had killed Chris to help him, and he would help her now. That's what siblings did.

"Bring the car around to the bank."

"What for?"

"Just do it, okay?"

She hung up, then slowly opened the door to the trailer. She listened for any sounds of movement, any indication the trio was leaving their current hiding place in search of another. She knew they could not see her. To do that, they would have to be peeking around one end of the trailer or the other, where she would also be able to see them. But they might be listening, just like she was.

She stepped onto the ground softly. With the gun held up to her shoulder, she made one slow step after another toward the trailer where she'd seen Marty go. There was no need to rush. The closer she could get to them before she had to fire, the better off she would be.

Connor watched Hannah step off the trailer, but not the way Hannah expected. He knew as well as she did that peeking around the side of the trailer would expose him. Since they weren't on the move, though, he had another option. He lay on his stomach, watched Hannah's left foot hit the ground and then her right.

"She's coming," he whispered to Marty, who looked toward the bank.

Seconds earlier, Dylan had made her way to a door along the side that was not visible from Hannah's vantage point. Marty watched as she removed a pair of bobby pins from her hair and huddled over the lock.

If this bank were still in use, picking her way past the deadbolt would have been pointless, since there was a second deadbolt that only turned from the inside. But Marty had said they were not using that lock. The crew were in and out of that door a lot, and it did not make sense to engage both deadbolts. If Dylan could get them past the one, they would be golden.

Connor got back to his feet. "We need to go. She's coming this way."

Marty nodded. They began to move quietly toward the bank. Halfway there, Connor could tell Dylan was still working to get them inside. "She'll get past that lock any moment now."

Then a shot rang out and, even though Connor knew Hannah had fired it, he instinctively spun around. She fired again.

"Dylan!" he shouted, as he and Marty broke into a sprint. "Get that door open now!"

When Hannah had fired the gun, Dylan too had turned to look, but she was already back at work.

She has to get through that lock, Connor thought. *She just has to.* This might have been Chris's last trip to London. It wasn't going to be theirs.

When they were only feet away, though, Connor worried she would need more time than she had and began considering other options. They could circle around the back of the bank. At least that way they could keep some distance from Hannah. It wasn't much of a plan—no better than darting across the road hoping to get into the hotel before one of them got shot. Still, it might be the only plan they had.

CHAPTER 48

BEFORE CONNOR COULD TELL Dylan to run, she jerked open the door, and all three of them barreled into the darkness inside as Hannah again pulled the trigger. The bullet hit the brick wall inches from the door.

Connor grabbed the handle and swung the door shut. He engaged both locks using only the light of the Emergency Exit sign above.

Marty flipped a switch to their right. A single exposed bulb came on overhead. They were in a tight room with peeling linoleum floors and cinderblock walls. Clearly, this utilitarian space had not received the same care the rest of the bank had. An assortment of film equipment was stacked up along the walls: light stands over there, a dolly and tracks over here, foldout chairs and clapboards and props of all kinds. There was little room left for the three of them to stand.

"What do we do now?" Marty said. He sounded scared, short of breath. They had not run far, but it was far enough to take a toll. Good thing they hadn't tried to make it all the way back to the hotel. Connor wasn't sure Marty would be able to do it without stopping to rest.

The room had two doors. Both were closed. The first was the one they had come through, and the second, by all indications, led farther into the bank. Going through that door seemed like the next logical step. Then Connor saw something mounted to the wall beside it.

It was partially obscured by camera equipment, so Connor couldn't be certain he saw what he thought he did until he got close. "We got a phone here!"

From the look of it, the phone had to be twenty years old, at least.

"Really?" Dylan said, coming up behind him.

"Yeah. I think we're going to be okay."

He picked up the receiver, ready to dial 999. There was no dial tone. He tapped the cradle twice. Still nothing.

"They probably disconnected it when the bank closed," Marty said.

"Maybe we should just stay here until morning," Dylan said. "At least we're safe."

"I wouldn't count on that," Marty said. "Maria trusts Hannah with everything."

"So what?"

"So Hannah has a key."

"She can't get through that," Connor said, indicating the second deadbolt.

"She has a key to the front door."

Jax was lying in bed with Laura when he heard a loud bang from outside. It sounded like a gun. "What was that?"

She shrugged, and maybe he should have let it go, too. But he slid his arm out from underneath Laura's pillow and went to the window.

She rolled over. "What are you doing?"

He parted the curtains just enough so he could see out. His room had a clear view of the bank and the trailers surrounding it. At first, everything seemed normal. "Maybe it was a car backfiring," he said.

"I'm sure that's all it was. Come back to bed."

Then movement between a trailer and the bank caught his

attention. It was Dylan. What was she doing?

"Jax, I'm getting cold."

"Hold on," he said without taking his eyes off the window.

A moment later, the door to another trailer opened. Out of it stepped Hannah. Although he couldn't be certain from here, it looked like she might be carrying a gun.

After that, things started happening quickly. Two more people appeared from behind the same trailer that had first concealed Dylan. Jax squinted as he tried to get a better look at them, realized it was Connor and Marty.

"What do you see?"

"Shhh," Jax said, waving a hand in Laura's direction, indicating she should stop talking.

Hannah stretched both arms out in front of her, and because of her stance the thing she was holding looked even more like a gun now. But Hannah—with a gun? Then there was another bang and a corresponding flash from the thing in Hannah's hands and Jax no longer had any doubt he was right.

"Holy shit!"

"What?" Laura said, rising from the bed and wrapping the sheet around her. "What is it? Another car? Is someone out there joyriding or something?"

Jax didn't answer because he didn't hear her. All of his attention was focused on the scene playing out across the street.

Dylan pulled open the bank door. She, Connor, and Marty raced inside as Hannah fired again. They pulled the door shut behind them. Hannah grabbed the handle, but nothing more happened.

"They locked it," Jax said to himself. "Good for them."

"Who locked what?" Laura said, finally joining Jax at the window.

She tried to take his hand, but now he was moving, too. He grabbed his jeans off the floor, quickly slid them on. "Call the police," he said, pulling on his shoes.

"The police? What for? Is Lance back?"

"It's not that. It's Hannah."

"Hannah?"

Jax grabbed his shirt. Sliding it over his head, he said, "Send them to the bank." Then he rushed out the door.

"Where are you going?" Laura shouted after him.

"Just call the police!"

Dylan opened the door that would take the trio from the room they were in to an equally utilitarian hallway. There were several other doors that led off it and a staircase at the far end.

"That will take us into the lobby of the bank," Marty said, referring to the staircase. "If Hannah decides to come down here after us, that's the only way she can do it."

"Maybe we should stay where we are," Dylan said. "If we hear her coming, we can just go back out the way we came in."

"What if she has Jami watch that door?" Connor asked. "What if he has a gun, too?"

"I have an idea," Marty said.

CHAPTER 49

HANNAH WAITED BY THE side door until she saw Jami's rented BMW pull into the parking lot. When the car came to a stop, its headlights aimed straight at the front of the bank, she stepped around the corner and waved her hands in the air to draw his attention.

The car started to move again. Hannah returned to her previous position. Jami pulled up beside her and rolled down his window. "What's going on?"

"Connor and Dylan know what happened."

"They can't know," Jami said incredulously.

"They know enough. They know I killed Chris, and they were talking about sticking around to find out why. That would be bad for both of us. I need you to stay here in case they come out this door. I'm going through the front. Once I take care of this problem, I'm going to need you to help me get them in the car, okay?"

"Where did you get that?" Jami said, surprised to see the gun in her hand.

"Props." She did not have to tell him they were shooting the movie with real guns. He knew at least as much as she did about what happened on a film set. Probably much more.

"All right. Go take care of it. I'll be here."

Hannah nodded.

"Bring the gun back with you," he said as she walked away. "We're going to have to get rid of it, too."

Hannah resisted the urge to tell him she was not an idiot, but did not acknowledge the comment in any other way, either. She climbed the stairs at the front of the bank, pulled the keys out of her pocket, and unlocked the door. Once inside, she moved carefully through the darkness. The light would make them easier to see, but it would make her easier to see, too. She wanted to get as close to them as she could before firing again. She knew how many bullets she had loaded into the gun and how many she had already used. She had only four bullets left, which left her little room for error.

After she determined they were not hiding behind the sofas in the middle of the lobby or underneath the desks on the far end, she made her way through the door that would take her behind the teller windows. There was still a splattering of fake blood on the wall from the scene they had shot earlier that day.

She could use that to her advantage, she thought. She would just have to get Connor and Dylan back to the lobby before she killed them. That way, if she and Jami ran out of time to clean up, the real blood would likely be mistaken for more of the fake stuff and be taken care of by the crew that cleaned the set before it was reset.

Hannah moved from one teller window to another, approaching each at such an angle that it would be hard for Dylan to take her by surprise again. She then moved to the manager's office, which, in addition to the room in the basement, was being used to house an assortment of film equipment. This time, she did turn on the light. There were too many nooks and crannies in here where someone might hide. As soon as she determined this room was unoccupied, she turned it back off.

There were still two other offices and several closets to check before she could be confident Connor, Dylan, and Marty were not up here. She intended to search all of them. However, before she could, she heard two gunshots come from behind the door that led to the basement.

That couldn't be Jami. He didn't have a gun. Nor could he have gotten through the side door where Hannah had left him. What the hell was going on down there?

Hannah ran to the door, pulled it open. The staircase and hallway beyond it were dark, lit only by the faint glow from the Emergency Exit sign. She flipped the light switch. Nothing happened.

But she had been in near total darkness since entering the bank. Her eyes had adjusted. Even from where she was, she could see Connor and Dylan slumped against the walls halfway between the stairs and the storage room. Their heads hung forward, their shirts soaked with blood.

Marty was standing over the bodies, holding a gun. When he saw Hannah, he dropped it. "Don't shoot. I did this for you."

She descended two steps and stopped. "For me?"

"Okay, I did it for me. If I didn't, you were going to kill all three of us, right?"

Hannah descended another two steps, still with her gun raised, but now looking at Connor and Dylan instead of Marty.

"I have enough of my own problems. I didn't want to die for them. I don't even know them."

Another two steps. Hannah was now closer to the bottom of the staircase than the top.

"I'll even help you get rid of the bodies," Marty said. "You can't do it on your own. I'm in this as deep as you are now. Please, put the gun down."

Hannah stepped off the last stair. She moved closer to Connor and Dylan.

"Why did you kill Chris, anyway?"

Hannah stopped her approach, turned her attention back to Marty. "I didn't want to. He was my friend."

"So why did you do it?"

Hannah debated telling him, but it didn't seem like there was anything to lose. Connor certainly couldn't use it against her. Not now.

She let the gun fall to her side, keeping her finger on the trigger. "I guess if there's anyone who would understand, it would be you."

Marty responded with a quizzical look.

"You said you needed this job because you had debts."

"Right. Normal things. Car payment, house payment, credit cards. So?"

"Remember how you felt when Chris threatened to get you fired?"

"You didn't kill him because he threatened to get *you* fired, did you?"

"No." Hannah pulled her phone out of her pocket, brought up a picture of a small child, and showed it to Marty. "His name is Henry. He's my brother's son. He's two years old. That's why I did it. For my brother and for him."

"I don't understand."

"I'm getting there." She put the phone back in her pocket. "You know I used to have a drug problem?"

"I . . ."

"It's okay. I know how the rumor mill works around here. Before I got clean, that wasn't the only problem I had. I had a lot of them. I owed people money, and not the kind of people who would come to repossess my car if I didn't pay them. Jami helped me out, got me out of trouble. But I just did it again. And again. And again. Jami lives large; he says it's expected." She shook her head. "I don't know. Either way, between his lifestyle and his new baby, he was strapped. His wife told him if he gave me one more dollar, she was leaving him. So he found another way to help me."

"Chris?"

"Jami managed his money. It was easy to take just a little. He always planned to put it back later, but I still didn't stop. I kept using, and Jami kept paying back my dealer, until suddenly the little bit he took in the beginning had become a lot. Finally, Jami put his foot down. He said if I didn't sober up, he wouldn't have anything else to do with me."

"That's why you got clean?"

"Sort of. At first, I told him he could go fuck himself. Then my dealer beat the crap out of me when I couldn't pay him, and I showed up at my brother's door once again asking for his help. This time, I was finally ready to go into rehab.

"Chris was as happy about it as Jami was. We all go way back. That's why he got me this job. After I helped him get his."

Another quizzical look from Marty.

Hannah had previously suspected Connor would have figured out she and Lance were working together. The PI seemed to be good at making connections other people had missed. Maybe she had been wrong. That or he hadn't had a chance to tell Marty about it.

"It doesn't matter. He was trying to help me get my life on track. That's all that matters. But that's not the only reason I wanted the job. I knew I had put Jami in a bind. He took that money out of Chris's account for me, and I wanted to help him put it back before Chris found out. Then Chris started talking seriously about this being his last movie. Sure, he'd been talking about it for a while. This was different.

Jami said he sounded serious. He started making plans, looking into his account himself. That's how he found out what Jami had done.

"He didn't tell me about any of this. Probably because he didn't know what Jami had used the money for. But he told Jami he was flying back to the US and would be reporting him to the police, and I guess Jami told me because he didn't know who else to tell."

"That's why you killed him," Marty said.

"I had to. Jami did everything he did to help me. I couldn't let him go to jail for that, and I couldn't let that kid grow up without a father, either."

"Did Jami help you kill him?"

"No. He didn't know until he got here. He was in the air when I did it. He was hoping if he could get to London before Chris left, he could talk some sense into him."

"Why didn't you try to talk to Chris?"

"You saw how he was acting the day he died. What if he didn't listen to me? That seemed like too much of a risk. I cared a lot about Chris. However, if it was going to come down to him or my brother, I was going to choose my brother."

CHAPTER 50

JAX BOLTED ACROSS THE street and headed straight for the bank. He did not stop to ask himself what he was doing or whether it was a good idea. Maybe—he would later speculate—he had played an action hero so many times now, it had become part of who he was.

He was almost at the steps that would take him to the main entrance when Jami appeared from around the corner. "Jax? What are you doing here?"

Jax did not stop to answer. He slugged Jami across the jaw hard enough to knock him off his feet and kept running. Whatever Hannah was up to, her brother had to be involved.

He leapt up the stairs two at a time. He did not wonder until he reached the top whether the door would be locked, and he was inside before he had time to think about what he might have done if it was.

Before Hannah arrived, Marty had found two squibs and a gun among the assortment of props in that basement room. While he attached the first to Connor's chest, Dylan crept up the stairs to see if Hannah had indeed come in through the front door.

"She's here," Dylan said when she returned, and Marty strapped a squib to her as well.

He loaded two blanks into the gun, detonated the squibs, and pulled the trigger twice. "Handy to have an FX guy around for something like this," he said dryly as Connor and Dylan took their positions on the floor. Then he turned off the light and unscrewed the bulb in the hallway, trusting the darkness to better conceal the truth and the glow from the Emergency Exit sign to provide just enough visibility.

Let's hope Hannah buys it, Connor thought. He could feel every muscle in his body tensing up with each step she took down the stairs. He was certain that at any moment she would figure out the ruse and put a pair of bullets in him and Dylan for real. So far, however, she hadn't.

She told Marty everything Connor wanted to know. Judging by her voice, she was standing only feet away. Close enough to grab, but this wasn't the time. Not yet. If he tried, she would kill him as soon as he moved. Sooner or later, though, she would turn her back on him, Marty would snap his fingers, and Connor and Dylan would spring into action.

That was the plan, anyway, until Hannah said, "Happy now, Connor?"

Connor felt his heart skip a beat. Did she know he was alive?

A foot kicked him hard in the hip. "Get up. Both of you."

Reluctantly, he opened his eyes and saw Dylan had done the same.

Hannah had moved far enough back that Connor could no longer reach her.

"You knew?" Connor said as he pushed himself up the wall.

"Of course I knew. You thought this little act of yours was going to fool me?"

"Why did you say all that, then?"

"After all the trouble you went through staging this scene, I thought the least I could do was tell you the truth before I killed you. Now, upstairs! All of you!"

Dylan shook her head at Connor, but he didn't see what choice they had. Although Hannah might prefer to kill them upstairs, she would do it down here if they forced her hand. At least if they complied, they would buy themselves a little time.

The sound of footsteps in the lobby drew everyone's attention, and suddenly another person was standing in the doorway, a dark-on-dark shadow. Connor thought it had to be Jami until he spoke.

"Hannah," Jax said. "What the hell are you doing?"

Perhaps Hannah also thought it was Jami, because she had hardly even glanced at the man until that moment. Startled, she spun around.

Connor knew it was now or never. He lunged on top of her, and they fell to the floor as one. Connor grabbed the wrist holding the gun and slammed it against the linoleum floor until she let go.

"I'll go after Jami," Dylan said, already heading up the stairs.

"I'll come with you," Marty replied, following.

Jax grabbed Dylan's arm as she passed. "What is all this? What's going on?"

She jerked away. "Hannah killed Chris." Then she was on the move again.

Connor continued to struggle with Hannah. She squirmed and kicked and reached for the gun. She shouted for Connor to get off. She told him he would regret getting involved in this case. But Connor had no intention of letting her up, and once Jax joined him, pinning her wrists to the ground, the little chance she had of regaining control of the situation was gone.

"Call the police," Connor said to him.

"Laura already did that," he replied. "They should be here any second."

They just had to keep her under control until then.

CHAPTER 51

JAMI WAS NOWHERE TO be found. He was gone, along with his car. But the police put out an All Points Warning, and he didn't make it any farther than the airport.

Hannah and Lance were charged in the UK with murder and attempted murder, respectively. Jami was extradited to the US, where he was charged with embezzlement. Connor and Dylan were called as witnesses in all three trials.

They were exhausted from flying back and forth over the Atlantic. But the coverage of the trials had brought their firm, Red Sky Investigators, some much-needed attention and more work than they could handle, which allowed them to pick and choose the cases that interested them.

Sometime in the midst of all that excitement, Connor and Dylan had met with Hudson at Cafe de Flore one last time to discuss the case.

Over coffee and pastries, he had admitted that he had hired Connor's firm because he was afraid of being blamed for the murder if the police ever found out he had been blackmailed into hiring Chris. He had offered this confession unprompted and then said, "You already knew all this, didn't you?"

"What do you mean?" Connor asked.

"You took my computer."

Connor almost choked on his croissant. "Excuse me?"

"We didn't—" Dylan began.

"Not you, personally. You were in the UK. Somebody who works for you did. Probably that guy who came to visit me in my office. Am I right?"

Neither Connor nor Dylan responded.

"Who else would steal it and later return it? You didn't trust me." Then, for the first time, his perpetual frown turned into a smile. "It's okay. I might have done the same thing if I was a younger man." He tossed a pair of twenties on the table to cover the bill. "It taught me a valuable lesson."

"What's that?" Dylan asked as Hudson stood up and slid his chair back into place.

"I was worried about the cost of divorcing my wife, but I'm not happy—I suppose that's obvious—and I shouldn't stay with her. No matter how much she will get, it's far less than what it might cost me if I give someone like Lance the opportunity to blackmail me again."

That divorce was not the only one this case brought about, either. Jax, who had found a new appreciation for life after nearly being killed, and his wife, who no longer wanted to be married to somebody who might draw a person like Lance to her door, divorced amicably, which finally freed Jax up to propose to Laura. When he called to report the news to Connor, he also told him, "You'd better come to my wedding."

Connor assured him he would, then hung up. There were dozens of case files spread out on the conference table before him. They had yet to pick their next job, and it wasn't going to happen tonight. Olin and Dylan had already gone home. He turned off the light and stepped into the lobby.

"Good night, Connor," said Lucy McBeal, the receptionist Connor had once thought they might never hire.

"You're still here?"

"I didn't want to leave before you did in case anyone came in."

Like most days lately, today had been a revolving door of people looking for their help. Lucy had done a great job of keeping it all organized—gathering the basics, fielding their questions, making sure the right case notes landed in the right file. She also did a great job at keep away the riffraff and reporters, whom Connor and Olin had had enough of many times over.

No doubt, she was exactly what they needed.

Lucy grabbed her purse and left with Connor.

"See you tomorrow," Connor said as they parted ways in the parking lot.

"Bright and early."

If anybody else had replied like that, Connor would have thought they were being glib. But in addition to being well organized, Lucy was chirpy and cheerful in a way that almost made it feel like she had stepped right out of a Disney movie.

As Connor got to his car, he found he was still thinking about the files spread out across the conference table. He hadn't come across anything that piqued his interest. Neither had Olin or Dylan. He wondered how long it would be until they did. In the end, the only thing he could say for sure was, whatever case they took, he was confident they would solve it like they had solved so many others.

Find out what happens next in *Reckless.*

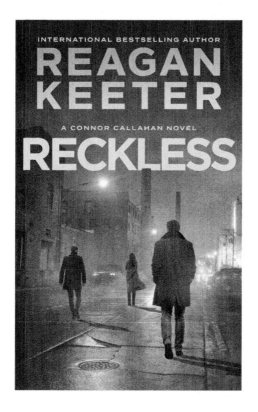

GET AN EXCLUSIVE COPY OF *THE LAYOVER*

Connor Callahan is back in this exclusive novella that takes place three years after his parents were abducted and prior to his first case in Atlanta. When he sees a man discreetly tag a stranger's suitcase with a black magic marker, he sets out to discover what is going on. It's a decision that will thrust Connor into a conflict far more dangerous than he could have imagined, and when it's over he will know one thing for sure: You're not always safer on the ground.

When you join my readers club, you will immediately get a free and exclusive copy of *The Layover*, not available elsewhere.

I usually e-mail once or twice a month with things I think you'll find interesting, such as behind-the-scenes stories, new releases, and fan discounts. Of course, you can unsubscribe at any time.

Join the readers club by signing up at
read.reagankeeter.com

ALSO BY REAGAN KEETER

THE CONNOR CALLAHAN SERIES
Gone

A Good Plan

STANDALONES
The Redwood Con

Misery Rock

99 Souls (as Gabriel Burns)

ABOUT THE AUTHOR

Reagan Keeter is the author of multiple Amazon bestsellers and a National Indie Excellence Awards finalist. He has worked as a writer and editor at Georgia newspapers. From Georgia State University, he earned his undergraduate degree in Journalism and from Southern Polytechnic State University his master's in Technical and Professional Communication. He lives with his wife and their two dogs in Atlanta, Georgia.

You can connect with him via:
His website: reagankeeter.com
Facebook: https://www.facebook.com/AuthorReaganKeeter/
Twitter: @ReaganKeeter
Email: reagan@reagankeeter.com

Printed in Great Britain
by Amazon

22704902R00162